Erle Stanley Gardner and The Murder Room

>>> This title is part of The Murder Room, our series dedicated to making available out-of-print or hard-to-find titles by classic crime writers.

Crime fiction has always held up a mirror to society. The Victorians were fascinated by sensational murder and the emerging science of detection; now we are obsessed with the forensic detail of violent death. And no other genre has so captivated and enthralled readers.

Vast troves of classic crime writing have for a long time been unavailable to all but the most dedicated frequenters of second-hand bookshops. The advent of digital publishing means that we are now able to bring you the backlists of a huge range of titles by classic and contemporary crime writers, some of which have been out of print for decades.

From the genteel amateur private eyes of the Golden Age and the femmes fatales of pulp fiction, to the morally ambiguous hard-boiled detectives of mid twentieth-century America and their descendants who walk our twenty-first century streets, The Murder Room has it all. >>>

The Murder Room
Where Criminal Minds Meet

themurderroom.com

Erle Stanley Gardner (1889–1970)

Born in Malden, Massachusetts, Erle Stanley Gardner left school in 1909 and attended Valparaiso University School of Law in Indiana for just one month before he was suspended for focusing more on his hobby of boxing that his academic studies. Soon after, he settled in California, where he taught himself the law and passed the state bar exam in 1911. The practise of law never held much interest for him, however, apart from as it pertained to trial strategy, and in his spare time he began to write for the pulp magazines that gave Dashiell Hammett and Raymond Chandler their start. Not long after the publication of his first novel, *The Case of the Velvet Claws*, featuring Perry Mason, he gave up his legal practice to write full time. He had one daughter, Grace, with his first wife, Natalie, from whom he later separated. In 1968 Gardner married his long-term secretary, Agnes Jean Bethell, whom he professed to be the real 'Della Street', Perry Mason's sole (although unacknowledged) love interest. He was one of the most successful authors of all time and at the time of his death, in Temecula, California in 1970, is said to have had 135 million copies of his books in print in America alone.

By Erle Stanley Gardner
(titles below include only those
published in the Murder Room)

Perry Mason series

The Case of the Sulky Girl
  (1933)
The Case of the Baited Hook
  (1940)
The Case of the Borrowed
  Brunette (1946)
The Case of the Lonely
  Heiress (1948)
The Case of the Negligent
  Nymph (1950)
The Case of the Moth-Eaten
  Mink (1952)
The Case of the Glamorous
  Ghost (1955)
The Case of the Terrified
  Typist (1956)
The Case of the Gilded Lily
  (1956)
The Case of the Lucky Loser
  (1957)
The Case of the Long-Legged
  Models (1958)
The Case of the Deadly Toy
  (1959)
The Case of the Singing Skirt
  (1959)

The Case of the Duplicate
  Daughter (1960)
The Case of the Blonde
  Bonanza (1962)

Cool and Lam series

The Bigger They Come (1939)
Turn on the Heat (1940)
Gold Comes in Bricks (1940)
Spill the Jackpot (1941)
Double or Quits (1941)
Owls Don't Blink (1942)
Bats Fly at Dusk (1942)
Cats Prowl at Night (1943)
Crows Can't Count (1946)
Fools Die on Friday (1947)
Bedrooms Have Windows
  (1949)
Some Women Won't Wait (1953)
Beware the Curves (1956)
You Can Die Laughing (1957)
Some Slips Don't Show (1957)
The Count of Nine (1958)
Pass the Gravy (1959)
Kept Women Can't Quit (1960)
Bachelors Get Lonely (1961)
Shills Can't Count Chips (1961)

Try Anything Once (1962)
Fish or Cut Bait (1963)
Up For Grabs (1964)
Cut Thin to Win (1965)
Widows Wear Weeds (1966)
Traps Need Fresh Bait (1967)

Doug Selby D.A. series

The D.A. Calls it Murder (1937)
The D.A. Holds a Candle (1938)
The D.A. Draws a Circle (1939)
The D.A. Goes to Trial (1940)
The D.A. Cooks a Goose (1942)
The D.A. Calls a Turn (1944)
The D.A. Takes a Chance (1946)
The D.A. Breaks an Egg (1949)

Terry Clane series

Murder Up My Sleeve (1937)
The Case of the Backward
  Mule (1946)

Gramp Wiggins series

The Case of the Turning Tide
  (1941)
The Case of the Smoking
  Chimney (1943)

Two Clues (two novellas) (1947)

Spill the Jackpot

Erle Stanley Gardner

An Orion book

Copyright © The Erle Stanley Gardner Trust 1941

The right of Erle Stanley Gardner to be identified as the author of this work has been asserted in accordance with the Copyright, Designs and Patents Act 1988.

This edition published by
The Orion Publishing Group Ltd
Orion House
5 Upper St Martin's Lane
London WC2H 9EA

An Hachette UK company
A CIP catalogue record for this book is available from the British Library

ISBN 978 1 4719 0882 8

www.orionbooks.co.uk

Chapter One

THE NURSE SAID, "Doctor Crabtree wants to see you before you see the patient. Will you follow me, please?"

She walked ahead. Professional efficiency emanated from her in the rhythmic pound of her heels, the rustle of a starched uniform. She turned right, pushed a door open, and stood holding it.

"Mr. Lam," she announced.

I walked in, and she pulled the door shut behind me.

Dr. Crabtree had a thin nose with penetrating pin-point eyes. Looking at him, you had the impression of staring at a long, straight line with a dot on each side.

"Mr. *Donald* Lam?"

"That's right."

Long, cold fingers wrapped themselves around my hand. "Sit down."

I sat down, said, "My plane leaves in forty-seven minutes."

"I'll try to be brief. You've come to get Mrs. Cool?"

"Yes."

"What do you know about her condition?"

"Not much. She had flu and pneumonia. The doctor in Los Angeles suggested this sanitarium for a long rest."

"Did he tell you why?"

"No."

"You're her partner?"

"An employee."

"She operates a detective agency?"

"Yes."

"And left you in complete charge?"

"Yes."

1

"She has a very high opinion of you, Mr. Lam, a regard which amounts to affection."

"The pay checks don't show it."

He smiled. "Well, I want you to know about her condition. I don't want to alarm her unnecessarily so I'm not telling her. But *if it should become necessary*, I want you to get her Los Angeles doctor to tell her."

"What about her condition?"

"You knew, of course, how much she weighed?"

"Not exactly. She told me once that everything she ate turned to fat. She said she could go on a diet of pure water and put on weight."

The doctor took it literally. "Oh, hardly," he said. "What she undoubtedly meant was that her digestive enzymes are highly efficient, and she—"

"Squeezes the last drop of nourishment out of every bite of food."

"Well, something like that."

"That's Bertha," I said. "She would."

He studied me for a minute. "I've given her a rigid diet to follow."

"She won't follow it."

"It's up to you to see that she does."

"I can't. I've got my hands full."

"She's let herself get in a deplorable condition so far as weight is concerned."

"She just doesn't care," I said. "She tried to keep thin until she found her husband was two-timing her, then she let him have his friends, and she had her potatoes and desserts. Anyway, that's what she once told me. After he died, she kept right on eating."

"Well, she's down to a reasonable size now, and she *must hold that weight*. After all, you know, her heart isn't going to stand up forever under the strain of carrying around an enormous burden of flesh such as she was carrying. There's not only the extra exertion due to the added weight, but each pound of fat requires yards of capillaries to keep it supplied with blood."

"Have you talked with Mrs. Cool about that?"

"Yes."

"What does she say?"

I could see indignation in his eyes. "She told me I could go to hell—I mean literally, Mr. Lam."

"I'm not surprised."

He pressed a button. The nurse promptly opened the door.

"Mr. Lam is calling for Mrs. Cool. She's ready to leave?"

"Yes, Doctor."

"Very well."

"The bill paid?" I asked him, taking the statement he'd mailed to the office out of my pocket.

He avoided my eyes. "It's been settled. Mrs. Cool made a protest, and we adjusted the—er—fees."

I followed the nurse down a long corridor and up a flight of stairs. She paused before a swinging door. I pushed it open, and Bertha Cool said, "Get the hell out of here! I've paid my bill, and I won't have any more thermometers— Oh, it's Donald! You're a sight for sore eyes. Come on in, lover. Well, don't stand there staring like that. Come in. Pick up my bag, and let's get the hell out of this place. Of all the—well, *what's* the matter?"

I said, "I hardly knew you."

"I hardly know myself. I lost it while I was sick, and the doctor says I can't put it back on. Nuts to him. Do you know what I weigh, Donald Lam? A hundred and sixty. Think of it. I can't wear a single stitch of clothes I've got to my name."

"You look fine."

"Bosh! That's some more of that hooey the doctor's been handing out. Told you to flatter me, didn't he, Donald? Did the old croaker tell you confidentially that my pump couldn't stand the strain?"

3

"What gave you that idea?" I asked.

"I'd be a hell of a detective if I couldn't read the mind of a string bean like him. Asking about when the plane got in, when I expected you to get here, and telling the nurse that he'd like to see you as soon as you arrived. Bosh! Stuff and nonsense! What are you doing with the agency, lover? Are you making any money out of it? Bertha's been under a big expense, and we've simply *got* to watch every penny. And do you know what that income-tax man did? My God, Donald, it's all right to be patriotic, but I don't want to pay for their whole damn rearmament program. I—"

I picked up the bag and said, "The plane leaves at ten o'clock. I have a cab waiting outside, and—"

"A cab! Waiting outside!"

"Yes."

"Well, why didn't you say so? Here you've been chinning while the taximeter is clicking off money. Is that any way to help me meet expenses? You're a nice enough boy, Donald, but you think money grows on bushes. The way you throw it away, you—"

The nurse held out her hand as Bertha Cool was striding out of the door. "Good-by, Mrs. Cool, and good luck."

"Good-by," Bertha said, without looking back. She went marching down the corridor at double-quick.

I said, "He isn't charging us for waiting time."

"Oh," she said, and slowed her pace.

We went down the stairs, and the taxi driver took Bertha's bag.

"Airport?" he asked.

"Airport," I said.

Bertha settled back against the cushions. "What about that Gilman case, Donald?"

"It's closed."

"Closed? How am I going to make any money when you close the only decent case—"

"We found her. He paid us a bonus."

4

"Oh."

"We've got another case."

"What?"

"I don't know. A Mr. Whitewell wrote the office to have a representative meet him in Las Vegas tonight."

"Did he send any money?"

"No."

"What did you tell him?"

"I wired him I'd meet him."

"Didn't ask for an advance?"

"No. We go right through there anyway. I can stop over without it costing anything extra."

"I know, but you could have got some expense money out of this Whiteside, and—"

"Whitewell."

"All right, whatever his name is. What's he want?"

"He didn't say." I took his letter from my pocket. "Here's his letter. Notice the stationery. They could use it instead of sheet metal to build airplanes."

She took the letter. "Well, I'll stop off with you."

"No. You're supposed to rest for a week or two."

"Bosh. I'll talk with him myself."

I didn't say anything.

We got to the airport with fifteen minutes to spare. We sat around and waited for the plane. After a while it came skimming in from the east, taxied across the field, and was serviced.

A loudspeaker blared out that passengers for the west would be taken aboard the plane. A gate slid open.

The men who had been filling the plane with gasoline and giving it a routine check-up got back out of the way. The stewardess opened the plane door, and a uniformed attendant pulled away a barrier. Bertha and I got aboard. There were already half a dozen through passengers on the plane. Bertha settled herself, heaved a deep sigh, and said, "I'm starved. Donald, run back and get me a chocolate bar."

"No. There isn't time." .

"Don't be a sap. There's two minutes yet."

"I think your watch is slow."

She settled back against the cushions with a sigh. The man who was seated by the window turned to give her a surreptitious glance.

"Everything all right?" I asked.

"All right, except my knees are wobbly. There isn't any food in me. I'm a dishrag. Those doctors drained me dry."

The man next to me held out a watch and tapped the dial. It was still three and a half minutes of time for departure. "I happen to know," he said, "that this is right—to the second."

Bertha twisted her neck around. I said, "Yes, I knew her watch was a little slow. You see, mine is *exactly* right. I set it at the airport this morning."

I took out my watch and showed him. It was the same as his.

He started to say something, then changed his mind, and looked back out of the window.

They started the motors, and the engines clicked the props around at idling speed. A late passenger came bustling out to climb aboard the plane. He acted as though he'd made it by the skin of his eyeteeth. He settled down in a seat and waited for the plane to start. When it didn't take right off, he seemed surprised.

Bertha Cool looked at her watch and then turned around to glare at me. Two minutes and fifteen seconds later, the plane started taxiing down the field.

After we got up off the ground, and the roar of the motors settled into a low, monotonous hum conducive to sleep, Bertha started to doze. The man who was beside me leaned across so that his lips were close to my ear and said, "You didn't misunderstand about the time, did you?"

"No."

He laughed. "You'll pardon me, but I'm interested in psychology."

"It's an interesting subject."

"You've been at the Springs Sanitarium?"

"She has."

"I heard what she said about the doctors and the wobbly knees. Seems husky enough."

"Yes."

He studied me for a few seconds, then settled back, and looked out of the window. After another half hour he turned to me again. "She's reducing?"

I shook my head.

He went back to his window for a while, and I settled down. A little later, I heard him turn and could feel that he was staring at me. I opened my eyes. He was watching me in frowning concentration. He shifted his eyes hastily.

I beckoned him to lean over and said in a low voice, "The doctor wants her to reduce. She's had flu and pneumonia. She's taken off about a hundred pounds. The doctor wants her to keep it off. She's never denied herself anything. She loves to eat. Now, leave me alone and let me sleep."

He seemed surprised at first, then he got the idea, and laughed. "You're all right," he said.

I dozed off for a few minutes, then woke up as we were coming in to a landing. The man next to me leaned over and tapped my knee.

The motors were throttled down now, and he lowered his voice, and asked hastily, "How long had she been so much overweight?"

"I don't know."

"You're going to have a hard time to keep her from putting it right back on."

"*I'm* not. It's her funeral."

"You're not related?"

7

"No."

He seemed disappointed for a moment, then said, "Perhaps I can help you, and at the same time try an interesting experiment in psychology. I'll bet it's been some time since any man has noticed her as a woman. I'll make up to her a bit at this stop, and you watch and see what happens."

"Don't do it on my account."

"I'd like to. It will be interesting."

"Okay. It's your party."

The plane glided into a smooth landing, skimmed over the paved runway, past the hangars, to come to a stop in front of the big administration building and passenger depot. The stewardess said, "Ten minutes at this stop." The motors were shut off, and most of the passengers trooped out.

"How do you feel?" I asked Bertha.

"I'm weak as a kitten."

"You have to expect that after your illness."

"I'm starved to death."

"Going to get out?"

"I think I will. I want some chocolate bars."

She got out, and walked into the depot, saw the cigar counter and newsstand, marched across, and bought herself two chocolate bars.

The man who had been seated next to me strolled over to her and said something. Bertha stared at him with those diamond-hard eyes of hers. He looked her over approvingly, started to move away, then turned back, and said something which made Bertha smile.

I bought a newspaper and read through the headlines. After a few minutes, the man who had been talking with Bertha moved over to stand at my shoulder and said in a low voice, "Want to make a bet?"

"No."

He laughed. "It'd be a cinch. I'll bet you anything you want she doesn't eat that second candy bar."

I folded the newspaper. "She paid a nickel for it, didn't she?"

"Yes."

"Then she'll eat it."

Chapter Two

THE PLANE DIPPED DOWN over the desert, skimmed low over a dazzling white surface spotted with clumps of sage and greasewood. The shadow cast by the big ship seemed inky black as it scudded along over the ground below. Then the wheels touched the ground. The plane settled, and taxied up to where attendants were waiting.

"This is it," I said to Bertha.

The man who was seated next to me said, with some surprise, "Are you getting off here?"

"Yes."

"So am I."

Bertha smiled at him. "That's nice. Perhaps we'll be seeing you."

"Staying long?" the man asked me as we settled ourselves in the automobile which would take us to town.

"I don't know."

"Business?"

"Yes."

Bertha Cool was up in the front seat beside the driver. The man leaned over so his lips were close to my ear.

"I take it then you aren't acquainted here in Las Vegas?"

"No."

We rode on for a while, then he said, "The Sal Sagev Hotel is a nice place to stay. Name's hard to remember until you realize that it's just Las Vegas spelled backwards. This certainly is a great town. Reno gets the advertising, but Las Vegas has just as much color as Reno. Sometimes I think more. It's more distinctive, more individual."

"I've been to both places."

"Well, you know what it's like then. I get a kick out of it."

Bertha Cool turned in the seat. "This desert air certainly makes you feel good."

The man next to me said with a little bow, "It certainly makes you *look* good. You're the picture of health."

"My war paint," Bertha said.

"That sparkle in your eyes didn't come from a drug-store, and if you have any make-up on, it's simply gilding the lily. Persons who have your smooth, fine skin texture don't need make-up."

It had been a long time since Bertha had heard anything like that. I looked for her to tell him off. Instead she tried a smile. It melted into a simper as she turned around to face the windshield.

At the Sal Sagev Hotel, Bertha Cool inscribed her scrawl on the register. The man said, "That's interesting. I'm to meet the representative of a man by the name of Cool."

Bertha looked at him. "You're Whitewater?" she asked suddenly.

"Whitewell," I amended.

He stared in surprise. "But—but—I—" He turned to me. "Are you Lam?"

I nodded.

"Don't tell me that B. Cool is a woman."

Bertha said, "I run the agency under the name of B. Cool because it saves a lot of explanation."

Whitewell said, "Let's go upstairs and talk. Your room, Mrs. Cool?"

"Yes," she said, "in ten minutes."

His room was a floor below our rooms. After he'd left the elevator, Bertha said, "He's nice."

"Uh huh."

"Refined—sort of distinguished looking."

"Uh huh. Aren't you going to eat that chocolate bar?"

"Not now, lover. I have a little headache. I'll save it. Run along to your room, but be sure you're back in ten minutes. I don't want to keep Mr. Whitewell waiting."

"I'll be there."

I washed up, and got to the door of Bertha's room in exactly nine and one-half minutes. Whitewell came down the corridor just as I knocked.

Bertha let us in. She smelled of hand lotion and toilet water. "Come right in, Mr. Whitewell," she said. "Come right in and make yourself comfortable. Donald, sit over there in that chair."

We sat down. Whitewell glanced quizzically at me, and said, "He isn't exactly the type I'd expected."

Bertha dragged a coy smile out of moth balls, draped it over her face, and said, in a voice that sounded kittenish, "And *I* surprised you, too, didn't I?"

"Very much. I simply can't picture a dainty, refined woman in such a business. Don't you find it sordid?"

"Oh, not at all," Bertha said in stilted tones of mealy-mouthed politeness. "It's really *very* interesting. Of course, Donald takes over the sordid part. What was it you wanted us to do?"

"I want you to find a young woman."

"Donald's good at that. He just finished one of those cases."

"Well, this is a little different."

Bertha asked cautiously, "Are you her father?"

"No. I'm the father of a young man who is very much concerned—too much concerned, in fact."

We waited for him to go on. He crossed his knees, clipped the end off a cigar, and asked, "Mind if I smoke?"

"Oh, *please* do," Bertha said. "I like to see a man smoke a cigar. It's so thoroughly masculine."

He lit the cigar, carefully dropped the match into a tray, and said, "I have an only son, Philip. I run an advertising agency. Philip is coming in with me. I'm going to incorporate the business. I intended to give Philip a half interest as his wedding present."

"That's nice."

"You see, he didn't care much about settling down in an office. Perhaps I've been too indulgent. But when he fell in love, it changed all that. He was simply crazy over this young woman. She worked as secretary to one of the officials in an airplane factory and is strong for work and self-reliance. She imbued Philip with her ideas, and he suddenly decided he wanted to take his coat off and dig in. It was a miraculous transformation."

"Must have made you feel pretty good."

"It did—in a way—but—"

"Didn't you want him to marry her?"

"At first, I didn't want him to marry anyone until he'd become settled in a career. He's twenty-eight, and has never done anything except play and travel. I could never get him interested in hard routine work."

"I see. What's happened to the woman?"

"Two days before the wedding, on the tenth, to be exact, she disappeared."

"Leave any notes or anything?"

"Not a thing. She simply vanished into thin air, and hasn't been heard from since."

"If you didn't want him to get married, why not let it go at that?" Bertha asked. "She had some reason for leaving. It's probably something that would make her—well, even less desirable as a daughter-in-law."

Whitewell made a little gesture with his hand. "I've thought of all that."

"What's the answer?"

"Philip. I told you she'd completely changed him. Frankly, I'm opposed to the match. But the circumstances surrounding her disappearance are such that I simply *have* to find her—for Philip's sake if for nothing else. Philip isn't sleeping; he isn't eating. He's going around in a half daze, losing weight, and looking like the devil."

Bertha said, "All right, Donald will find her."

He turned to me.

"Tell me all you know," I said.

"As I've said, Corla was employed as secretary to one of the executives in the Randolf Aircraft Company. She lived with another girl in an apartment. On the day of her disappearance, she seemed moody and distraught. The girl with whom she was living tried to find out what was the matter. Corla said everything was all right.

"About ten minutes past eight, on the morning of the tenth, she started for work. She showed up on the job. Her employer said she seemed the same as usual, except she was very quiet. She'd already given notice that she was going to leave as soon as they could find someone to take her place. She and Philip were going to defer their honeymoon until later. Corla was exceedingly efficient as a secretary, and her employer had tried on several occasions to get her to remain on the job. I'm mentioning this because I want you to understand how thoroughly conscientious she was in regard to her work. Even if something had happened to make her take a run-out on Philip, she wouldn't have left her employer in the lurch."

"Go ahead," Bertha said.

"She took dictation until about ten o'clock, then she started transcribing. Among the letters she had taken was a very important and confidential communication, dealing with a new model plane. Also there were some interoffice memos which were important and confidential.

"Her boss stepped out of the office after he'd finished his dictation to have a brief conference with one of the other executives. The conference lasted about twenty minutes. When he returned, he noticed that Corla was not at her desk. A sheet of paper was in the typewriter. She'd started to write the first letter, but had only transcribed a few words. She'd stopped typing in the middle of a sentence.

"Her employer thought she'd gone to the restroom. He went on into his office, sat down at his desk, and started work. About fifteen minutes later, he thought of another letter that had to go out, and pressed the buzzer for Corla. When she didn't show up, he went out to the outer office and found things just as they were when he had come in.

"About ten or fifteen minutes later, he summoned one of the other secretaries and sent her into the restroom to see if Corla was ill. Corla wasn't there. They've never found a trace of her from that time on. Her handbag was lying on her desk. There were fifty-odd dollars in it in currency, every cent the girl had in the world. She didn't have a bank account. Her lipstick, powder, rouge, keys, everything, were in that bag."

"The police were notified?" I asked.

"Yes. They didn't do anything."

"Any clues?"

"Only one."

"What is it?"

"According to her roommate, Corla had been feeling radiantly happy up until twenty-four hours before her disappearance. I have, therefore, tried to find out something about what happened in that last twenty-four hours. The only thing that I can find that's at all unusual is that the morning prior to her disappearance she received a letter. Now, that letter was from someone named Framley in Las Vegas, Nevada."

"How is that known?"

"The landlady distributes mail to the apartments. Her maiden name was *Franley*—with an 'n.' Her story is that she wouldn't think of scrutinizing the mail received by her tenants except for the sole purpose of ascertaining which letter goes to which apartment."

"No, of course not," Bertha said sarcastically. "She wouldn't *think* of looking over their mail."

Whitewell smiled briefly, said, "She claims that the name, Framley, in the upper left-hand corner was so much like her own maiden name that she thought for a moment it had been written by some of her family. Then she saw that it was an 'm' instead of an 'n' in the name."

"And she noticed it was from Las Vegas?"

"Yes."

"What address in Las Vegas?"

"She doesn't remember."

"Remember the first name, whether it was a man or a woman?"

"No, only that it was from Framley, Las Vegas. That, of course, is a very slender clue, but it's the only clue we have. There's nothing in the facts surrounding her disappearance to help us."

"How about her notebook?" I asked. "The shorthand notebook with the notes on the important and confidential—"

"Lying right there on her desk," he said. "If that had been missing, I could have got some action from the F.B.I., but there's absolutely nothing to indicate that her position had anything whatever to do with her disappearance. Apparently it's purely a private matter."

"And you think there's a person named Framley in Las Vegas who knows something about her disappearance?" Bertha asked.

Whitewell said, "Yes, Mrs. Cool. There's a Helen Framley who lives here in Las Vegas. That is, she's been here for the last few weeks."

"You've been to her?" I asked.

"What makes you think I've been to her?" he inquired cautiously.

I said, "Once you'd located her, you'd hardly pay money to a detective agency unless you'd already tried getting the information yourself—and failed."

He didn't answer immediately. He took the cigar out of his mouth, studied it for several seconds, then shifted his position in the chair, and said, "Frankly, I did. It happens that I have some friends here, the Dearbornes. Ever heard of them?"

"I don't know anyone in Las Vegas," I said.

He said, "Mrs. Dearborne is a *very* close friend. Her daughter, Eloise, is quite attractive—for a long time I had hoped that Philip would realize just how attractive."

"He hasn't?"

"Well, they're friends. I had hoped that friendship would ripen into something deeper. I think it would have if it hadn't been for Miss Burke."

"Anyone else in the Dearborne family?"

"Ogden Dearborne, a young man who's employed in the powerhouse at the Boulder Dam. Amateur aviator. Owns a quarter interest in a plane."

"That's all?"

"Yes, just the three."

"And you got one of them to look up Helen Framley?"

"Yes. Ogden made an investigation. I called him on the telephone, asked him to try and find out about a person named Framley. If he could locate such a person, to try and find out what this person knew about Corla. He learned there was a Helen Framley in the city."

"Did he locate her?" Bertha asked.

"Yes. He found Helen Framley—and that's all the good it did him."

"What happened?" Bertha asked.

"Miss Framley told him she hadn't written any letter, that she had no idea who Corla was or where she was, and didn't want to be questioned about anything pertaining to her, that she'd never even heard of Corla Burke."

"Was she telling the truth?" Bertha asked.

Whitewell said, "I don't know. Ogden seemed to think she was. There's something very evasive and mysterious about the young woman. That's why I wanted a professional detective on the job."

"How about the police?" Bertha asked. "You said they weren't interested?"

He moved his shoulders. "Just another missing person

so far as they're concerned. They're going through the motions of trying to locate her, but that's all. They insist that a certain percentage of young women who disappear that way are either going to have a baby or are running away with some man. They seemed to think Corla was really in love with someone else, had decided to marry Philip because he looked like a good catch, and then had changed her mind."

"Would he be a good catch?" Bertha asked.

"Some mothers have so considered him," Whitewell said dryly.

"And you want Donald to break through on this Framley girl?"

"I want him to find out what happened to Corla, why she disappeared, where she is now."

"Just what do you want him to find?" Bertha asked.

"I want to establish that her disappearance was voluntary. I'm hoping the reason back of it will not only set my son's mind at rest, but make him realize the advantages of strengthening his friendship with Eloise Dearborne. After what's happened, I feel Corla wouldn't be exactly the sort I'd want as a daughter-in-law—too much notoriety—this disappearance business— Bah! She's a nice girl, but the Whitewells can't stand for anything like that."

Bertha said, "Donald will turn Helen Framley inside out. Girls fall for Donald, and fall hard."

Whitewell looked approvingly at Bertha. "I'm very well satisfied indeed," he said, "that your organization is exactly what I want—although I'd hardly expected to find a woman at the head of a detective agency, nor such an attractive woman."

I asked, "Have you a picture of Corla Burke?"

He nodded.

"I'll want it, also a description, also an introduction to Ogden Dearborne. You can telephone him and tell him I'll be out. Ask him to tell me anything I want to know."

Whitewell thought for a moment, then said, "Yes, I guess that will be the best way."

"And the address of Helen Framley if you have it."

"I'll write that out for you."

"Got that picture handy?"

He took two photographs from his inner pocket, and passed them over. One of them was a small-sized studio photograph of a girl with light hair, a slightly turned-up nose, and wistful eyes. The other was a snapshot. The shadows were pretty dark. The camera had been slightly out of focus, but it showed a girl on the beach in a bathing-suit. The camera had caught her just as she was reaching to throw a beach ball. She was laughing, and her mouth showed even rows of regular teeth. Her eyes were too shaded and blurred to give expression, but there was something in the poise of the figure the camera had caught, a dashing verve, a zest for life. Such a girl would never be quiescent, would never settle down. She was thoroughly volatile. She'd make mistakes as she went through life, but she'd keep moving.

I put the pictures in my pocket. "Don't forget to call the Dearbornes and tell them that I'll be out to see Ogden."

"I could run you down there and—"

"No. I'd prefer to go by myself."

"All right."

"Donald," Bertha said, "works very fast."

Whitewell said, "I think I am to be congratulated." He was looking steadily at Bertha as he spoke.

Bertha lowered her eyes. I'd never seen an expression on her face like that in all the time I'd been with her. She looked coy.

"What's all this going to cost me?" Whitewell asked.

Bertha's face changed as though someone had jerked off a mask. "Twenty-five dollars a day and expenses."

"Isn't that high?"

"Not for the service we give."

"I understood a private detective—"

"You're not hiring a detective, but an agency. Donald will be out on the firing line. *I'll* be in the office, but very much on the job."

"At that figure," Whitewell said, "it seems to me you should guarantee results."

Bertha's eyes glittered into his. "What the hell do you take me for?" she asked.

He said, "There's got to be some limit."

Bertha said, "We'll keep the expenses down."

"How about expenses for entertainment?"

"There won't be any. And we'll want two hundred dollars in advance."

Whitewell started making out his check. "If you can either find her or get proof that she left of her own free will within a week, I'll give you a bonus of five hundred dollars. And if you can find her, I'll make it an even thousand."

Bertha looked across at me. "You get that, Donald?"

I nodded.

"Well, get out and start working. I may have been cooped up in a sanitarium for six months, but I don't need any help to sign a receipt."

Chapter Three

PURPLE SHADOWS WERE CREEPING across the desert. The air was clear as gin, dry as a piece of new blotting paper. It was early spring, but none of the men wore coats, except an occasional tourist.

Las Vegas keeps to the traditions of western towns by having one main street which shoots the works. A few cash-and-carry grocers and businesses that people will search out hang on to the side streets. Two main districts branch out at each end of this main street: one of them a two-mile-long collection of tourist camps containing some of the best air-conditioned auto cabins in the country. At the other end, like the arm of a big Z, is the stretch of houses where women sit around—waiting.

The length of the main street is sprinkled with gambling-casinos, eating-places, hotels, drugstores, and saloons. Virtually every form of gambling runs wide open. The whir of roulette wheels and the peculiar rattling clatter of the wheels of fortune were distinctly audible on the sidewalk as I walked along, taking stock of the place.

After I'd soaked up a little atmosphere, I found a taxicab, and gave the address which Whitewell had written out for me.

The house itself was rather small, but it was distinctive. Whoever had designed it had tried to break away from the conventional styling which characterized the other houses on the street.

I paid off the cab, walked up three cement steps to a porch, and rang the bell.

The young giant who came to the door had blond hair, but his face was the color of saddle leather. He looked out

21

at me from gray, sun-bleached eyes, said, "You're Lam from Los Angeles," and, at my nod, gripped my hand with lean, strong fingers.

"Come in. Arthur Whitewell telephoned about you."

I followed him into the house. The smell of cooking came to my nostrils. "My day off," he explained. "We're having dinner at five. Come on in. Try that chair over by the window. It's comfortable."

It was comfortable. It was the only really comfortable chair in the room. The whole house was like that. Little economies paved the way for a splurge on one or two items that would count. The house didn't have the stamp of poverty, but it bore unmistakable evidences of persons who wanted better things, and would make every sacrifice to possess one or two objects that would be symbols of what they wanted.

Ogden Dearborne was lean as a log, but he moved with quick, easy grace. You could see his job was outdoors in the desert, and he was young enough to have a boyish pride in his deeply bronzed skin.

A door opened. A woman came in. I got up, and Ogden said, "Mother, may I present Mr. Lam of Los Angeles—the one Arthur Whitewell telephoned about."

She came toward me, smiling graciously.

She was a woman who was still in the running. She'd taken care of her figure and her face. She might be in the late forties, perhaps in the early fifties, but she *might* have been in the thirties. She knew the pinch of self-denial, this woman. She didn't eat everything she wanted and try to keep her figure by wrapping her body with elastic. She had kept her figure by self-discipline—by going hungry.

She was brunette with eyes that glittered like polished, black marble. Her nose was long and straight, and the nostrils were so thin they seemed almost transparent.

She said, "How do you do, Mr. Lam. Anything we can do for a friend of Arthur Whitewell will be a privilege.

Won't you make our house your headquarters while you're in Las Vegas?"

It was one of those invitations that was a symbol. If I'd said yes, someone would have had to sleep on the back porch. I wasn't expected to say yes. I said very gravely, "Thank you very much. I'll probably be here only a few hours, and I'll be busy. But I appreciate your invitation."

The girl came in then. It was as though they'd been standing outside the door, timing their entrance, each one careful not to interfere with the impression the others would make.

Mrs. Dearborne went through the formula. "Eloise, I wish to present Mr. Lam of Los Angeles, the person Mr. Whitewell telephoned about."

Eloise was unmistakably the daughter of her mother. She had the same long, straight nose. The nostrils weren't quite as paper thin. Her hair was a deep auburn. Her eyes were blue, but there was the same hard leanness, the same purpose of living, the same impression of self-discipline. These women were hunters, and they had just that feline touch which the woman hunter always has. A cat, sprawling out in front of the warmth of a fireplace, looks as softly ornamental as the fur thrown about a woman's throat. The padded feet move noiselessly, and softly. But the claws are there, and it's because they're kept sheathed, they're so deadly dangerous. A dog doesn't conceal his claws, and they're only good for digging. A cat sheathes its claws, and they possess needlesharp efficiency in the problem of sustaining life by death.

"Won't you sit down?" Mrs. Dearborne asked when I had muttered the conventional formula.

We all sat down.

You could see that whatever was discussed was going to be discussed jointly—not that they distrusted Ogden's ability to report, but these people weren't the kind to trust anyone else. They wanted firsthand information. They'd all come to attend the conference. They'd planned it that way.

I said, "I'll only stay for a minute. I want to find out about Helen Framley."

"I really know virtually nothing," Ogden said.

"That's good. Then you won't have to skip over any of the details."

He smiled. "Well, I went up—"

"I think, Ogden, Mr. Lam would like to have you begin at the beginning."

"Yes," Eloise said, "your call from Arthur Whitewell."

He didn't even bother to communicate his acceptance, simply adopted their suggestion as a matter of course, something that went without saying. "I received a call from Arthur Whitewell. He was calling from Los Angeles. We've known the family for some time. Eloise met Philip in Los Angeles a year ago. He's called at the house several times. She's been entertained in Los Angeles. Arthur, you know, is Philip's father. He's—" Ogden flashed a quick glance at his mother, evidently failed to get a go-ahead signal, so said instead, "He comes through here quite frequently and drops in to spend an evening."

"What did he say over the telephone?" I asked.

"Said that a someone named Framley had sent a letter to Corla Burke. He wanted me to find this Framley and ask about what was in it. Said it had seemed to upset Miss Burke.

"I didn't have anything whatever to work on. It took me half a day to locate this party. She's living in an apartment, has only been here for two or three weeks. She said she didn't know anything about it, that she didn't know any Corla Burke, that she hadn't sent any letter, and, therefore, couldn't help me in the least."

"Then what?"

"That's all there is."

"Did Miss Framley seem frightened or evasive?"

"No, just frankly told me she didn't know anything at all about it. Seemed rather bored."

"Do you know Corla?" I asked.

His eyes shifted, not to his mother this time, but to Eloise. "I've met her. Philip introduced me."

"You knew, of course, that she and Philip were planning on getting married?"

Ogden said nothing. Eloise said, "Yes, we knew."

I said, "Whitewell gave me the address of Miss Framley's apartment. I presume he got that from you?"

"Yes."

"Do you know whether she's still there?"

"I believe she is—at least as far as I know. I haven't seen her since that time, but she gave me the impression of being settled."

"When did Arthur—Mr. Whitewell get to town?" Mrs. Dearborne asked.

"He came in on the plane with me this afternoon."

"Oh."

Eloise asked, "Do you know if Philip was planning to join him?"

"I haven't heard."

Mrs. Dearborne said confidently, "Arthur will be down after dinner."

There was just a subtle accent on the word dinner.

"What about Helen Framley herself?" I asked Ogden.

He said, "She's typical," and then gave a little laugh.

"Of what?"

"Of a type you'll find here in town."

"What sort of type?"

He hesitated as though trying to find words.

Eloise said promptly, "A tart."

Ogden said, "A man came in while I was talking with her. I think—well, he doesn't seem to be her husband, but—"

"He's living with her," Eloise interposed. "Is that what

you are trying to tell Mr. Lam, Ogden?"

"Yes," he blurted.

"After all, Ogden, Mr. Lam has to have the facts, you know."

"He's got them now," Ogden said, embarrassed.

I looked at my watch, said, "Well, thanks a lot. I'll see if I can get anything out of her."

I got up.

They all three arose. I had neither the time nor the inclination to go through the polite patter.

I said, "Well, thanks for the help. I'll talk with her," and started for the door.

Ogden let me out.

"You don't know how long Arthur Whitewell intends to be here?"

"No."

"And you didn't hear him mention whether Philip was coming?"

"No."

"If there's anything I can do, I hope you'll let me know. Good night."

"Thank you, I will. Good night."

It was four-thirty when I climbed the steps to Helen Framley's apartment and rang the bell. I rang a couple of times, then tried the apartment next door. A woman pushed her head out so quickly that I knew she'd been standing at her door listening. Evidently, she could hear Helen Framley's bell over in her apartment.

"I beg your pardon," I said. "I'm looking for Helen Framley."

"She lives in that apartment next door."

"I know, but she doesn't seem to be home."

"No. She wouldn't be."

The woman was somewhere in the forties. Her glittering, black eyes had the fidgets. They darted to my face, then away, then back, then made a quick survey of the hallway, and came back to me again.

"Know where I might find her?"

"Do you know her when you see her?"

"No. I'm investigating her nineteen-thirty-nine income tax."

"Can you fancy that—" She half turned and called over her shoulder, "Paw, did you hear that? That woman pays an income tax!"

A man's voice from the inside of the apartment said, "Uh huh."

The woman moistened her lips, took a deep breath. "Well, Lord knows as how I'm not the one to pry into a neighbor's business. Live and let live, that's my motto. Personally, I don't care *what* she does as long as she's quiet about it. I was telling my husband just the other day. The Lord knows what the world is coming to when a girl like this Framley girl can turn night into day, have men friends calling at her apartment, and stay until all hours of the night. Heaven knows what she *does!* She certainly doesn't work, and she's never up before eleven or twelve in the morning. And *I* don't think there's a night in her life she goes to bed before two o'clock. Of course, you understand I'm not saying anything against the girl, and heaven knows she's decent-appearing enough, perfectly quiet, and all that. But—"

"Where can I find her?"

"Well, mind you, I'm not one to say anything. Personally *I* can't afford to play those slot machines. They tell me they're so arranged that it's just like throwing money away. Yet three afternoons now when I've walked past the place, I've looked in and seen that girl standing in front of the slot machines at the Cactus Patch, dropping one coin after another, working the handles just as fast as she could pump her hand up and down.

"She hasn't a job, and I don't know as she's *ever* had a job. But for a girl to live a life like that—such a nice, decent-appearing girl, too—and then you tell me she pays an income tax! Well, Ah-h-h-h-l declare! How-much-did-she-pay?"

That last question was shot out at me so fast the words all ran together.

I heard steps behind the woman. A man with round shoulders, a shirt open at the neck, an unbuttoned vest flaring away from the hollow chest, pushed reading glasses up out of the way onto his forehead, and stared at me owlishly. "What's he want?" he asked the woman.

He was holding a newspaper between his thumb and forefinger. It was open at the sporting page. He had a little drooping, black mustache, and seemed comfortable and relaxed in his bedroom slippers.

"He wants to know where he can find that Framley girl."

"Why don't you tell him?"

"I *am* telling him."

He pushed her to one side, and said, "Try the Cactus Patch."

"Where's that?"

"On the main stem, a casino, big bank of slot machines. You can't miss it. Come on, Maw, mind your own business and let the girl mind hers."

He pushed the woman to one side and slammed the door.

I didn't have any difficulty finding the Cactus Patch. It preserved a fiction of having the bar and the casino in two different establishments; but both opened on the street through wide doorways, and there was a glass partition between the two. The casino had a big wheel of fortune right up in front, then a couple of roulette wheels, a crap table, and some stud poker games. There was a bingo parlor in back of that. Over on the right was a whole bank of slot machines, a double row standing side by side and containing possibly a hundred machines in all.

There were a few scattering customers here and there.

It was too early as yet for the bulk of the tourist trade to come in, but the crowd was the mixture that can be found only in a Nevada town.

Here were professional gamblers, panhandlers, touts, and some of the higher-class girls from the red-light district. A couple of the men at the bar were probably miners. Three chaps who were at the wheel of fortune might be engineers from the Boulder Dam. A small sprinkling of auto tourists wandered aimlessly around the place.

Some of these tourists were from the west and more or less familiar with Nevada. Some of them were seeing it for the first time, and their reaction to the wide-open gambling, the shirt-sleeved camaraderie of the crowd was one of gawking wonderment.

I got a dollar changed into nickels, went over to the slot machine, and started playing. It seemed as though every time the wheels clicked to a stop a lemon would be staring me in the face.

A woman was playing a two-bit machine halfway down the bank of machines. She was in the thirties, and her face was touched up like a desert sunset. She didn't register as Helen Framley. I was down to my last nickel, when two cherries clicked coins into the metal pay-off cup. Just then, a girl came in.

I said to the machine in a voice loud enough to be distinctly audible to the girl, "Don't get generous now."

She turned, looked me over, walked past without saying anything, and dropped a dime in the ten-cent machine. She got three oranges, and dimes cascaded into the cup in a jingling tune.

I could have made her Helen Framley; but she stood looking at the machine with a dazed expression of "What-do-I-do-next?" so I decided at once she was no old hand at the game. She played another dime.

A jaunty chap with quick, restless eyes and head that seemed perfectly poised on a muscular neck paused in front of the quarter machine. I watched his hands as he dropped the coin and slammed down the lever. Not a wasted motion. Everything was as smoothly graceful as though his arms had been pistons working in an oil bath.

The girl over at the dime machine called, "Oh, I must have broken something."

Her eyes shifted over toward me, but the other chap was nearest. He beat me to it. "What's the matter?"

She said, "I dropped a dime in the machine. And I guess I must have broken something. Dimes spilled out over everything—all over the floor."

He laughed easily, and moved over toward her. I noticed particularly the broad, supple shoulders, the straight line of his back, and the thin waist and narrow hips.

"You didn't break the machine—not yet. But if you keep on being lucky, maybe you will. You just won a jackpot."

He glanced over at me, and winked.

"Wish she'd show *me* how it's done," I said.

She laughed uncertainly.

The young chap got down on his hands and knees, picked up a couple of dozen dimes, scooped a handful out of the cup, and said, "Now, let's make certain there aren't any back up in there."

His fingers explored the cup.

"Nope. Everything's swell."

I caught the reflection of light gleaming from a dime on the floor. I picked it up, handed it to her, and said, "Don't overlook this one. It may be lucky."

She thanked me with a swift smile, said, "Well, I'll see if it is."

I felt someone watching me, turned around, and saw an attendant, wearing a green apron with change pockets in it, eyeing us in scowling suspicion.

The girl dropped the dime into the machine, and jerked the handle. The woman who had the gaudy face was walking out past us. She coughed as she caught the eye of the green-aproned attendant.

Apparently, it was a signal.

He came walking swiftly toward us as the whirling dials of the slot machine went "clack"-"click"-"bang"-"chunk"-"jingle"!

A tinkling shower of dimes spilled into the metal cup and overflowed into her hands.

The attendant busied himself at a machine right behind us.

The young man said, "That's the way." His laugh was easy. "Go to it, sister. You're playing a run of luck. Only you don't know it. I'll see what I can do on the two-bit machine while you tickle the dimes."

He dropped another quarter in the two-bit machine, spun the lever, and called to me, "How *you* doing, stranger?"

I said, "I've got this machine fed up to a place where it's bound to start paying off. It's so full of nickels now, it's ready to bust."

I put in a nickel and pulled the lever.

The three discs whirled in a bewildering kaleidoscope. With a click the left-hand disc stopped. A half second later, the middle one snapped into position.

I saw two bars.

The third one jarred to a stop.

A metallic click emanated from the inside of the machine, and the floodgates opened. Nickels poured out into the cup, out from the jackpot, dancing a merry jig as they spilled over my hands and dropped to the floor.

I grabbed a double handful, but they kept coming. I pushed coins down into my side pockets, cleaned out the cups, and then started looking for nickels on the floor.

The attendant said, "Perhaps I can help."

He leaned over me. Suddenly his hands shot out, and his fingers gripped my wrists.

"What's the idea?" I asked, and tried to fight free.

He said, "Come on, buddy. The manager wants to talk with you."

"What are you talking about?"

"Do you want to come the easy way, or do you want to come the hard way?"

I tried to shake myself loose and couldn't. I said, "I'm going to get these nickels on the floor. They're mine."

"*Just* a minute," he said.

His fingers slid up my sleeve, felt around my forearm.

I jerked one arm free and made a swing. He brushed the blow aside, stepped in and grabbed the lapels of my coat, pushed down so that my coat was halfway down my arms, holding them pinioned. For the moment, I was helpless. The weight of coins in the side pockets became swinging pendulums of weight which struck against me as I moved.

Back of me I could hear sounds coming from a machine, and a light tinkle as a shower of dimes hit the metal cup. A moment later, there was another clack, and this time twenty-five-cent pieces cascaded out.

The attendant twisted his fingers into my coat collar, and, getting his weight behind me, gave me a push which sent me over toward the other machine.

"Okay, buddy," he said to the man, "I'll take a look up *your* coat sleeves."

"Mine?" the young chap said.

"Yours."

I said, "What's the matter with this guy? Has he gone crazy?"

The man who was standing at the two-bit machine weaved slightly back and forth, just an inch or two at a time as he shifted his weight on the balls of his feet.

The girl said, "I'm going to quit," and started for the door.

The attendant said, "Just a minute, sister," and grabbed. She eluded him. People were crowding around.

The attendant said, "You three crooks are going to get

yours right now. The law has a date with you."

"Not with me," I said.

He moved his right shoulder. I saw a blur of motion. Something hit me on the side of the jaw. The blow jarred me all the way down my spine.

"Try that, wise guy," he said.

My eyes were jarred out of focus; but I started both fists swinging and waded in. A left landed somewhere on his face. A right grazed his temple, then a mule kicked me. I went back against the machines and felt as though a ten-story building was using me for a basement.

I looked through eyes that kept showing double distorted images of what was happening. I saw the attendant lash out with a quick right, and the weaving shoulders of the other man slid past the blow and inside. I saw his back grow rigid. I heard a meaty sound as though a butcher had slammed a leg of lamb down on the chopping-block. The attendant's head shot up in the air. His feet left the floor. For a moment, it seemed as though he was taking off like a skyrocket, and I looked to see him go through the roof.

He rocked the whole bank of slot machines as he hit.

I heard a policeman's whistle, then some big man had me by the arm. He slammed me around some, and I tried to fight back.

A man's voice came through to my consciousness. "—one of them. We've had an eye on 'em for two weeks now. They've looted the place clean. Working a cup. It's a racket."

"Come along," the law said. A big hand twisted my coat collar and jerked.

I wanted to talk, but I couldn't get words to come the way they should. The girl who had been playing the machines and the man who had hit the attendant had gone. The attendant lay on the floor. His eyelids were quivering, and I could see the whites of his eyes beneath those fluttering lids.

There were faces gathered around in a circle of open-mouthed curiosity.

The hand twisted my coat, hard. I took a deep breath and managed to start talking, but the words sounded funny, as though I was listening to someone else say some of the things I wanted to say.

"I'm from Los Angeles. I haven't been in Las Vegas for an hour. I came in on the Salt Lake plane. I never saw this place before. I played a dollar's worth of nickels into the machine, and hit the jackpot with the last nickel."

There was silence. Gradually my head was clearing. The man who was holding me glanced at a newcomer who looked as though he might be the manager of the place. The manager said, "Talk's cheap. These crooks always have a swell alibi cooked up." But his voice didn't have quite the ring of assurance it should have had.

The green-aproned attendant who lay sprawled out on the floor stirred, got up on one elbow, and looked past us with glassy eyes that seemed to stare right through the wall of the building.

The manager bent over him. "Now listen, Louie, we can't muff this. Are you all right?"

The attendant mumbled something.

"Look, Louie, we've got to be sure now. Is this one of them? Is this the guy?"

The manager pointed at me.

The groggy attendant said, "That's him. He's the brains of the gang. They're cup-and-wire workers. I've seen 'em before. This guy's the leader. The others came in first an' cased the joint."

"Come on," the law said to me. "You're going places."

My head had cleared now. "This," I said, "is going to cost somebody money."

"Okay, let it cost. Come on and take a ride. We want to show you our city. Coming in on the afternoon plane the way you did, you haven't had a chance to see it."

The big hand of the law caught my coat again, started pushing me toward the door.

The manager said, "Wait a minute, Bill," and to me, "What's your name?"

"Lam—Donald Lam. I'm in business in Los Angeles."

"What sort of business?"

"I don't care to tell you that."

They laughed then.

I said to the officer, "You'll find a card in the wallet in my right-hand hip pocket, but don't read it out loud."

The officer pulled a wallet out of my pocket, opened it, and took a look at my identification card as a private detective. That sobered him. He showed the wallet to the manager. I saw the manager's face change expression.

"Did you say you came in on that Salt Lake plane?"

"Yes."

He said, "Bring him over here, Bill."

The curious faces melted away from in front of us and closed in behind as though they had been wisps of fog, clinging to a road. The manager picked up a telephone, got his number, said, "Was there a Donald Lam came in on that plane from Salt Lake today? . . . There was? . . . A chap in the twenties, regular features, wavy hair, weight about a hundred and twenty-seven pounds, about five-feet-five. . . . The hell! . . . Okay, thanks."

He hung up the telephone, said to the officer, "Bring him upstairs, Bill."

He opened a door. We climbed stairs to a cool office which looked out through broad windows on the constantly increasing activity of the town's main stem. We all three sat down. The manager picked up a telephone and said, "Get Louie up here right away."

He hung up the telephone, and almost immediately I heard steps on the stairs, then the door opened, and the attendant, still looking punch groggy, came into the room.

"Take a good look at this chap," the manager said.

The attendant took a good look at me, said, "He's the new guy they ran in to make the clean-up. That means he's the brains of the gang. He was cupping the machine."

"How do you know?"

"I could tell by the way he was standing, the way he leaned against the machine."

"You didn't *see* any cup?"

"Well, no. But he was with the other two, talking with the girl."

"Where are the other two?"

The attendant blinked his eyes and started to turn his head. Then he stopped quickly as though something hurt him when he tried to turn his neck.

"They got away."

The manager said impatiently, "What the hell? I hired you because you said you could handle this stuff. You're supposed to know all the rackets and all of the gangs who work 'em."

The attendant was getting the cobwebs out of his brain. "Listen," he said, "that guy's a prize fighter. I didn't make him at first. Then when he threw that punch, I recognized his style. That's Sid Jannix. He was in line for a title once, but they framed him. He's good—plenty good." He looked at the officer, and then at me, and said, "This guy is the brains—but he's a new one on me."

"This is a hell of a time to say so," the manager said. "Why didn't you grab their cups so you'd have some evidence?"

The attendant was silent.

"Was that what you were trying to do when you grabbed my wrist and felt up my arms and jerked my coat off?" I asked.

The manager's face kept getting darker. The attendant didn't say anything.

After a moment, the manager said disgustedly, "Okay, Louie, get the hell out of here."

Louie left without a word.

The manager turned to me. "Now," he said, "this is too bad."

"For you."

"For one of us," he admitted. "I'm in so deep, *I'm* not going to quit. Suppose you tell me about you."

"What about me?"

"Who you are, what you're doing here, and how I know *this* isn't a racket."

"What isn't a racket?"

"The whole play. You can't stick me without bringing your life's history into court, anyway, so you may as well spill it now."

I said, "I'm a private detective. I'm here on business. I'm employed by the B. Cool Detective Agency. Bertha Cool and a client are up in the Sal Sagev Hotel right now. Give her a ring if you want to. Bertha Cool's been in a sanitarium for months. This is her first day out. I've been running the Los Angeles office. I'm here to try and find a certain person. The person was out when I called. I killed time playing the slot machines." They tried to interrupt me, but I droned right on. "I put in a dollar without getting a smell. The last nickel gave me two cherries. I scooped out the winnings, and the next nickel hit the jackpot. I never saw either of those other two people in my life, and I don't know a damn thing about the slot-machine racket. I'm telling you all this because I don't want you to be able to stand up in front of the jury and say that I didn't co-operate by giving you everything. It's your move now. Go ahead."

The manager looked at me for a minute, then picked up the telephone, and said, "I'm calling your bluff."

"Go ahead."

He called the Sal Sagev Hotel. "You got a Bertha Cool registered there?" he asked. "That's right, from Los Angeles. Let me talk with her."

He held the phone a moment, then suddenly said to the officer, "Better make this official, Bill, just in case."

"Uh huh," the officer said.

His thick fingers enveloped the telephone. He swallowed the receiver in his big hand, and raised it up to his left ear. Watching his face, I could tell when Bertha came on the line.

"This is Lieutenant William Kleinsmidt of the Las Vegas police. You've got a man working for you whose first name is Donald? . . . 1 see. . . . What's his last name? . . . How about a description?"

He held the phone and looked at me as though checking things off. Once he grinned, and I knew that Bertha's description would have the unmistakable salty tang that characterized all of her utterances.

"And you operate a detective agency in Los Angeles? Thanks very much, Mrs. Cool. . . . No, he hasn't done anything. I was just checking up, that's all— Well, just a minute. Hold the phone."

He clamped the palm of his right hand over the transmitter, looked up at the manager, and said, "It checks. She wants to talk with him."

The manager heaved a weary sigh. "Put him on."

The officer handed me the phone. The hard rubber was hot and moist where his big hand had been touching it.

I said, "Hello."

Bertha said, "What the hell have you done now?"

"Nothing."

"Baloney!"

I said, "I got a line on our party."

"Talked with her?"

"No."

"Well, that isn't going to get us any bonus."

"I know. She wasn't in."

"Well, what the hell have you been doing?"

I said, "I've been out to see the other people. Then I

went to see this party. She was out. I dropped in to a casino while I was waiting, and played the slot machine."

"Did what?" Bertha screamed over the telephone.

"Played the slot machine."

"What did you do that for?"

"Because this party that I'm looking for is supposed to hang around the slot machines in that joint."

"Now you listen to me, Donald Lam," Bertha yelled. "You don't have to play slot machines in order to find a woman. The trouble with you—" Suddenly her voice changed. "How much did you play?"

"Nineteen nickels without even getting a smell. I didn't even—"

She interrupted me. "And it serves you right. Don't try to charge *that* as an expense. Whenever you do any gambling, it's on your own. I'm not interested. You're—"

"And then," I interrupted, "I won three nickels with the last play."

"And then shot the three nickels I suppose," Bertha said sarcastically.

"And the last nickel," I said, "hit the jackpot."

There was silence. Then Bertha's silky voice said, "How much did you win, lover?"

"I don't know, because about that time the law came down on me. I'm supposed to have been milking the slot machines."

"Now you listen to me, Donald Lam. You're supposed to have brains. If you haven't got brains enough to keep yourself out of jail, you're fired. Can't you realize that we have to work fast?"

"Sure," I said, and hung up.

The manager looked at Lieutenant Kleinsmidt. "How does the description check, Bill?"

"It checks. She says he's a pint-sized parcel of dynamite with the nerve of a prize fighter and a punch that wouldn't jar a fly loose from a syrup jug—but he's always trying."

The manager heaved a sigh that seemed to come from his boot tops. "All right, Lam, how much?"

"For what?"

"For everything. A complete release."

"I couldn't set a price."

"You're crazy. You probably work for ten dollars a day. Fifty dollars would square everything. You—"

"You heard what Bertha told the officer."

"I'll make it a hundred, even money."

I got up and smoothed my clothes down. The nickels in each of my side pockets sagged the cloth of the coat. "What's your name?" I asked.

"Harvey Breckenridge. I want you to understand, Lam, there's nothing personal about this. When you're running a place such as we run, we have to contend with—"

I shoved my right hand out at him. "All right, Mr. Breckenridge, no hard feelings. After all, it's just a matter of business. I'll have my lawyer get in touch with your lawyer."

"Now listen, Lam, let's be reasonable. There are slickers who go around the country milking the slot machines. They cost us thousands of dollars every year. We keep laying for them, but they're damned hard to catch. Louie, this attendant of mine, came to me a week ago looking for a job. He said he knew all the gangs who are in the game. He was boxing champion in the Navy, and he's a little too handy with his fists. He just lost his head, that's all. I guess the guy's slap-happy. Now, why not be reasonable and—"

"I'm the one that's reasonable," I said. "You're the one that isn't. I've been exposed to ridicule. I've been humiliated. Not only that, but you called up my employer and forced me to explain the circumstances to her. She'll—"

"Oh, hell, take five hundred dollars in cash and sign a receipt and we'll call it square."

I said, "No hard feelings. It's just a matter of business," and started for the door.

He didn't say anything.

At the door, I turned. "Understand, Breckenridge, I'm not trying to stick you. If I hadn't been working on a case that was very important, I wouldn't have cared so much. But you asked me my name in front of all those people."

"That didn't hurt you any."

"The girl who was playing that dime machine was the one I was tailing. I'll have a hell of a time doing anything with her now."

That rang the bell. He said, "Hell," with more disgust in his voice than I've heard since the Republicans lost the election. "Come back and sit down."

I walked back and sat down. Lieutenant Kleinsmidt was staring at me. I said to Breckenridge, "The law's in this, too."

"What do you mean?" Kleinsmidt asked.

"You."

"The hell I am. I won't pay you a damn cent."

"You're in it just the same."

"I was following instructions," Kleinsmidt said.

"Whose?"

"His." He jerked his head toward Breckenridge.

Breckenridge said, "How much, Lam?"

"Ten thousand or nothing. I'd prefer to have it nothing."

They looked at me.

I said, "I may be here for a while. I may want some co-operation. You fellows made things hard for me while I was getting started. I just want you to understand that. You can make up for it later. That would be all I'd want."

Breckenridge held his face in a poker mask. "You kidding us?"

"No. It's on the square."

Breckenridge pushed back his chair, shot his hand across the desk, and said, "That's damn square, Lam. Shake."

I shook hands. When Breckenridge released my hand, I

saw Kleinsmidt's big paw out in front of me. I shook it, too. It was moist and hot, and it had bone-crushing strength.

"Exactly what do you want?" Breckenridge asked.

"First," I said, "I want to talk with Louie. I want to know what he knows about the girl who was playing the machines."

• Breckenridge said, "Personally, I think Louie is full of prunes. He drifted in here from San Francisco, telling me about how he'd worked in the resorts and knew all the gangs that were working on the slot machines. Evidently, he was a good man with his mitts in the Navy. That's the trouble. They've jarred his brain loose from its moorings. He's punch drunk."

I rubbed my sore face. "He's got a good wallop," I admitted.

They laughed.

The manager picked up the interoffice phone, and said, "Send Louie back up here."

Lieutenant Kleinsmidt said, "We meet lots of your kind who don't want to co-operate. We don't waste much time with them. You're different. Anything you want, just ask for it. I'll see that you get it."

Louie came back in.

Breckenridge said, "Louie, this guy is one of the family. Give him anything he wants. All of his drinks are on the house. As far as you're concerned, he owns the joint."

I could see the surprise in Louie's eyes.

I got up and said, "Thanks. I'll have a talk with Louie."

Louie looked past me to Breckenridge. "You mean *anything?*" he asked.

"Anything in the place," Breckenridge said.

Louie shifted his eyes to me.

"Come on," I said. "I want to look at the inside of a slot machine, and I want to find out how they're fixed."

Louie began to fit his clothes a lot better. "I can show

you the whole dope," he said. "There ain't anybody in the West that knows more about 'em than I do. I know all the gangs, and there ain't one of 'em can slip anything over on me. What's more, the way I handle my mitts, I don't need to take no run-around. When I see 'em cupping a machine, I give 'em the old one-two before they can ditch the evidence and—"

The manager coughed, a dry, significant, sarcastic cough.

Louie quit talking abruptly.

"Come on," I said, and pushed toward the door. I looked back over my shoulder. Breckenridge gave me a slow, solemn wink, put his thumb and forefinger to his temple, and made little circles.

"Got a machine I can play with?" I asked Louie. "I want to take it to pieces. It's five-fifteen now. I have half an hour."

"Yeah. Down in the basement," Louie said.

"All right, let's go down to the basement then."

We went down the stairs, across the casino to a back door, and down into a cool basement. Louie switched on lights. "What you want first?" he asked.

"How do they fix 'em?"

He said, "There's lots of ways. They drill 'em right here and stick in a piece of piano wire. Then the machine don't lock off after each play, and they can keep pulling the handle until they milk the machine dry.

"Or they can drill 'em, stick in a wire, and pull down the trigger that releases the gold award. Or they can take a cup and slide it up through the pay slot. They play until they get a win, and the fingers start to work. Then they shove the cup up in the fingers. That keeps 'em from closing, and they can milk all the money that's in the tube out through the pay cup."

"What's the tube?" I asked.

"Say, you don't know much about slot machines, huh?"

"Not a thing."

He looked at me, and seemed rather sheepish. He said, "I guess I stepped on my foot. No bad feelings over the sock I gave you?"

"Only my face is sore, not my feelings."

"Say, guy, you're all right. Here, let me show you something about a machine."

Louie pointed to a workbench. A slot machine was sitting on this bench. It took him only a few moments to unlock the back, take it off, unfasten a couple of catches, and lift out the internal mechanism.

"Here you are," he said.

"How does it work?"

"Simple. You drop the coin. That pulls back this little finger. You press the lever. That gives the power that starts 'em going. Here's a little time clock—right down here. That spins around, and when it comes to the first notch, that stops the first wheel. Then a bit later, the second stops, and then the third. Now, a slot machine has five clicks. The first three are the wheels. The fourth is the lock off, and the fifth is when the pay-off snaps. If you don't get those five clicks, your machine's gone flooey. Get me?"

I looked at the three dials with the strings of different figures.

"Those pictures don't mean nothing," Louie said. "The whole thing comes from these notches in the back. You can see where this shovel slides into the slot in the first one, then the second, and then the third. It's the notches that count, and the notches are in the back."

"And how about this tube?"

"That tube is always filled with coins. After it gets filled, the overflow goes into the jackpot and down into the box in the machine. You've got two jackpots. After the first pays off, the second comes into the pay-off position and the coins begin feeding into the first one again."

"Then once the wheels have started spinning, the clock in back determines the time when they're going to stop?"

44

"That's right. It's a question of timing. That's what it is in everything: golf, baseball, tennis, fighting—anything."

I studied the mechanism of the machine.

Louie said, "Timing! That's the way I won the championship bout in the Navy."

He danced out into the middle of the cement floor, ducked his head down, raised his left shoulder, and started making jabs at an imaginary opponent, ducking and weaving around, dancing lightly on the balls of his feet, the leather soles of his shoes making a peculiar shuffling sound as they slid over the cement. I let him go because I wanted to study the machine.

"Now, lookit," Louie said.

I looked up.

"He comes at me with a hard left twice, like this, see?" And Louie lashed out with his left. "You get me?" he asked anxiously, pausing in his shuffle to look over his shoulder, his left arm still outstretched.

"I get you, but let's get back—"

"All right, then the third time I'm waiting for it. I throw up a block. And what happens? He outguesses me. His right comes across like a pile driver. I manage to duck and—"

"Snap out of it!"

But Louie started dancing again, all around the cellar, his feet stirring up a continual fog of dust as he weaved his shoulders, lashing out quick blows and battering out a blow-by-blow account of his fight. I couldn't stop him. He was in the ring and I couldn't get him out. I finally gave up and waited for him to finish. He ended up right in front of me.

"Come on over here. I want to show you. I won't hurt you, just get yourself in position. That's right. Now shoot out a right at my chin. Go ahead. Shoot it out. Don't be afraid. Just give me the works."

"I'm afraid I could never do it," I said.

45

"Shucks," he said modestly. "It's easy."

"That fall *you* took upstairs doesn't seem to have hurt you at all."

The eager glow of animation faded from his eyes, left him as only a shell.

"Shucks," he said, "that was Sid Jannix. I seen him fight once. He's good—awful good. But he ain't too good. I could have taken him if I'd known who he was sooner, but you know how it is, buddy. You get careless in this business. You get so you don't want to miss a punch. You try to get set, and get in just the position you want before you turn it loose. You can't get set on Sid Jannix. You can't get set on any pug that's up on his toes. He just threw a fist at me, that's all. Now let me show you something, buddy. You don't hit right. You hit with your arms. You can't do that. You gotta sink your body in back of the blows. Here, let me show you."

"I want to look at this slot machine."

"Okay, buddy, sure. I ain't tryin' to butt in. I just thought I'd teach you something, that's all."

"Thanks," I said.

"What else do you want to know about the machine, buddy?"

"What are your chances of winning?"

"Pretty good. Of course, if you was to play a hundred dollars right across the board, you'd probably only get forty of it back. That sixty would represent the profit for the house. But, in playing that hundred, you might feed five bucks into the machine without getting over fifty cents back. Then you might play fifty cents, and get four dollars back—see? That's the way it works. Guys don't play slot machines the way they play the stock market, putting a bunch of dough in it. They just come in and try 'em out to see if they're lucky. Or in a restaurant if they get some change in nickels, they put ten or fifteen cents into the slot machines. Then maybe they get hot and pull all the nickels out of their pocket and play 'em. They'll get a few wins, and they play back their winnings. That's why they keep machines around restaurants rollered so heavy. They don't have to let the customer win. Up here, we figure it's good advertisement to hear the coins jingle in the pay-off cup once in a while; but that's not saying we can afford to donate to charity."

"What do you mean by a machine being rollered?"

He pointed to a bulky piece of metal clamped over one of the sprockets and screwed into place. "See the roller on that first wheel?"

I nodded.

"Well, that's a roller. That's on one of the oranges. Now, you see there's three oranges on the first wheel, four on the second, and six on the third. That makes a man feel good. You see, the machine stops just that way. One—two—three. Now suppose he gets an orange on the first, and an orange on the second. He's got time to do a little thinking before the third wheel clicks, and if it's an orange, he thinks he made it come just by thinking about it. That's why there's so many oranges on the third wheel. Six out of twenty. Get me? There's twenty figures on each wheel. Well, with six oranges on the third wheel, there's about one chance out of three that it'll stop on an orange *after* you've got the first two oranges. That's the trick. Getting the first two oranges.

"Now that's where the roller comes in. Ain't you never played a slot machine and seen a pay-off figure sorta hesitate in front of the window, and then shoot on by, and the wheel lock with a hell of a heavy click on the next figure? Well, buddy, when that happens, you've been rollered off. Take this machine, for instance. There's three oranges on the first wheel. That means you got about one chance in seven of gettin' your first orange. All right, we put a roller on this orange slot, and that means there's only two oranges left. Get me? Two oranges out of twenty. That means you only stand one chance in ten of getting your first orange. You might not think there was much difference between one chance in seven and one chance in ten, but when you're givin' a machine steady play, it sure shows up in the old bread basket."

I looked the machine over. "How do they tamper with them?"

"They carry a little drill, and they drill a hole right through here. See? Now you notice these rivets here? Well, they plug up that little hole with a fake rivet head. Then if a man looks at the machine, he don't see nothing wrong. Get me? A man don't never bother to count the rivets in a machine. Just one extra rivet don't show up at all."

"Then what?" I asked.

"Then after they get the machine bored and riveted, they'll come back. Usually, they have a gang of three or four. There's usually a hell of a good-looking jane in the gang. They pretend to be liquored up, and they're having a great time. They get all excited and crowd around the machine. And one of the good-looking janes will slip that false rivet out. They got a piece of stiff wire that they stick in that hole, and it's got a little twister on the end, and they turn it. Now, if they've drilled that hole in the right place, when they turn that wire, it pushes this metal finger back, and they can keep on playing the machine without putting no coin in. If the machine ain't got a cheese knife—or if the cheese knife has been disconnected."

"What's a cheese knife?" I asked.

"Well, that's something that rolls over the nickel. It won't release unless it first slides over the round part of a nickel. But they're pretty delicate, and they're always jamming, so lots of places take 'em off. Then lots of times they get stuck and won't work at all."

"You said something about a cup."

"That's different," he said. "That goes up in the pay-off mechanism. They stick it up through the cup where the coins come out, and when those little metal fingers that release just so many coins start working, they slip this cup up and jam 'em open. Then the coins start spilling out until they empty the tubes."

"You keep the machines here rollered?" I asked.

"Sure, they're rollered. Particularly those near the front of the line. You get me? We figure that the customer that just drops by the slot machine and only puts in four or five nickels is the guy that's going to quit after he's put in those four or five nickels. He's just playing to be doing something. May be a tourist who wants to say he's been out in the wild West where they have gambling running wide open. Get me?"

"But why not let those people win occasionally? I think that would be good bait."

"Nope," he said. "The percentage is against you. They've only got four or five nickels in their pocket to lose. They ain't going to change fifty-cent pieces or dollars into nickels. They're just going to play with what they've got. All right, we let 'em win on a couple of cherries, and maybe sometimes on three oranges. But the heavy stuff is all rollered off. There ain't no percentage in letting a man win five bucks on a jackpot if the limit he'd let *you* win is twenty cents. Get me?"

I nodded.

"Now then, the machines toward the back we don't roller so heavy. The people that get back that far are the slot-machine addicts. They get a fad for it, just like drinking whisky or anything else. They keep thinking that the next machine farther down is going to be a little hotter. Well, they *are* hotter. They stand more chance there, and those people stand a chance of making a big winning. That brings 'em back.

"You get me? Suppose a party keeps working his way down the slot machines? Well, we've got four or five nickel machines, then a dime machine, then a nickel machine, then a two-bit machine, then two nickel machines, and another two-bit machine. Well, by the time he's got down toward the end of the line, he's paid a bunch of money to us. Because those first machines are all rollered so heavy, he can't win nothing big. Now then, what do we care if we give him an even break on the last machine? We're already working on velvet. Maybe if he wins a jackpot, he'll put the coins in his pocket and walk out, but don't worry. He's a slot-machine addict, and next day, he'll be back. And the next and the next and the next. That's why I figured you for a crook when you won the jackpot on that nickel machine up near the front. Ordinarily, your jackpot has two bars on the first wheel. That gives you one chance in ten. Then there's one on the middle wheel, and one on the third wheel. Get it? One chance in twenty on each of those wheels, and one chance in ten on the first wheel. Now, on that nickel machine, we'd rollered off one of the bars on the first wheel, so figure how much chance you've got of hitting a big jackpot. Right away, I thought you was slicking the machine."

"What about that girl?" I asked.

"The jane, brother, was a slicker."

"How do you know, Louie?"

"How does a guy know anything? Shucks, I had her spotted ever since I came here."

"How long's that been?"

"About ten days or two weeks. She's been a slot-machine fiend. She played it on the square at first, all right. That's where she threw me off guard, and she's such a cute little trick. She certainly did play me for a sucker. She'd play those machines. I don't think she was doing much more than breaking even. So I'd look the machines over after she left, and there wouldn't be nothing wrong with 'em. Well, she fooled me all right. She drilled a couple of machines after I'd classed her as okay. She'd been milkin' them for a couple of days, and then she and this boy friend of hers showed up for the big clean-up tonight. They were going to cup 'em dry. And if it hadn't been for you winning that big jackpot on the machine that was rollered off, I'd have had 'em."

"Where you from?"

"N'Orleans originally. I came here from San Francisco. I looked over the machines, and seen about half of 'em was drilled. I went up to Harvey Breckenridge and told him he was a sucker, that they was milking him dry. So after I'd talked with him awhile, and showed him the machines, he give me the job of taking charge of the joint. I told him I knew all the mobs that was working the machines. And I did, too. I didn't know Sid Jannix had gone into the machine racket, and this jane is a new one. But all the regulars I know. You understand they ain't so bad here in Las Vegas as they are in California."

"Why not?"

"Because it's illegal in other states. Here in Las Vegas it's legal."

"What's that got to do with it?"

"Be your age, buddy. Be your age. Suppose the machines is illegal, and you catch a guy cupping the pay-off? Well, you kick him out in the street and cuss him, but you don't arrest him, because he ain't stealing nothing, and the reason he ain't stealing nothing is because you ain't got no machine, and the reason you ain't got no machine is because the law says you can't have it. Get me?"

"I get you."

"Anything else you want to know?"

"You don't know that girl's name?"

"No."

"How does she play the game? Is she on the make?"

"You mean with men?"

"Yes."

He thought for a while, scratched the fringe of dark, woolly hair around his ears, and said, "Now you got me, buddy. Y'understand Las Vegas is different from other places. Girls come here to get a divorce. They have to wait to establish a residence. It ain't a long time, when you just think of it as so much time out of a year, but when you stay here, it gets pretty long. The girls get lonesome, and if a good-looking guy gives 'em the eye, they figure what the hell. They ain't got nothing else to do, and they fall. Back in their home town, they'd give him the icy stare, but out here, they want something to break the monotony and they're just getting a divorce so they figure it's sorta in between drinks, and a little cheating don't count. You get me?"

"I get you."

"So when you ask me, is a woman on the make, I can't tell much unless she's pretty heavy on the make, because out here they're all more or less on the make. You get me?"

"Can you remember anybody who's been in with her?"

"No, I can't. But wait a minute. I do, too. I remember one girl that was in with her yesterday, a knockout."

"Can you describe her?"

"She had red hair. I don't remember what color her eyes were, but she was all strawberries an' cream, and when she moved, she moved as easy as jelly on a plate."

"Fat?" I asked.

"No. That's it. She wasn't fat. She was thin like, but she wasn't stiff. Lots of women go on a diet and starve themselves until their joints get frozen stiff, and they move like wooden jumping jacks. This girl just walked like she was all double-jointed. I noticed her particularly."

"Anything else about her?"

"No."

"How old?"

"In the twenties maybe."

"How many times has she been here?"

"She was here a couple of times with this girl. Say, wait

a minute. I remember something about her, too. She was a bunny-nose."

"What do you mean?"

"You know the way a bunny moves his nose? Well, she had thin nostrils, and when she'd get a little excited, they'd twitch. I remember now, I noticed that. She was a good-looking jane. Boy, I could have gone for *her* in a big way."

I gave him my hand. "Thanks, Louie," I said.

"Not at all. And no hard feelings over the sock I gave you?"

I shook my head.

"Honest," he said, "you was a pushover. Now mind, I ain't throwing no slams at you, buddy. I'm just telling you. You didn't have any neck hold at all. When you're fighting, you want to keep your neck muscles so that when a punch gets by your guard and you have to take it on the button, you can roll it off. You get me?"

"No," I said, "and I haven't time to go into it right now. But I'm coming back some day and let you show me."

His face lit up. "Do you mean that, buddy? Gee, that'd be swell. I need to get in practice a little, and I'd like to show you. First we start out with the old one-two—" And he got the fighter's crouch again, and his feet started shuffling over the cement.

"Okay," I said hastily, "I'll be back," and headed for the door. My watch gave the time as five minutes before six.

Chapter Four

I CLIMBED THE STAIRS to Helen Framley's apartment once more. My face was sore now. The tips of my fingers showed there was a bump on the right side of my jaw, and another just below my left cheekbone. I didn't think they'd show badly, but they hurt.

I rang the bell and waited.

There was no answer.

I rang again.

Abruptly the door of the adjoining apartment opened. The woman who had talked with me before, said, "Oh, it's you. I think she's in now. I thought you were ringing *this* apartment. What's the matter? Won't she answer?"

I said, "Give her time. She may not have heard the bell."

"Humph! I can hear it in my apartment as plain as my own bell. I certainly thought you were ringing *my* bell. Perhaps—"

The man's voice called impatiently from the back of the apartment, "Maw, get away from that door and quit prying into other people's business."

"I don't pry into other people's business."

"No, not much."

"I thought he rang my bell, and—"

"Get away from that door."

The door slammed.

I rang Helen Framley's bell again.

Her door opened a cautious inch. I could see the brass chain which kept it from opening wider, could see cool, slate-colored eyes looking at me, and then heard her exclamation of surprise. It was the slot-machine girl. "How did you find me?"

"May I come in?"

"No— Certainly not— What do you want?"

"It doesn't have anything to do with what happened at the Cactus Patch—and it's important."

She hesitated a moment as though turning something over in her mind, then slid the guard chain back out of its catch.

She studied me curiously as I walked on in.

"Don't pay any attention to the face," I said. "It'll come back into shape after a while."

"Did he hit you hard?"

"I guess it was hard. I felt like a flock of tenpins when a bowler makes a strike. I've often heard them explode all over the alley, and now I know just how they must feel."

She laughed, said, "Come on in here and sit down."

I followed her into a little living-room. She indicated a chair. I sat down.

"Weren't you sitting here?" I asked.

"No. I was sitting over here."

The chair was warm.

"Mind if I smoke?"

"I should say not. I was smoking when you came in."

She picked up a cigarette from an ash tray which was by her chair.

I said, "I'm going to put the cards on the table."

"I like people who do that."

"I'm a private detective."

Her face became cold and white, frozen into a stiffly starched look of courteous attention.

"What's wrong with that?" I asked.

"N-n-nothing."

"Don't you like private detectives?"

"It depends on—on what they're after."

"I'm after information about a friend."

"I—I'm afraid I can't help you. I—"

I heard a hinge squeak. She flashed a quick glance past

me, then shifted her eyes and kept silent, waiting for something.

I said, without turning my head, "You might just as well come on over and join the party, Sid."

I heard quick motion behind me, sensed someone standing close to the back of my chair. "Get *all* your cards on the table, brother," a man's voice said.

"All of them that concern you *are* on the table."

I turned around and looked at him then. It was the man in the plaid sport coat who had been playing the quarter machine, and I noticed now he had just the trace of a cauliflower on his right ear. He was uneasy—and dangerous.

"Sit down," I told him, "and join the party. I'm not holding anything back."

He said, "You happened to stumble into the Cactus Patch at a queer time tonight. Maybe it was just luck— and then—"

I said, "Don't talk so loud. The woman in the next apartment is curious."

"I'll say she is," Miss Framley said.

The man in the plaid coat sat down. He said, *"We're* not going to say anything for about five minutes. During those five minutes, you're going to do a lot of talking."

"There'll be just about four minutes of silence then," I said. "My name's Donald Lam. I'm working for the B. Cool Detective Agency. I'm trying to locate Corla Burke. I have reason to believe Miss Framley knows where she is."

His face twitched. "What you want to locate her for?"

"A client."

"Ain't *you* smart?"

"I'm not trying to be, but I'm not dumb enough to go around telling the names of our clients to anyone who happens to ask."

He said, "Well, Miss Framley doesn't have any idea where Corla Burke is 'cause she don't know any Corla

Burke."

"Why did Miss Framley send her a letter then?"

"She didn't."

"I know people who say she did—people who are in a position to know."

"Well, they're cockeyed. She didn't send any letter."

Miss Framley said, "I don't even know who Corla Burke is. You're the second person who's asked me."

Sid flashed her a quick glance. "Who was the first one?"

"An engineer out at the dam."

His eyes glittered. "Why didn't you tell me about him?"

"Why should I? I didn't know what he was talking about even. He got the wrong number somewhere." She turned to me and said, "And I presume he's the one who tipped you off, and that's why you're here."

"What was this man's name?" I asked.

"The one who asked me the first time?"

"Yes."

She started to answer, then glanced at Sid Jannix, and hesitated perceptibly.

"Go on," he said.

"I don't know his name. He didn't give it to me."

"You're lying."

She flared up. "Why should I lie to you, you big baboon? My God, do you want to know every agent that comes to the door trying to sell a new vacuum sweeper?"

He turned to me and said, "What gave you the idea she'd written a letter?"

"Some people thought she had."

"Who were they?"

"People who reported to the agency. The agency sent me out."

"Who were the people?"

"You'd have to ask the agency."

He said to Helen Framley, "But you didn't write any letter?"

"No, of course not."

He turned back to me. "What was that you called me—what name?"

"I don't get you."

"When I first came out, you said something—"

"Oh, I called you Sid."

"Where'd you get that name?"

"Isn't that your name?"

"No."

"Pardon me, my mistake. What is it?"

"Harry Beegan."

"Sorry."

"Who told you to call me Sid?"

"I thought that was your name."

He scowled at me, said slowly, "Get this straight. My name's Harry Beegan. My nickname is Pug. I don't want to be called by any other name."

"Okay, that's fine by me."

He turned back to Helen Framley. There were lights in his eyes, little lights coming and going, like the reflection of sky in a mountain pool when the wind blows it into little ripples. "If I thought you was two-timin' me," he said, "I'd—"

"Get it out of your head once and for all," she said, "that you can frighten me, and I'm not your slave. I'm living my own life. Ours is a business partnership, and that's all."

"Oh, yeah?"

"You heard me."

He swung back to me. "I want to know some more about this client of yours."

"You can ask Bertha Cool about that. She's at the Sal Sagev Hotel."

"That client here in town right now?"

"You'll have to ask her about that."

"I think," he said, "I'm going to take quite an interest in that client of yours."

"I wouldn't," I told him, "not after what Kleinsmidt told me about you."

"Who's Kleinsmidt?"

"The big cop who collared me at the blowoff."

"How did you happen to horn in on that?"

"I didn't. I walked in and won a jackpot."

He said, "You weren't dumb enough to tap a nickel machine when the ten-cent and two-bit machines were all ripe, were you?"

I said, "I had nickels so I played nickels."

I saw that he was studying me with a puzzled look on his face.

"Did you take out a phoney rivet and leave it out?"

I said, "I don't know about any phoney rivets. I put in nickels and didn't win anything until a couple of cherries showed up. The next time I hit the jackpot right on the nose."

"Then what?"

"Then the attendant moved over, and we started arguing."

"Go on."

"Then the manager showed up, and the law. The law was named Lieutenant William Kleinsmidt. They took me up to the office and turned me inside out."

"Find anything?"

"A bunch of nickels and—"

"You know what I mean. Piano wire, drill, cups, or any of that stuff?"

The girl said, "Pug, I believe he's on the outside."

"Don't be too sure," Pug said without taking his eyes off of me. "What did they find?"

"They found," I said, "that I'd hit Las Vegas a couple of hours ago on the plane. They found that I hadn't been here before for six months, that I'm a private detective, that I'm employed by Bertha Cool, and that Bertha Cool was in the Sal Sagev Hotel waiting for me to make a report."

Pug looked me over carefully. "Wouldn't it be a scream," he said, "if you *were* telling the truth?"

I said, "Kleinsmidt thought I was telling the truth."

"He's dumb."

"And Breckenridge, the manager, thought I was telling the truth."

"Do you mean to say you just blundered in there and didn't know the machines were fixed?"

"The woman next door told me I could find Helen Framley hanging out around the slot machines at the Cactus Patch."

They exchanged glances. Pug gave a low whistle.

"How did she know?" the girl asked.

"She said she'd seen you there several times as she walked past."

"I wish she'd mind her own business for a change," the girl said savagely. "She told you about Pug being in here, too, just now, didn't she?"

I nodded, then said, "She didn't have to. I knew he was in the closet."

"Yes, you did," Pug said derisively.

I said, "The chair was warm. The girl was smoking a cigarette. Her cigarette was in the ash tray over by that other chair. She leaves lipstick on the paper. The cigarettes in this ash tray didn't have any lipstick."

Pug said, "By God, he *is* a detective."

"Do I get what I want about Corla Burke?"

"We haven't anything, Honest Injun," the girl said.

"You don't know anything about her?"

"No, honest—except what I read in the newspapers."

"You read what the newspapers had to say?"

"Yes."

"Las Vegas newspapers?"

She glanced at Pug, then let her eyes slide away from his. Pug said to me, "Forget it. You ain't goin' to cross-examine her."

"I can ask her questions, can't I?"

"No."

I said, "I don't think there was anything published in the Las Vegas newspapers. The Los Angeles papers didn't give it a big play. The man she was to marry wasn't prominent enough to make it a subject of general interest. It was just another disappearance."

"Well, she says she doesn't know anything about it."

"Except what she read in the papers," I pointed out.

Pug's scowl creased his forehead. "Listen, guy, you've gone far enough, see?"

I said, "I don't see."

"Well, maybe something will happen to improve your eyesight."

I said, "It costs money to get me working."

"What's that got to do with it?"

"It means that the people who have hired my agency to find Corla Burke are willing to spend money."

"Okay, let 'em spend it."

"And," I said, "if a Los Angeles grand jury got the idea there was something back of that disappearance, it would call witnesses."

"That's fine. Let 'em go ahead."

"The witness who testified before the grand jury would be testifying under oath. Any lies they told would be perjury, and you know what that means. Now, I'm here as a friend. You can tell me whatever it is you know, and I'll try to find Corla Burke. I could leave you out of it—if I got results. If you appear before the Los Angeles grand jury, the situation might be different."

"Forget it. I don't want to appear before no grand jury."

I lit a cigarette.

Helen Framley said, "Well, I'll tell you. I—"

"Skip it," Pug said.

"Shut up, Pug. I know what I'm doing. Let me tell it."

"You're talking too much."

"No, I'm not. I'm not talking enough. Now, listen, Mr. Lam, I'm just like any other woman. I'm curious. Well, after this Mr. Dearbor—this engineer started asking me questions, I made up my mind I'd find out what he was talking about, so I wrote to a friend in Los Angeles to get clippings from the newspapers."

"Now," I said, "we're doing a *lot* better. How about the clippings?"

"They were mailed to me."

"What did you learn?"

"Nothing you don't know. Just the stuff that was in the newspapers."

"I haven't seen the papers," I said. "I was only employed on the case a short time ago. You got those clippings with you?"

"They're in the bureau drawer."

"How about letting me see them?"

"Lay off," Pug said.

"Oh, forget it, Pug. There's no reason why he shouldn't see the newspaper clippings."

She jumped to her feet, eluded Pug's reaching hand with a swiftly graceful motion, vanished into the bedroom, returned after a moment with some newspaper clippings. I glanced through them. They had been cut from a newspaper and fastened together with a paper clip. The line along the edge of the paper was in irregular waves as though the cutting had been done very hastily.

"Could I take these for a few hours?" I asked. "I'd bring them back in the morning."

"No," Pug said.

I handed them back to her.

"I don't see why not, Pug," she said.

"Listen, babe, we ain't going to help the law in this thing. If that girl took a powder, she had her own reason for doing it. Let's mind our own business and keep our own noses clean."

Pug turned to me. "I don't exactly get you," he said.

"What about me?"

"That slot machine. There was something funny about it. You don't work that racket?"

I shook my head.

"Not even as a side line?"

I said, "Listen, when it comes to slot machines, I'm a babe in the woods. There's one in the Golden Motto—the restaurant where I eat in Los Angeles. It isn't supposed to be there, but it's in one of the private dining-rooms, and the regular customers know about it. Bertha Cool goes crazy at the way I throw money away on that machine. Every time I go in, I look through my pockets for nickels. Ordinarily, I only play fifteen or twenty cents. I don't think I've ever won anything out of the machine except a couple of small pay-offs."

He said, "Serves you right. Machines that are in restaurants that way are after a quick take. They don't go for steady customers. They put rollers on the sprockets so winning two cherries and a bell is darn near as hard as winning the jackpot or the gold medal award."

I said, "Other people seem to win on it two or three times a week. The woman who runs the place will tell me about some of the salesmen who are pretty lucky on it."

"They're supposed to win?"

"They've won the jackpot three or four times."

"You never saw 'em do it?"

"No. That's what the woman who runs the restaurant says. She tells me about 'em every so often."

He gave a contemptuous snort and said, "That's kindergarten stuff. She's probably telling the salesmen about how there's a private detective who keeps the machine milked dry by playing twenty-five cents to half a dollar and always coming out a heavy winner."

Helen Framley said to me, "You certainly have nerve."

"Why?"

"Standing up to Pug the way you do. Most people are afraid of him. I guess that gets your goat, doesn't it, Pug?"

"What?"

"To have this man so independent?"

"Aw, nuts."

"I didn't mean anything, Pug."

"Well, see that you don't."

She turned slate-gray eyes on me again. "You must get around a lot. You know, get to know different types."

"Not much."

"What are you going to do with Corla when you find her?"

"Talk with her."

"Then are you going to tell the man who was going to marry her?"

I grinned and said, "I'll tell my boss. She'll tell our client. Our client will use the information any way he damn pleases. I don't care what he does with it. He pays Bertha Cool, and Bertha Cool pays me money. That's all there is to it."

Pug said, "It's like I tell you, babe. Everybody in this world is on the make. You've got to take it where you can find it."

She grinned across at me. "Pug thinks I'm developing a conscience."

"On the slot-machine racket?"

"Uh huh."

Pug said, "Forget it, babe."

She said, "The machines are all dishonest. They're stealing from the customer. Why shouldn't we lift some from the machine?"

"It ain't stealing," Pug said. "It's just taking back some of the public's investment—and we're the public, ain't we? As far as the slot machine is concerned, we are. They use mechanical devices to keep the machines from paying off, and we use mechanical devices to make 'em pay off. It's fifty-fifty."

I said, "I think this man, Kleinsmidt, is going to be laying for you. He—"

"Oh, sure," Pug said. "We've got to blow. They always told me never to try working Nevada with all the protection they've got here, but I had to have a crack at it. California's different. Take Calermo Hot Springs for instance. You can always get a good play there. That's the worst of it. Good play means competition. I remember one time we tried to work a resort right after another gang had pulled out. The owners had been checking up on the machines, and when they found how small the take was, they had some private detectives come down to see what was happening, and who was doing it."

Helen Framley laughed nervously, and said, "That's where I got my complex on private detectives. They almost nailed us."

"It wouldn't have done 'em any good," Pug said.

"They might have made a lot of trouble."

"They could have talked," Pug admitted, "but that's all."

"Well, I don't like it, Pug. I wish you'd get something else lined up."

"This is plenty good, babe, *plenty* good."

I said casually, "I'm going to have to get back to Los Angeles."

Pug said, "You're acting awfully funny about this thing. You wouldn't by trying to hand us no line, would you?"

I shook my head.

Pug frowned and stared at me with his eyes sharp with suspicion. Abruptly, he said, "Get your things together, babe."

"What do you mean?"

Pug's eyes grew hostile. "There's just a chance this guy's trying to stall us along until the law can get us spotted.

Where you got those coins?"

"In my—you know."

"Okay," Pug said, "beat it out and get 'em changed. If they raid the joint, we don't want to have a lot of dimes and nickels and quarters on hand. And you, buddy, you better be going. Like you said, you've got a lot of things to do."

"I'd like to ask a few more questions."

Pug got to his feet, came over, and put his hand on my shoulder. "I know you would, but we're busy. We've got things to do. You know how it is."

"Now, Pug, don't you hurt—"

"Forget it, babe. Get that stuff together and get it changed into currency. This guy's leaving right now, and you've got work to do."

Her eyes studied Pug for a minute, then came over to mine. Abruptly she smiled, walked over, and gave me her hand. "You're one swell guy," she said. "I like guys with nerve. You sure have plenty."

"Go on. Get in that bedroom and get that stuff together," Pug said sharply.

"On my way."

Pug started me toward the door. " 'By," I said to Helen Framley, "and thanks. Where can I reach you if I want to get in touch with you?"

It was Pug who answered the question, and his eyes were cold. "That, buddy, is the thing I was going to tell you when I got you outside, but I might as well tell you now. You can't."

"Can't what?"

"Can't get in touch with her."

"Why not?"

"For two reasons. One of 'em is that you won't know where she is, and the other one is I don't want you to. Get me?"

Helen said, "Pug, don't be like that."

Pug said, "On your way," and gripped his fingers around my elbow. The push which he exerted was gentle but insistent. Over his shoulder, he said, "You get into that bedroom, babe, and make it snappy."

Pug opened the door. "So long, guy," he said. "Nice meeting you. Don't come back. Good-by."

The door slammed.

I looked at the door of the adjoining apartment and saw that there was a ribbon of light coming out from under the door.

I tiptoed gently down the stairs.

I walked out and stood in a doorway, watching the sidewalk, and waiting. The street lights were on now.

After a while, I saw Helen Framley walking down the street, a neat little package that would attract attention anywhere.

I sauntered along behind.

She went into one of the casinos, and started playing the wheel of fortune long enough to register with the gang around the place as one of the players. Then she went over to the cashier's desk, opened her purse, pulled out an assortment of nickels, dimes, and quarters and got them changed into currency. She came out, crossed the street, went to another casino, and repeated the operation. When she came out of that place, I was waiting for her.

"Hello," I said.

There was sudden fear in her eyes. "What are you doing here?"

"Standing here."

"Well, you mustn't be seen talking with me."

"Why not? I have a couple of questions I wanted to ask you privately."

"No, no, please. You can't."

"Why not?"

She looked around her apprehensively. "Can't you understand? Pug's jealous. I had an awful time with him after you left. He thinks I—thinks I was too nice to you, that I was trying to protect you."

I fell into step at her side. "That's all right. We'll walk along the street and—"

"No, no," she said, "not this way. Here, walk the other way if you've got to walk. Turn to the right at the corner. Get down that dark side street. Gosh, I wish you wouldn't take chances like this."

I said, "You wrote a letter to Corla Burke. Why and what did you say?"

"Why, I never wrote her in my life."

"You're certain?"

"Yes."

"You didn't send her a letter a couple of days before she disappeared?"

"No."

I said, "She was blond. I don't think she was the type to do things on impulse exactly. Like to see her picture?"

"Gosh, yes. You got one?"

I guided her into a lighted doorway and took the pictures from my pocket. They were a little cracked where Louie had pushed wrinkles in my coat when he jerked it back from my shoulders and down my arms.

"See. She looks quick on the trigger, but she's a thinker."

"How can you tell that?"

"From the lines of her face."

She said, "Gosh, I wish I knew things like that."

"You do. You unconsciously size up a person's character as soon as you meet him. Perhaps you know someone with thin nostrils and—"

"Yeah, but I size 'em up wrong about half the time. Gosh, the double crosses I've had handed me, just because I play wide open. I take a good look at 'em and either like 'em or don't. If I like 'em, I go the whole hog. Say, listen— Your name's Donald, isn't it?"

"Yes."

"Okay. Now listen, Donald, we've got to cut this out. Pug's awfully mean when he gets jealous, and he certainly is on the prod tonight. The way he was feeling when I left, he's almost certain to get restless and start following us. That's the trouble with Pug. He won't stay put. When he gets nervous, he gets all excited."

"Where can I get in touch with you, Helen?"

"You can't."

"Isn't there some way I could reach you, some friend to whom I could write—"

She was shaking her head emphatically.

I gave her one of my cards. "There's my address," I said. "Will you think it over and see if you can't figure out some way I could keep in touch with you? Some place I can get you in case it should be important to have your testimony?"

"I don't want to give any testimony. I don't want to be dragged into the limelight and have a lot of questions asked me."

"You can trust me. If you shoot square with me, I'll play square with you."

She slipped my card in her purse. "I'll think it over, Donald. Perhaps I can drop you a card, letting you know where you can get in touch with me."

"Do that little thing, will you?"

"Perhaps—Donald, can I tell you something—and have you play ball?"

"What?"

"I wasn't telling you all the truth up there."

"I was afraid of that."

"Listen, I want to go some place where we can talk, and Pug may be down any minute."

"The hotel lobby or—"

"No, no, some place right close. Here, come over in this—Now listen, Donald, I want to know exactly why you thought I was holding out."

I said, "I just thought so. And I have evidence that you sent a letter to Cora Burke."

"I haven't lied to you. I just haven't told you all the truth. I'm going to give you a break. I wanted to up there, but I couldn't on account of Pug. I didn't know what to do. I finally decided that *if* you had the nerve to be waiting for me when I came out, I'd tell you—maybe."

"What is it?"

"She *did* write to me."

"That's better. When?"

"The day before she disappeared, I guess it must have been."

"And you'd written to her?"

"No, I hadn't. Honest and truly. I'd never seen her in my life. I didn't know anything about her."

"Go ahead."

"Well, that's just about all there is to it. I had this letter delivered to me. It was addressed to Helen Framley, General Delivery, Las Vegas. The post office just happened to catch it, knew that I had an apartment here, and changed the address so that it was delivered to this address."

There was a night light in a grocery store on a side street. It gave sufficient illumination to see things—more or less clearly. I stopped her in front of the window. "Let's see it."

"If Pug ever knew—"

"What business is it of his?"

"Really," she flared, "it isn't. I told him at the start it was just a business partnership. He's insanely jealous. Of course, he keeps wanting more—and then he hates the law. He says that it's very evident there was some other Helen Framley in Las Vegas, just passing through, and that I got a letter intended for her. I don't know. I can't make it out, but Pug says I mustn't stick my neck out."

"The letter."

"You promise you won't—"

"Hurry up," I said. "You haven't got all night. Neither

have I. Let's see it."

She opened her purse, took out an envelope, and handed it to me.

I put it in my pocket.

"No, no, you mustn't do that. I'll need the letter. Pug will ask me about it as soon as I get back. He'll want to burn it."

"I'll have to go where I can read it and study it for a clue."

"Donald, you can't. You've got to just glance at it. I can tell you what's in it. I— Oh, my God!"

I looked up, following the direction of her startled eyes.

Pug was standing on the corner of the main thoroughfare, looking up and down the street.

She grabbed my arm. "Quick. Get back here—" Pug turned, looked down the side street, saw us, took a dubious step forward as though trying to see better, and then came rapidly toward us.

"What will we do?" she asked. "You run. I'll stick it out. Run fast around the corner, and I'll delay things until— No, no, you can't. Donald, he's dangerous. He's half crazy. He—"

I held her arm as I walked toward him.

I couldn't see his face clearly. The hatbrim shaded the expression in his eyes. The light on the side street was dim. A car swung around the corner behind us. Its lights illuminated his face in a harsh glare of white light. The features were hard with hatred.

Helen Framley saw that face and pulled back at my arm, twisting me half around.

Pug didn't say anything. His eyes were on my face. He reached out with his right hand, caught the girl by the collar of her jacket, and sent her spinning across the sidewalk.

I swung for his jaw.

I don't know whether it was the poor light or whether

he was too mad to see what I was doing, or sufficiently disdainful not to care. He didn't try to block or dodge. My blow caught him on the chin. Unconsciously I'd remembered something of what Louie had told me about throwing my body muscles into a blow. I hit him so hard I thought my arm was broken.

It didn't even jar his head back on his neck. It was as though I'd swung on the side of a concrete building. He said, "You double-crossing, two-timing stool pigeon—" His fist crashed into my jaw.

It was his left. It jarred me back on my heels. I knew his right would be coming across. I tried to get out of the way and stumbled, off balance, which threw my shoulder up. His right caught me on my shoulder and sent me out across the sidewalk into the gutter.

The car swerved. Headlights blazed at us. I thought the machine was going to run over me. I got up and Pug was coming toward me, not hastily, just with a quiet deadliness of purpose.

The car was stopped now. I heard a door slam, steps behind me. A voice said, "No, you don't."

Pug didn't pay any attention to the voice. His eyes were only on me.

I thought I saw an opening and lashed out.

The big bulk of a body moved past me. I heard the thudding impact of a fist against flesh, and then Pug and a big man were whirling around in a tangled circle. The big man's shoulder hit against me and flung me off to one side. Before I could get back, Pug had broken free. I saw his shoulders weave, then the broad back and huge shoulders of the big man interposed themselves between me and Pug.

Something sounded like a fast ball thudding into a catcher's glove. The big man came back hard, and took me down with him.

I heard people shouting. A woman screamed. There were steps—running toward us.

Someone bent over us. I squirmed to get free. The automobile lights showed Pug's face, still hard with cold hatred, bending over. He jerked the inert body of the big man to one side as though it had no weight. He leaned over me. His left hand grabbed my shirt and necktie. He started to lift me.

Someone was back of him. I saw a club making a glittering half circle, and heard the thud on the back of Pug's skull. The hand that was holding my shirt loosened its grip. I fell back against the bumper of the car.

By the time I straightened, there was a swirl of activity back in the crowd. I heard the sound of grunting breaths, the sound of another blow, then feet running, this time away from me.

The big man who had gone down and taken me with him struggled to his knees. His right hand swung back to his hip. I saw blued steel glittering in the light reflected by the automobile headlights. I caught the man's profile as he raised the gun and turned his head. It was Lieutenant Kleinsmidt.

A man pushed through the little crowd. "Everything all right, Bill?" he asked.

Kleinsmidt said thickly, "Where is he?"

"He got away. I gave him a full swing with the club, but it didn't stop him."

Kleinsmidt struggled to his feet.

I was tangled up with the bumper of the car. I had to get a hand on it to pull myself up. Kleinsmidt grabbed me, spun me around, and said, "Oh!"

I said, "I'm sorry, Lieutenant," and added with a flash of inspiration, "I tried to hold him for you."

"You sure have guts," he told me, and rubbed his jaw.

"What you want him for, Bill?" the man with the club asked.

"Slot-machine racket," Kleinsmidt said, and then added as an afterthought, "Resisting an officer."

"Well, we can get him."

Kleinsmidt said to me, "Know where he lives?"

I brushed dirt off my clothes. "No."

"Which way did he go?" Kleinsmidt asked.

Half a dozen people were eager to volunteer information. Kleinsmidt looked back at the car for a moment as though hesitating, then started out on foot, and took the other man with him. The little crowd went streaming along behind to see the fun.

I limped away into the darkness. Seven o'clock, and Bertha would be waiting.

Chapter Five

I WENT OVER to the Apache Hotel, drifted into the lobby, found a seat, took the letter Helen Framley had given me from my pocket, and looked it over carefully.

It was written on a good quality stationery, but the sheet was an odd size. The top edge held little irregularities so small as to be almost imperceptible unless you looked for them carefully. The paper spilled a faint trace of scent. I couldn't tell what kind it was. There was a certain suggestion of cramped angularity about the handwriting.

The letter read:

Dear Helen Framley:

I'm grateful for your letter, but it's no use. I can't go through with the marriage now. It wouldn't be fair to him. The thing you suggest is unthinkable. I'm getting out of the picture. Good-by.

Corla Burke

I studied the envelope in which the letter had been enclosed. It was a stamped, air-mail envelope. The General Delivery address on the outside was in that same handwriting as the body of the letter. Someone at the post office had crossed this out and written in the street and number of Helen's apartment.

I put the letter back in the envelope, put it in my pocket, then thought better of it. I took the letter back out of the envelope, put it in my inside coat pocket, put the envelope in the outside pocket on my coat, and walked back to the Sal Sagev Hotel.

Bertha said, "Donald, what the hell have you been doing?"

"Working."

"You've been fighting again. You're a mess. Here take this clothesbrush. No, tell me first, what did you find?"

"Clues."

"Well, don't be so damned reticent. Tell me what happened."

"I heard this girl was a slot-machine addict. I would either have had to stick around until three or four o'clock in the morning waiting for her to come in, or go out and find her around the slot machines."

"Well, you don't need to *play* slot machines just because you're waiting."

"You look conspicuous if you hang around and don't play 'em."

"Go ahead and look conspicuous. Who cares? After all, lover, we're in business for money, not to conform to what Las Vegas, Nevada, thinks the well-dressed detective will wear. Don't you think for a minute you're going to put any gambling expenses on the expense account."

"I won't."

"What happened?"

"There was a fight."

"You don't need to tell me that. You've been leading with your face again."

"Does it look bad?"

"Terrible."

I walked over to the full-length mirror. A table had been moved so it was possible to see my reflection clear across the room. On the table, still in its original silver foil wrapper, was Bertha's second chocolate bar. There was quite a bit of dust on my clothes. My face had a queer lopsided look to it.

Bertha asked, "What was the fight about?"

"The first one was because someone thought I was

tampering with the machines."

"And you fought over that?"

"No. I got arrested."

"I gathered as much. What happened after that?"

"I saw the girl again. Where's Whitewell?"

She said, "He's due here any minute. He got a telegram. His son's on the way here. He's waiting for him to come in."

"From where?"

"Los Angeles."

"How's he coming?"

"He's driving. There's been some business emergency and Philip's bringing his father's right-hand man with him, someone who's been in business with him for years."

"Does Philip know what his father's doing here?"

"I don't think so, but I think the father's going to take him into his confidence."

"You mean he's going to let him know about us and what we're here for?"

"I think he is. Donald, isn't he the *nicest* man?"

"Uh huh."

"The most observing. He has wonderful taste."

"Uh huh."

"He's a widower, and I wouldn't be surprised if he was just a mite lonely. Not that he's thinking of marriage. He values his independence too highly, but he isn't entirely self-sufficient. He's something of a child down underneath. All men are. They want to be mothered, particularly when things go wrong."

"Uh huh."

"Donald Lam, are you listening to me?"

"Yes, of course."

"Well then, make some contribution to the conversation other than that inane grunting."

"Don't you want me to agree with you?"

"When a man's as nice as Mr. Whitewell, you should be

able to add something to what I'm saying."

"I couldn't. No one could."

Her lips were a thin, straight line. "Sometimes, you little devil, I hate the ground you walk on!"

"Aren't you going to eat your chocolate bar?"

"You may have it."

"I don't want it. What's the matter with it?"

"I don't know. That other one gave me sort of heartburn. Have you had dinner, lover?"

"No. I've been busy."

"Well, Mr. Whitewell suggested that we should eat together—that is, if you came back. He said," and she let her mouth soften into the suggestion of a simper, "that he wanted his son to meet me. He seemed particularly anxious."

"That's nice."

Knuckles tapped on the door.

"Open it, lover."

I opened the door. Whitewell stood on the threshold. Slightly behind him was a boy who was quite obviously his son. There was the same high forehead, long, straight nose, well-shaped mouth. The father's eyes were keen with a slightly humorous twinkle. The boy's were the same color, but didn't have the keenness nor the twinkle. They looked as though the boy might be slogging his way through life without getting much pleasure out of it. Back of the boy was a man in the forties, bald, thick, competent, and built like a grizzly bear.

Whitewell said, "Philip, this is Donald Lam. Mr. Lam, my son, Philip Whitewell."

The tall young man gave me an inclination of the head, extended his hand, gripped mine politely but without fervor. "Very pleased to meet you, I'm sure."

"Won't you come in?" I asked.

The father made quite a ceremony of it. "Mrs. Cool," he said, "may I present my son, Philip. Philip, this is the

78

woman I've been telling you about."

Philip looked at her curiously for a moment before he bowed, and said, "Mrs. Cool, I'm very pleased to meet you. Father has been talking about you a lot."

The thick man who seemed to have been forgotten, grinned, pushed a hand out to me, and said, "My name's Endicott."

"Lam," I said.

We shook hands. Whitewell whirled, and said, "Oh, pardon me," and then to Bertha, "And may I present Paul Endicott. He's been with me for years. The real brains of the business. I only take in the profits and pay the income tax. Paul does the work."

Endicott grinned, the good-natured grin of a man who is too healthy, big, and powerful to ever let anything bother him.

Bertha beamed all over her face. She actually got up out of her chair to be the perfect hostess, telephoned room service, and had some cocktails sent up.

Whitewell said to me, "I suggested to Mrs. Cool that we might all dine together when I found that my son was coming. Have you been looking the town over?"

"Yes."

"Find out anything?"

"A little."

"Get a line on Miss Framley?"

"Yes."

"You didn't talk with her, did you?"

"Yes."

He studied me for a minute as though I'd said something he hadn't expected to hear. Then he said with a little laugh, "I've taken Philip entirely into my confidence. Philip knows that Mrs. Cool is running a detective agency, and that I've employed her to find what happened to Corla Burke. He knows that you're working for her, so if you've found anything that's at all significant as a clue, you don't need to hold it back."

I took the envelope from my pocket, showed it to young Whitewell, and asked, "Is this her handwriting?"

He took the envelope in eager fingers, stood looking down at it with expression veiled out of his eyes.

"That's her writing," he said at length.

Whitewell, Senior, grabbed at the envelope. "You were right, Mrs. Cool," he said, "the boy's a fast worker."

"I told you he was."

Whitewell ran his fingers down inside the envelope. There was a puzzled look on his face when he failed to find a letter.

"Wasn't there a letter in this?" he asked.

"I guess so."

"But that would have been a clue."

I nodded.

"Where's that letter now?"

"Miss Framley hasn't got it."

"She hasn't got it!"

"No."

"What did she do with it?"

I shrugged my shoulders.

"Did she remember what was in it?"

"I don't know."

Bertha Cool said, "*Why* don't you? Weren't you talking with her?"

"Yes, but her boy friend didn't like my technique. He used me as a punching-bag."

"You look it."

Whitewell said, "We'll have him arrested."

"We won't need to. When he was trying to put the finishing touches on me, a cop interfered."

"What happened to the cop?"

"He looks as bad as I do."

Bertha Cool and Whitewell exchanged glances.

"Well," Whitewell said, "you can get after Miss Framley

now and find out about that letter."

"Better let things cool down a little."

Bertha frowned as though something was puzzling her. Then she said, "Donald, go down to your room and get on a clean shirt. Get some of that dust out of your clothes. Do you have another suit with you?"

"No."

"Well, do the best you can with that."

Endicott said, "It looks like we'll have time to get off a few telegrams, Arthur. Philip, you'd better come along, too. Will you excuse us, Mrs. Cool?"

Most of the dirt brushed out of my clothes, but my tie was badly ripped, and my shirt collar crumpled and dirty. I got on a new shirt and tie, held hot towels on my face until I'd got rid of some of the soreness, combed my hair, and went back to Bertha's room.

When the door had closed she turned to me. "That's the first time I ever knew you to do that, Donald."

"What?"

"Show the white feather. Not that Bertha's blaming you, lover, because she isn't. But I just can't understand why you're not out after that letter."

I took the letter out of my pocket and handed it to her.

"What's that?"

"Corla's letter."

"Where did you get it?"

"From Helen Framley."

"Then you lied to Whitewell?"

"No. I didn't tell him *I* didn't have it. I said the girl didn't have it. She didn't. She'd given it to me."

Bertha's little glittering eyes blinked at me. "What's the idea?"

"Read it."

Bertha read the letter, looked up, and said, "I don't get it. Why hold out on our client?"

"Have you," I asked, "got that letter Whitewell wrote?"

81

"The one you gave me?"

"Yes."

"Why?"

"Let's take a look at it."

Bertha said impatiently, "Let's do nothing of the sort. Let's talk about this Burke matter."

"I think we can find out more about it by looking at Whitewell's letter."

"What do you mean?"

"Look at the letter," I said. "It's written on a fine grade all-rag bond. The watermark is Scribcar Bond. Notice the dimensions of the sheet. Notice the way it's folded. See what I mean? That sheet of paper is part of a business letterhead. Someone cut off the top of the letterhead with a sharp knife."

Bertha blinked her eyes. After a moment, she said, "I think I'm beginning to get it, but keep right on telling me."

"Whitewell didn't like the idea of his son marrying Corla Burke. He got Corla into his office. He made her some proposition that she accepted. She agreed to get out, but she wanted to save her face. She was to get out under circumstances that would make it appear she *might* have been forcibly removed, or been running away from something she was afraid of."

"Then why the letter?" Bertha asked.

"The letter," I said, "clinches it. It's the pay-off, so far as we're concerned. Corla Burke didn't know any Helen Framley. Helen Framley didn't know any Corla Burke. But Arthur Whitewell had friends here in Las Vegas. Those friends were in a position to look around and find some girl who would make a good plant. Whitewell had this letter written as a second string to his bow, a safety anchor out to windward."

"That's something I don't get."

"Remember, he's Philip's father. After all, he has Philip's best interests at heart. That's why he interfered in the first place."

"Naturally."

"A man like that wouldn't want to see his son suffer unduly. If it was just a blow due to having the woman he loved walk out on him, Philip would get over it. The father knew that. But if Philip got the idea in his head the girl had been kidnaped or was in danger and he was failing her, he'd never get over it. It would be such a long-drawn nervous strain that it would change his entire career. Evidently, that's what's happening."

"Well?"

"And the father was shrewd enough to know that it might happen. Remember, he's an amateur psychologist. He certainly wouldn't have overlooked that possibility."

"I get you now. He couldn't have pulled this letter out of his sleeve then and said, 'Look, son, what I've found.' He'd have to have the letter planted some place where a private detective agency could find it."

"That's right. That letter shows that Corla Burke left under her own power. He wants us to find that letter, and is willing to pay us for doing it. Then he'll show it to his son."

Bertha blinked her eyes and said, "All right, lover, if it's a run-around, we'll just play ring-around-the-rosy with him. We'll run around in circles, draw a per diem for six days, find this letter on the seventh so we can still get a bonus, and teach him not to play us for suckers. Was that your idea, lover?"

"Not exactly."

"What then?"

"It's going to work out about that way. If I accuse him of writing the letter and getting rid of Corla Burke, I can never tell whether he did it or didn't—"

"Donald Lam, what do you think you're doing? He's a client. You can't accuse him of anything."

I said, "No, but if we hold this back for a little while, he'll start putting pressure to bear here and there to see that the letter does get delivered into our hands. When he starts moving around, he's got to get out in the open enough so we can catch him red-handed."

"Then what?"

I said, "We'd know more about it then."

"Donald," she said, "you're going overboard again. You're thinking about Corla Burke's broken heart."

"I'd like to see her get a square deal. She's up against a wealthy man who evidently has used some form of blackmail."

"What did he do?"

"I don't know. I don't think she'd have quit for money. I think Whitewell's the sort who would put her on the wheel and break her a bit at a time, body and soul. He'd torture anyone who got in his way."

"Donald, how *can* you say such things? He's a nice man."

"He's nice when he wants to be, but he's ruthless when it comes to getting what he wants."

"Aren't we all?"

I smiled and said, "Some of us are."

"I suppose that's a dirty dig."

I kept quiet.

Bertha said, "Open that suitcase, lover, and look in the zipper compartment. His letter's in there."

I got out his letter, held it up to the light. It was Scribcar Bond. I held the two sheets side by side. Corla Burke's letter had been written on his stationery. The upper part of the letterhead had been folded over and cut off with a sharp knife.

Bertha Cool said, "Well, fry me for an oyster!"

I folded Corla Burke's letter and put it in my pocket.

"What do we do next, lover?" Bertha asked.

"I want to check up on the Los Angeles end. How long's Whitewell going to stay here?"

"I think for a day or two."

"Want to go to Los Angeles with me tonight?"

"No. Bertha's rather tired, and I like this desert climate. I think it would be better to—"

"There's a train at nine-twenty," I said. "I'll get reservations on it."

Chapter Six

THE COCKTAILS DIDN'T HELP things any. Philip Whitewell became moody and showed his heartbreak. His father kept looking at me as a poker player looks at a man who shoves a stack of blues into the middle of the table after announcing a pat hand on the draw. Bertha, trying to hover over us like a dove of peace and keep things running smoothly, showed signs of cracking under the strain.

It was a new role for Bertha, as foreign to her as the relatively slim silhouette she presented. Whitewell had somehow managed to hypnotize her. She was suddenly conscious of the fact that she was a woman. How that was going to affect her business judgment remained to be seen. When Bertha Cool's newly discovered romantic streak ran up against her business cupidity, it was going to be a major collision.

Personally, I was sitting tight, playing them close to my chest, quite willing to talk about politics and armament—but I'd quit talking about Corla Burke.

We had dinner. The night was warm. Insects buzzed around the street lights in spinning circles. Doors and windows were all open. The natives and a goodly sprinkling of the tourists went around in shirt sleeves. You weren't aware of perspiration—except when you leaned back against a cushion so the air couldn't get to you. Then you'd feel your shirt was damp when you pulled away. Other times, the dry air evaporated perspiration just as fast as it formed.

Whitewell did the honors with the check. While he was waiting for change, Philip said to me, "Lam, I have a lot of confidence in you."

"Thanks."

"You'll find Corla?"

"Your dad's the one who's employing us," I said.

"But I don't understand. He wants you to find Corla. Don't you, Dad?"

Whitewell said, "Yes, Philip, if it can be done with a reasonable expenditure of time and money."

"But don't you see, Dad? It can't be a matter of money. There's something back of it, something sinister, something terrible—"

"Well, let's not discuss it while our dinner is digesting, Philip."

"But you'll promise me that you'll keep Mr. Lam— That is, Mrs. Cool and Mr. Lam on the job?"

"That, Philip, you'll have to leave to my judgment." He looked across at me. "Lam, if you could find that letter and *if* that letter showed definitely that Corla had left voluntarily, I think Philip and I would be willing to accept that as a completion of your employment."

"I take it, you wouldn't want any ideas I might have about the letter?"

"I think the letter would speak for itself."

"But, Dad, you can't let it go at that. We must find Corla. We *must!*"

The waitress came with the change. Whitewell gave her an even ten percent tip, put the remaining money in his pocket.

"You didn't eat nearly as much as usual. Your appetite all right?" I asked Bertha.

"Yes. I just didn't feel as hungry. Not that I haven't a good appetite; but I just don't have that ravenous, all-gone feeling I had when I was—heavier."

Whitewell said to his son, "Ever seen one of these gambling casinos, Philip?"

"No," he said, craning his neck.

Whitewell looked at Bertha significantly. "Would you,"

he asked, "care to join us in a little gambling, or would you prefer to go to the hotel and have a conference with your assistant?"

Bertha caught his eye. "We're going to the hotel," she said.

As nearly as I could remember afterwards, it was then about eight o'clock. We went up to Bertha's room. She closed and locked the door. "Donald," she said, "you'd better let me have that letter."

I looked at my watch. "Don't you think it would be a lot better to have me complete my investigations?"

"About what?"

"About the letter."

"Donald, what the devil are you up to? What in the world do you want to go to Los Angeles for?"

"Various reasons. If you're going to stay here on account of the climate, someone should be running the Los Angeles office."

She let her little eyes glitter at me. "Damn you, Donald. You don't need to play them so close to your chest with me. Why do you want to get out of here?"

"It was just a suggestion."

She sighed. "All right, you obstinate little devil, go take your damn train."

"When will I see you?"

"I don't know. I like it here."

"The climate?"

"Of course, the climate. What else would I be sticking around this dump for?"

"I wouldn't know."

"I guess you wouldn't. Go ahead and get your train."

"Don't tell the Whitewells where I've gone until after the train leaves."

"What *will* I tell them?"

"Tell them I'm out making another investigation. I'll leave a note at the desk for you, telling you I have decided to take the train to Los Angeles, and you can wait here for me. I'll leave word to have the note delivered at nine-thirty, or you can ring up the office and ask if I left any message for you when I don't show up."

She said, "Mr. Whitewell may not like this."

"That's right," I agreed. "He may not."

She stared at me again as though trying to read my mind, then turned away with a gesture of irritation.

I unlocked the door, walked quickly down to my room, and tossed my wardrobe into a light handbag. Experience with Bertha had taught me the advisability of being able to travel with nothing more bulky than one light bag. I still had half an hour to kill. I killed it studying the letter and thinking back over conversations.

Chapter Seven

THE TRAIN PULLED IN on time. I climbed aboard and had fifteen minutes to wait. I had a lower berth. The cars were air-conditioned. It was still warm in the depot and after the desert heat, the air-conditioned cars seemed chilly. There wasn't anything else to do, so I undressed while the train was still in the depot, slid into my berth, found that a single blanket didn't feel at all uncomfortable, and dropped off to sleep. I didn't even know when the train pulled out.

Somewhere along the road, I dreamed there was a big earthquake. The track had twisted and turned like a tortured snake trying to crawl off a hot iron. The train buckled in the middle, slewed sideways. Cars were rolling over and over—

A voice kept saying in a hoarse whisper, "Lower nine—lower nine—lower nine," and I realized the earthquake was caused by hands tugging at the blanket.

I knuckled my eyes and said, "What is it?"

"Ge'mman has to see you right away."

"What the devil," I said, fighting against the sense of unreality and a growing irritation.

"Turn on the light in there," a voice said.

I sat up in the berth, and pulled the curtains aside.

Lieutenant Kleinsmidt was standing in the aisle with the white-coated, big-eyed porter at his side.

The car was rolling slowly along—gathering speed. Far up ahead I could hear the mellowed whistle of the locomotive drifting back across the roofs of the air-conditioned cars. The aisle was a dim mist of green curtains swaying with the motion of the train. Here and there, heads stuck out as curious passengers wondered what the commotion was about.

I stared at Kleinsmidt. "What's the idea?" I asked.

"You're going back, Lam."

"Back where?"

"To Las Vegas."

"When?"

"Right now."

I said, "Guess again. I'm going to be in Los Angeles at exactly eight-thirty in the morning."

He looked at his watch. "I got on at Yermo at two-thirty," he said. "We stop briefly at Barstow at three-ten. You're going to be dressed and off the train then."

"This is the kind of co-operation I get in return for giving you a break, I suppose."

He started to say something, changed his mind, said instead, "Start getting dressed, Lam," and added, "This is an official visit, and I'm talking in my official capacity. I mean it."

"How'd you get here?" I asked, accepting the situation and wriggling out of my pajamas.

He stood with one elbow propped against the lower part of the upper berth, looking down at me. "Airplane. There's a car following the train. We'll go back and—"

A man's voice from the upper berth asked irritably, "Why don't you get a ship-to-shore telephone?"

"Sorry," Kleinsmidt said.

The porter moved up "Beg pahd'n, ge'mmen, if you all don't mind."

"It's all right," I told him. "We'll be quiet."

I dressed in silence. Kleinsmidt's big hand reached in and took my bag as I finished packing.

He led the way down to the men's washroom. "What do you want out, Lam?" he asked.

"Toothbrush, hairbrush—"

He looked at his watch. "All right. I'll play valet."

I combed my hair and brushed my teeth, washed up, and reached for my shirt. Kleinsmidt handed it to me. He'd been holding it—looking at it.

I put my hairbrush, toothbrush, and tooth paste back in the bag. Kleinsmidt snapped the bag shut and wrapped his big hand around the handle.

"I can take it," I said.

"It's all right. I have it."

The porter came in. "Jus' a few minutes we'll be in Barstow, suh. We only stop there jus' a second. If you ge'mmen will be all ready to hop off."

Kleinsmidt nodded.

"Ah's openin' up at the rear," the porter said.

I lit a cigarette. "What's it all about?" I asked Kleinsmidt.

"Sorry, Lam, I'm not doing any talking right now."

"I'll say you're not. The way you're acting, a person would think you were breaking a murder case."

I could have bitten my tongue off as soon as I'd said it. The look on his face told me everything I needed to know. "How did you know there'd been a murder, Lam?"

"Has there?"

"That's what *you* said."

"Don't be silly. I told you you were going through as much agony as though there *had* been a murder."

"That isn't exactly what you said."

"The hell it isn't."

"You know it isn't."

"I know it is. I was merely using a figure of speech anyway. But that's no sign you can't tell me."

"We'll talk about something else until we get to Las Vegas."

The train slowed down. We walked back through the vestibule. The porter stood at the door, his hand on the catch. When the train came to a stop, he slammed up the platform, jerked open the door, jumped down the stairs, and stood staring. I could see the whites of his eyes.

The sharp tang of pure desert air knifed my nostrils. Even in the air-conditioned car I'd been conscious of sticky emanations oozing into the atmosphere from persons who were sleeping. Out in the desert, the cold, dry air, pure and sharp, dissolved those impurities from my lungs so rapidly it was like a stab.

I held a quarter out to the porter. He started to reach for it, then suddenly jerked his hand back and said, "No, suh. That's all right, suh. Ah ain' courtin' no bad luck— Ah means— Good mornin', suh."

I put the quarter back in my pocket.

Kleinsmidt chuckled.

I looked forward along the train. There was a wind blowing. Smoke and steam from the locomotive were whipped back, and tossed about to dissolve into fragments. Kleinsmidt walked ahead with my bag, seemed to know very definitely where he was going. Out beyond the station, I looked up at the sky. The stars were staring steadily down, close to me, unwinking and brilliant. It seemed there wasn't an inch of the heavens that wasn't blazing with pin points of light.

Typical of the vagaries of desert climate, the heat had given way to an intense, dry cold.

"Got an overcoat?" Kleinsmidt asked.

"No."

"Okay, the car's warm."

He walked across to where a car was parked. A man jumped out and pulled the rear door open.

Kleinsmidt saw that I got in first, tossed the bag in, and climbed in beside me.

"Let's go," he said to the driver.

We slid into smooth motion out from the railroad grounds in a wide, sweeping turn, up to the highway, and across a bridge. It was warmer inside the car, but there was the nearness of the stars; the vast space of the desert stretching away on each side, in front and behind, gave one a feeling of cold insignificance.

I said to Kleinsmidt, "Nice weather we're having."

"Isn't it."

"What's the idea? Am I being charged with some crime?"

"You're just going back, that's all."

"If I'm not charged with anything, you haven't any authority to take me off a train and take me back."

"That may be. However, the chief said to bring you back, and you're going back."

"What's the car?"

"One I rented down the line a piece. I have a plane parked down there."

I said, "Well, anyway, I'm glad we're friends. If we hadn't been, you might have got sore and decided not to tell me anything."

He laughed at that. The driver half turned, then pivoted his head back so his eyes were on the road.

The car roared into high speed, taking a series of dips in the road so fast I could feel the body lurch and sway on its springs.

I settled back into the corner and wrapped myself in silence. Kleinsmidt bit the end from a cigar and smoked. There was no sound save the noise made by the cold desert wind as it whistled around the car, and the sound of the motor. Once or twice we went through streaks of sifting sand hissing across the highway in long tendrils of drifting white.

The pitted crescent of an old moon came up when we had been traveling about half an hour, and a few minutes later the car slowed.

Ahead, a square of multicolored lights marked the location of a landing-field. The driver slowed the car, searched for a turn-off road with a spotlight, found it, and approached the field. Almost at once, I heard the roar of an airplane motor and saw lights come on on a plane.

Kleinsmidt said to the driver, "I'll want a receipt for this so I can turn it in on expenses."

The driver took the money Kleinsmidt gave him and scrawled out a receipt. Kleinsmidt opened the door, grabbed my bag, and we stepped out into the cold. The driver of the car backed it around and started back for the highway. The motor on the plane was turning over with clicking regularity. I could hear the coarse sand crunching beneath our feet.

Kleinsmidt said to me, out of the corner of his mouth, "They'd break me if they knew I'd done *any* talking. You're supposed to hit the chief's office without knowing anything about what the score is."

"Why?" I asked.

Kleinsmidt measured the distance to the waiting airplane, slowed his pace somewhat so he wouldn't get there too soon. "What time did you leave Bertha Cool in the Sal Sagev Hotel?" he asked.

"Why, I don't know. Yes, I do, too. It was shortly after eight."

"Where'd you go?"

"Down to my room."

"What'd you do there?"

"Packed up."

"You didn't check out?"

"No. I left that for Bertha to do. They'd have charged me for another twenty-four hours on the room, anyway, and Bertha's the treasurer. She knew I was going."

"You didn't say anything to anyone in the hotel?"

"No. Just took my bag and walked out. I put a note for Bertha on the desk."

"This one bag all the baggage you have?"

"Yes. What's the idea?"

He said in a low voice, "Somebody got killed. The chief thinks you may have had something to do with it. I don't know what makes him think so, but somebody gave him a bum steer. He thinks it's hot. Keep your head. Don't talk after we get in the airplane."

I said, "Thanks, Lieutenant."

"It's okay," he mumbled. "Just keep turning this over in your mind, and try and get an alibi."

"For what time?"

"From ten minutes to nine until the time the train pulled out."

"I can't do it. I got to the station about nine o'clock. The train pulled in at five minutes past nine, and I got aboard."

"The porter doesn't remember you."

"No. He was talking with someone. My bag was light, and I just climbed up the car steps. I was tired, and I undressed at once. I—"

"Save it," he said as the figure of the pilot loomed up in front of the plane.

"All ready?" Kleinsmidt asked.

"All right. Hop aboard."

We climbed into the low-ceilinged cabin of a single-motored plane. The pilot looked at me curiously, said, "You ever flown before?"

"Yes."

"Understand about your safety belt and all that?"

"Yes."

The pilot jerked down a curtain behind him, gunned the motor into a roar, and we started moving. After a few minutes, the wheels gave a series of short, sharp jolts, and then we zoomed upward and out across the line of colored lights. Ahead, the circling finger of an airway beacon cut through the darkness. Kleinsmidt tapped me on the knee, held his finger to his lips for silence, slid my bag over so that his leg was holding it tightly against the side of the cabin, out of my reach. He closed his eyes and almost immediately began to breathe heavily.

I didn't think he was asleep. Apparently, it was some sort of a trap to see if I'd try to get something out of my bag. I noticed he kept the edge of his foot pushing against the corner of the bag. He'd have felt it if I'd so much as touched the bag.

I thought back on it and remembered how he'd grabbed that bag as soon as he'd got aboard the train, and hadn't let it out of his possession since. Then I remembered how he'd examined my shirt in the washroom. Evidently, the chief of police had been given a very hot tip indeed.

Chapter Eight

CHIEF LASTER GLARED AT ME across his desk and said, "Sit down."

I pulled up a chair and sat down. Kleinsmidt settled himself over on the far side of the room, and crossed his legs.

Daylight was just breaking outside the building. The streamers of eastern clouds were a vivid crimson-orange, giving a reddish tinge to the landscape and even causing a slight russet coloring on the chief's face. There was just enough light outside to make electric lights seem sickly and pale, but not quite enough to dispense with artificial illumination.

Laster said, "Your name is Donald Lam, and you claim to be a private detective."

"That's right."

"Working for the B. Cool Detective Agency."

"Yes."

"Now, you hit town yesterday afternoon on a plane, didn't you?"

"Yes."

"Right away, you started stirring up a lot of trouble.'

"No."

He raised his eyebrows. "No?" he asked sarcastically.

"No. A lot of trouble started stirring me up."

He stared at me to see if I was cracking wise.

"Well, you involved Lieutenant Kleinsmidt in a fight, had an argument with the attendant in charge of the slot machines at the Cactus Patch, then had a street fight with a man by the name of Beegan, didn't you?"

I said, "The attendant over at the Cactus Patch took a swing at me. He called for the police. Lieutenant Kleinsmidt answered. As far as the other is concerned, a man made an unprovoked assault upon both Kleinsmidt and me. Kleinsmidt really got going and this man beat it—fast."

I glanced at the Lieutenant out of the corner of my eye. He was grinning. He liked that version of the fight.

Laster tried another approach. "You called on Helen Framley yesterday, didn't you?"

"Yes."

"How did you get her address?"

"A client of the agency gave it to me."

He started to say something, changed his mind, consulted some notes on his desk, looked up suddenly, and said, "Harry Beegan was her boy friend, wasn't he?"

"I wouldn't know."

"He acted like it?"

"I'm afraid I'm not qualified to judge."

"You were on that train for Los Angeles that leaves here at nine-twenty?"

"That's right."

"You got aboard by the skin of your eyeteeth, did you not?"

"I did not."

"What time *did* you get aboard?"

"As soon as the train pulled in."

"You mean you were waiting at the station and got aboard the train just as soon as it stopped?"

"That's what I said."

"Now, Lam, think that over carefully, because your answer may make quite a difference."

"To whom?" I asked.

"To you, among other people."

"I fail to see any reason for thinking over carefully what time I took a train."

"You're going to stick to that story?"

"That's right."

"You didn't catch the train just before it was pulling out?"

"No."

"You didn't board it after the train had been standing in the depot for some time?"

"No."

"You got aboard just as soon as the train came to a stop?"

"Oh, I waited for the other passengers to get off. That took a minute or two."

"But you were standing there by the train, waiting for the other passengers to get off—"

"That's right. What's all this leading up to?"

"I want to find out a little more about that train first. You were in the depot at nine-o-five?"

"I was at the depot by nine o'clock."

"Where in the depot?"

"I was standing out where it was cool."

"Oh," he said as though he'd trapped me into some damaging admission, "you weren't *in* the depot?"

"Did I ever say that I was?"

He frowned. "You were waiting outside?"

"That's right."

"How long before the train came?"

"I don't know. Five minutes, perhaps ten."

"See anyone you knew out there?"

"No."

The chief looked over at Kleinsmidt. "Bring the Clutmers in, Bill."

Kleinsmidt went out through a door that opened on a corridor. I said to the chief, "Now that I've answered your questions, perhaps you'll tell me what this is all about."

A moment later, the door opened, and the woman who had been in the apartment adjoining Helen Framley's walked into the room; a step behind her came her husband. They looked as though it had been a hard night. Their eyes were red-rimmed. The muscles on their faces sagged.

The chief said, "You know Mr. and Mrs. Clutmer?"

"I've seen them."

"When did you see them last?"

"Yesterday."

"What time yesterday?"

"I don't remember."

"Did you see them after eight-thirty last night?"

"No."

The chief said to Clutmer, "This man claims to have been hanging around the depot waiting for the nine-o-five train to come in. How about it?"

It was Mrs. Clutmer who answered the question. "That's absolutely impossible. I told you he couldn't have been there. The only way he could have caught that train was by the skin of his eyeteeth, because we didn't leave the platform until just as the train was ready to pull out."

"You're sure he couldn't have been there?"

"Absolutely positive. We had been talking about him, and I'd have noticed him if he'd been there."

"What time did you get to the depot?"

"Five or ten minutes to nine I think it was. We had to wait about ten minutes for the train to come in, and it was on time."

Laster looked at me. "There you are."

I said, "Mind if I smoke?"

He frowned. Kleinsmidt smiled.

Laster said to Mrs. Clutmer, "This man says he was on the outside of the depot standing out where it was cool, waiting for the train to come in. Now where were you?"

"We were right inside the depot for a while, and then we went out and stood on the platform outside. But we watched the people get off the train, and we watched the

101

people who got on. Not that I'm nosey at all, but I just like to know what's going on. I just use my powers of observation, that's all."

Laster turned to me.

"Well?" he asked.

I lit a match, held it to the end of my cigarette, and took a deep drag.

Mrs. Clutmer started volunteering information. "Helen Framley is pretty strong for this young man, if you ask me. I know for a fact that she and that boy friend of hers had a quarrel over this man last night."

"How do you know it was over him?" Laster asked.

"You could hear what they said in my apartment just as plain as day. They were talking very, very loud. Their voices were raised—almost shouting at each other. He accused her of falling for him, and she said that if she wanted to she would, that Beegan didn't have any mortgage on her. Then Beegan said he'd show her whether he had a mortgage on her or not, and said she'd spilled a lot of information she had no business giving. Then he used some kind of a funny expression—that is, he called her something."

It was Clutmer who furnished the gap in the information. "Called her a stool pigeon," he said dryly, and then lapsed into silence.

"You hear that, Lam?" the chief asked.

"I hear it."

"All right, now what have you to say?"

"Nothing."

"You're not going to deny it?"

"Deny what?"

"That they fought over you."

"I wouldn't know."

"And you still claim you were down at the depot?"

"I've told you where I was."

"But these people say you couldn't have possibly got

aboard that train immediately after it pulled into the station."

"I heard them."

"Well, what about it?"

"They're entitled to their opinion—that's all it is. I *was* on the train."

Mrs. Clutmer said, "I'm absolutely positive!"

Kleinsmidt said, "Just a minute, Mrs. Clutmer. You went down there to meet some people who were coming through, didn't you?"

"Yes."

"Friends from the East, I believe?"

"Yes."

"You were looking forward to seeing them?"

"Naturally. What do you suppose we went down there for?"

"And you were excited?"

"I don't think so."

"You knew what time the train got in?"

"Yes."

"What time did you leave your apartment?"

"About twenty minutes to nine."

"And walked to the depot?"

"Yes."

"That puts you there fifteen minutes before train time?"

"That's right. That's what I'm telling you. We were there. If anyone had been there, we'd have seen them."

"Why did you go to the depot so early?"

"Well, we wanted to be certain that we met the train."

"You knew it would be there for fifteen minutes? You were pretty excited over seeing these old friends of yours?"

"Well, we were looking forward to it."

"And as soon as the train pulled in, you started looking for them?"

"Well, we looked over the people all right."

"Where were your friends?"

"Standing right in the vestibule."

"And you had quite a little talk-fest there on the station platform?"

"We visited and chatted."

· "Your friends couldn't stop over?"

"No. They were going to Los Angeles on business. They were with some other people."

"And you visited until the conductor called out 'All aboard'?"

"Yes."

"Then they got back aboard the train?"

"Yes."

"Now, did you wait for the train to pull out, or did you leave then?"

"We left then, but the train pulled out right afterwards. We heard it pulling out just as we walked through the depot. And I may say this. We waited until after the porter had closed the vestibule."

"On the car in which your friends were riding?"

"Well—yes."

Kleinsmidt looked at the chief, didn't say anything.

The chief frowned at me, then looked at Mrs. Clutmer. His eyes shifted past her to her husband. "What's your name—your first name?"

"Robert."

"You were with your wife?"

"Yes."

"Do you agree with everything she says?"

"Well—well-l-l-l-l—in a way, yes."

"Where don't you agree with her?"

"Oh, I agree with her all right."

"Do you think there's any possibility this young man could have been at the depot and you not seen him?"

"Well, now there's just a chance—just a bare chance."

"Would it," I asked, "be too much to ask what this is all about?"

Mrs. Clutmer said, "Why, don't *you* know? They—"

"That'll do, Mrs. Clutmer. I'll handle this," the chief interrupted.

She glared at him and said, "Well, you don't need to snap a person's head off. I was only going to tell him—"

"I'll tell him."

"Well, he can read it in the papers. I guess there's no great secret about it. I—"

The chief made a motion to Kleinsmidt. He pushed his big frame up out of the chair, said to the Clutmers, "All right, folks, that's all."

"Let 'em go home," the chief said.

"You can go home now," Kleinsmidt told them.

"Well, I should say it was about time! The idea of getting a body up at midnight and keeping her—"

"Get 'em outside," the chief roared.

Kleinsmidt pushed them through the door and pulled the door shut behind them.

The chief turned to me. "Doesn't look too good for you, Lam."

"Apparently, someone was killed. Who was it?"

Lieutenant Kleinsmidt opened the door, entered the room, and pushed the door shut.

Chief Laster stared down at some notes in a leather-backed book which was open on his desk. Then he took a pen from his pocket and scribbled a few more notes.

He looked up, screwed the cap back on the pen, put it in his pocket, and said, "Harry Beegan was shot and killed last night sometime between quarter to nine and nine-twenty-five."

"Too bad."

They both looked at me. I didn't say anything more and didn't give them any facial expression to read.

"The girl he was living with seems to have skipped out," Chief Laster went on.

"Was he living with her?"

"Well, he was there a lot."

"There's quite a difference," I said.

"A very few minutes before he was killed—sometime within two hours let us say of the time of his death—you called on this girl. Beegan entered the picture. You had an argument. You left. Beegan accused the girl of having fallen for you. He was jealous. He accused her of going out to meet you. She swore she wasn't going to do anything of the sort. She went out. She met you. Beegan followed. You had a fight over the girl, I think it's fair to surmise that you arranged with her to run away from Beegan and meet you in Los Angeles. She left to keep that rendezvous."

"I don't follow your reasoning."

"You were working on a case. Your employer was here. You had planned to stay here for two or three days."

"Who says so?"

"It's a fair inference. Mrs. Cool is still here."

"The job I'm working on is finding someone who disappeared from Los Angeles. That's where the trail starts, and that's a mighty good place to pick it up."

He ignored me. "Suddenly last night out of a clear sky, you announced you were going to Los Angeles on the first available train. You left the Sal Sagev Hotel, which is right at the depot, with lots of time to spare. You had every motive, every incentive, and every opportunity to shoot Harry Beegan, and you know that as well as I do."

"He was shot in the girl's apartment?" I asked.

"Yes."

"How do you fix the time so accurately and yet still have an indefinite interim period?"

"The Clutmers were in their apartment until they went down to the station to meet some friends who were coming through. They left the train and walked directly back to their apartment. They hadn't heard anything at all—no sounds coming from the next apartment. They'd have heard voices raised in an argument. Unquestionably, they'd have heard a shot. That fixes the time of the murder absolutely within those limits."

"Unless the Clutmers are lying."

"Why should they lie?"

"Suppose they didn't like this man, Beegan, and had been waiting for an opportunity to do something about it? When was the body discovered?"

"Shortly before midnight."

"All right, suppose they came home, found Beegan either standing in the door of the girl's apartment or in the hallway or on the stairs? They had an argument. Or else they just walked into the apartment behind him and took a pot shot at him. If you list them as suspects, the killing could have been any time before the body was discovered."

"It sounds silly."

"Perhaps it does to you. It sounds silly to me to think that I'd have shot him."

"You wanted his girl."

"No more than I want a couple of hundred other attractive women."

"Enough to run risks of taking a beating."

"I was working."

"I know," he said, and ran the tips of his fingers along the angle of his jaw, "you have a great devotion to duty."

"When I work on a case, I want to crack it—the same as you do."

"Well, as far as that is concerned, the Clutmers are out of it. That means that the time of the murder stands. Now come on, Lam, let's be fair about this. If you were going to have a meeting with the girl, we'll find it out. If that's all there was to it, we'll forget it. But you know good and well that's why you wanted to go to Los Angeles. Now, isn't it?"

"I don't get you."

"You fixed it up with the girl to meet you in Los Angeles."

"No."

He said, "That denial just doesn't register with me."

"That's okay. Too bad you dragged me off the train."

"What do you mean?"

"I'm only a private detective," I said. "I don't want to tell you how to run your business, but if you had let me go on to Los Angeles and put a shadow on me and if I'd met the girl there, then you'd really have had something. As it is now, you can't prove I was going to meet the girl."

"It's a fair inference."

"Nuts!"

Laster said, "There's one other highly suspicious circumstance. When Kleinsmidt asked you if you knew where Beegan lived, you told him you didn't."

"That's right. I didn't."

"But you'd already been up to the apartment.'

"*He* didn't live there."

"His girl friend did."

"That wasn't what Lieutenant Kleinsmidt asked me."

"Aren't you being rather technical?"

"He asked me if I knew where *Beegan* lived."

"Well, you knew what he meant."

"And because I knew where his girl friend lived and didn't tell Kleinsmidt, you think I was holding out?"

"Yes."

"I saw no reason to drag the girl into it."

Laster said, "That's all for the present."

"I can go now?"

"Yes."

"I want to go to the Sal Sagev Hotel."

"Well, you can."

"I see no reason why I should walk. Remember, I was taken off a train to Los Angeles. I had my transportation and berth all paid for. What are you going to do about that?"

Laster thought for a minute, then said, "Nothing."

"I want to get back to Los Angeles."

"Well, you can't leave until we've finished our investigations."

"When's that going to be?"

"I don't know."

I said, "I'll report to Bertha Cool. If she tells me to go to Los Angeles, I'm going."

"I'm not going to permit it."

I said, "If I'm locked up, I won't go. If I'm not locked up, I'm going. How about having the Lieutenant take me to the Sal Sagev Hotel?"

Laster said, "Don't be silly. It's only a couple of blocks. You're a cool customer, Lam. Kleinsmidt told me as much, but—"

"Nuts. I'm giving you all the breaks. I could make you send me back to Los Angeles. I may yet, after I've talked with Bertha Cool. Right now, all I'm saying is that I want to go to the Sal Sagev Hotel."

Kleinsmidt got up from his chair. "Come on, Lam," he said.

There was a police car outside. Kleinsmidt was grinning as I got in.

"Well?" I asked.

"I told him to let you go through to Los Angeles, have the Los Angeles police pick up your trail, see if you met the girl, and if you did to pinch you both; otherwise, to leave you alone. He wouldn't listen to me. He said it was a cinch you were the one who shot him, that from all reports, you were a pencil-necked little chap who would spill everything you knew if we jerked you off the train, rushed you back here, and didn't do any talking on the way."

I yawned.

Kleinsmidt's car slid smoothly through the streets, deposited me at the Sal Sagev Hotel.

"How about you, Lieutenant?" I asked.

"What do you mean?"

"What were *you* doing last night between eight-forty-five and nine-twenty-five?"

"I was hunting for Beegan."

"Didn't find him, did you?"

"Go to hell," Kleinsmidt said, and grinned.

Chapter Nine

BERTHA COOL WAS DOZING. She was fully dressed, and her door was unlocked. After I'd opened it, I stood on the threshold, watching her stretched out in a chair, her head tilted slightly to one side, her breath coming rhythmically in gentle snores.

I said, "Hello, Bertha. Been to bed and getting up, or just waiting—"

She jerked her eyes open, and sat up in the chair.

There was no period of transition while she was groggy with sleep. One second she had been snoring gently, her lips puffing slightly outward with every exhalation. Now, she was wide awake staring at me with those hard, glittering eyes. "My God, Donald, if this isn't the damnedest town. Did they jerk you off the train?"

"Yes."

"They told me they were going to. I said I'd sue 'em for damages if they did. What did you tell them?"

"Nothing."

"You didn't give them any satisfaction?"

"Not that I know of."

"That lieutenant is all right," she said. "The police chief is a pill. Come in. Sit down. Hand me that package of cigarettes over there and hold a match for me. Suppose we have some coffee sent up?"

I handed her the cigarettes, held a match, went over to the telephone, asked for room service, and told them to send up a couple of pots of coffee with plenty of cream and sugar.

"You drink yours black, don't you, lover?" Bertha called.

"Yes."

"Well," she said, "never mind the cream and sugar for me."

I looked at her in surprise.

"I've begun to think it spoils the flavor of the coffee."

"Okay," I said, "never mind the cream and sugar. Shoot up a couple of pots of black coffee and make it snappy."

"Well," I said to Bertha, "what's the low-down?"

"I don't know. The blowoff came about twelve-thirty. They'd found the body about midnight, I think. There was a great hullabaloo. They wanted to know all about our case, who our client was, and where they could find him."

"Did you tell them?"

"Indeed I did not."

"Was it hard to hold out?"

"Not so bad. I told them that was a professional confidence. I might have had some trouble if it hadn't been that they discovered you'd gone to Los Angeles. That gave them all they needed to work on. They said they were going to catch the train by plane and bring you back."

"How late did they keep you up?"

"Most of the whole blessed night."

"Didn't they ever tumble to Whitewell?"

"After a while."

"How?"

"Snooping around."

"When did Whitewell get back here?" I asked. "Last night after I left?"

"That's the point, lover. He didn't."

"You mean you didn't see him at all?"

"No."

"When *did* you see him after that?"

"About four o'clock this morning."

"Where?"

"He dropped in here after the police had got done questioning him. He was very apologetic because he'd got us mixed up in it. He's an awfully nice man, Donald."

"What did he want?"

"What do you mean?"

"When he called in here at four o'clock this morning."

"Why, he just wanted to know how I'd stood the ordeal and wanted to apologize for getting me involved in a case which put me in such a position."

"And after he'd done all that, what did he want?"

"Why, nothing."

"He mentioned something more or less casually?"

"Oh, he wanted to know how much talking we'd do, and I told him he didn't need to worry, that you wouldn't divulge any information. He said he hoped particularly you wouldn't tell them anything about what case you were working on or about any letters. I told him he could go to bed and go to sleep with a mind free from worry."

"How about Philip? Was he with his dad?"

"No. That's why the father didn't come back here. He and Philip had some difference of opinion."

"Over what?"

"I don't know, lover, but I think it was over you."

"Why?"

"Philip seems to be very enthusiastic about you. He wanted his father to give you a free hand to go ahead and do anything you wanted to find Corla. His father said that was going to be too expensive, that as soon as you uncovered evidence showing that Corla had left of her own free will, that was all he could afford to do. Then Philip suggested she might have left because she was being blackmailed or something, and his father said that if that was the case, she wasn't the sort of girl they'd want in the family anyway; and I guess Philip's nerves were ragged. They had an argument, and his father walked away and left Philip alone in the casino."

I narrowed my eyes as I thought that over. "That would have been somewhere around eight o'clock, or a few minutes later?"

"I guess so."

"You didn't tell the law anything about that?"

"I told the law to mind its own business, and I'd mind mine," Bertha snapped. "The impertinent ignoramuses! Even wanted to know what proof I could give that I'd been here in the hotel all that time. Here I was waiting for Mr. Whitewell to show up, and because of that fight with Philip, he didn't come near me—"

"Where *did* he go?"

"He was very much upset. You know he's really attached to that boy, really and truly, worships the ground he walks on, and Mr. Whitewell was terribly upset. He even forgot about calling me and telling me he wouldn't be here. He didn't—"

"But where did he *go?*"

"He didn't *go* anywhere."

"You mean he came back to his room here in the hotel?"

"Oh, I see what you mean. No. He was very nervous. He walked around for a while, and then came back and tried to go to sleep. He and Philip and Mr. Endicott had a suite. Philip didn't show up until nearly eleven o'clock. The police found out Whitewell was my client and got him up for a grilling. Poor man. I guess he didn't sleep much last night."

"What do you know about the details of the killing?"

"Almost nothing. He was shot. That's all I know."

"What caliber gun?"

"I don't know."

"Did they find the gun in the apartment?"

"I don't think so."

"And no one heard the shot?"

"No. You know how that apartment house is. It's off on a side street, and there are just those two apartments over the store building. The store closes at six o'clock. Someone must have been looking for something in the kitchen. The doors of the cupboard beneath the sink had been pulled open and a couple of pans were on the floor. I understand there were a few drops of blood near the door which leads to the kitchen. I picked up a little information from the questions the officers asked, but they aren't giving out very much information."

"Well," I said, "it's a good thing he was killed. He had it coming."

"Donald, don't talk like that."

"Why not?"

"They'd hold it against you."

"They've got plenty to hold against me now, but it's not going to get them anywhere."

"Didn't the porter remember you, lover?"

"Apparently not."

"How about your ticket?"

"They didn't collect it."

"Nor your Pullman reservation either?"

"No. I just got aboard, climbed in, and went to sleep."

"It's queer the conductor didn't wake you up to take your ticket."

"That," I said, "is because the porter didn't see me. He didn't report to the conductor that anyone had got aboard with a ticket for lower nine."

"Isn't that going to make it rather tough?"

"Perhaps."

Bertha said, "Well, you're a brainy little devil. You can keep yourself out of jail all right, but we must do something to help Mr. Whitewell. Do you suppose this murder has anything to do with Corla Burke's disappearance?"

"I don't know yet. A lot of people could have killed Harry Beegan—and among them is my very estimable friend, Lieutenant William Kleinsmidt of the Las Vegas police force."

Bertha said, "Don't be a sap, Donald. If Kleinsmidt had killed him, he'd have admitted the shooting—posed as a hero— 'Fearless-officer-kills-desperate-criminal-who-has-ter-rorized-neighborhood,' and all that sort of bunk."

I said, "I'm not sold on it. I'm suggesting it as a possibility."

"I don't see where it's even possible."

"I do."

"Why?"

"Citizens don't like it when a cop is too handy with a gun. Kleinsmidt was looking for Pug, and Kleinsmidt was sore. Pug was handy with his fists, and wasn't in any mood to be pushed around."

"But Kleinsmidt could have claimed it was a self-defense no matter what had happened."

"Uh huh."

"Donald, that's not the way to treat me. What's wrong with what I'm telling you?"

I said, "Pug was unarmed. He was in his house. It was something which would pass for that with a jury. An officer is supposed to be able to take an unarmed man without anything more than a sap."

"But Pug was a good fighter."

"An officer is supposed to be able to take an unarmed man."

"What makes you think Kleinsmidt did it?"

"I don't."

"I thought you said you did."

"I said it was a possibility."

"Well, what makes you think it's a possibility?"

"The way the police are trying so hard to pin it on someone else."

"Meaning you?"

"Among others."

"Arthur Whitewell made me promise I'd let him know just as soon as you arrived in town."

"Did he know Kleinsmidt had gone after me?"

"I don't know. He knew someone was going to get you."

"Okay, give him a ring."

I handed Bertha the telephone. She cleared her throat twice and said into the telephone, "Would you ring Mr. Arthur Whitewell's room pull*eese*. Good morning, Arthur. This is Bertha. Oh, you flatterer! Donald's here— Yes— That will be splendid!"

She hung up, looked up at me, and said, "He's coming right up."

I sat down, lit a cigarette, and asked, "How long has this been going on?"

"What?"

"This Arthur and Bertha business."

"Oh, I don't know. We just started calling each other by our first names. After all, you know, we've had quite an experience together—this murder and the resulting investigation."

"How about Philip?"

"I haven't seen Philip except for a moment when the police were asking questions."

"Has Endicott gone to Los Angeles?"

"No. He's still here, but he wants to go."

"Whitewell planning to go?"

"Not for a few days. Give me a cigarette, lover."

I handed her a cigarette, held a match for her. Knuckles sounded on the door, and I opened it for Arthur Whitewell and Endicott.

"Well," Whitewell said, shaking hands, "this is hardly the way we'd anticipated it, is it, Lam?"

"No."

Endicott followed Whitewell's lead in shaking hands, but said nothing.

Whitewell stood over Bertha, smiling down at her. "I don't know how you do it."

"Do what?"

"Have virtually a sleepless night and still look as fresh as though you'd been in bed ever since ten o'clock. I can't get over marveling at your sheer vitality."

Bertha said coyly, "I wish I were one-tenth as good as you think I am."

I said, "I suppose you people have told your story to Kleinsmidt."

They nodded.

"He's been checking up. You'll hear more from him. He's a persistent cuss. I'd say he might be dangerous."

No one said anything for a few seconds, then Endicott said, "Yes, I have an idea you're right."

"Well, it might be just as well for us all to run over the facts and—" I broke off as I heard the pound of rubber heels in the corridor. Then as knuckles beat on the door, I said, "Even money that this is the law now."

There were no takers. I opened the door. It was Kleinsmidt.

"Come in," I said. "I wouldn't doubt if someone is going to suggest breakfast."

"Why, yes," Whitewell said. "An excellent idea. Good morning, Lieutenant."

Kleinsmidt didn't do any pussyfooting. "I have a little checking up to do," he said. "You, Whitewell, haven't told me everything that happened last night."

Whitewell said, "I'm afraid I don't understand."

"Weren't you down at the corner of Beech and Washington Streets at about nine o'clock last night?"

Whitewell hesitated. "I don't know," he said after a moment, "just how I am going to co-operate with you, Lieutenant. You seem determined to—"

"Quit sparring for time," Kleinsmidt said. "Were you or weren't you?"

Whitewell glowered at him. "No."

"You're positive?"

"Of course, I'm positive."

"You weren't there at any time, let us say, between eight-forty-five and nine-fifteen?"

"No, not at any time during the evening."

Kleinsmidt stepped back, jerked open the door, looked out in the hall, and nodded his head.

I said, "Brace yourself, Whitewell."

We heard the sound of quick steps in the corridor, then a girl stood in the doorway.

"Come in," Kleinsmidt said. "Look at the persons in this room and tell me whether any of them is the person you saw last night."

She stepped across the threshold. There was something proudly defiant about her, as though she knew that every hand would be turned against her, and had schooled herself to a pretended indifference. She didn't give the impression of having been aroused at an early hour to face this ordeal. Somehow, looking at her, you felt she hadn't been to bed and that she wasn't accustomed to going to sleep before daylight. There was a little too much color on her face, and her mouth was hard. But she'd taken care of herself, watched her figure, cared for her hands, was particular about her clothes—a woman in the late twenties who had learned never to let her guard down for a moment.

You knew what she was going to say before she said it. Her eyes moved in a swift half circle of appraisal, and then stopped on Whitewell. But before she could say anything, Bertha Cool was leaning forward on the edge of her chair. "No, you don't," she said to Kleinsmidt. "You're not going to pull any frame-ups here. If there's going to be an identification, you put the man in line with some other man of approximately the same age and build and—"

"Who's running this?" Kleinsmidt demanded indignantly.

"You may be running it, but I'm telling you how you'll have to do it if it's going to count."

"It'll count with me. How about it? Is that person here?"

She raised a finger and pointed it at Whitewell.

Kleinsmidt said, "That's all. Wait outside."

"Just a minute," Whitewell said. "I demand to know—"

"Wait outside."

She nodded and walked through the door, shoulders back, chin up, hips swinging with just enough exaggeration to indicate that she knew what we thought and was telling us what we could do about it.

The door closed. Kleinsmidt said, "Well?"

Whitewell started to say something.

"Wait a minute," I interrupted.

He looked at me with his eyebrows arched in the silent interrogation of one who is too well-bred to show annoyed surprise in any other way.

"You've already said it," I told him. "You weren't there. You can't add to that, and—" and I paused significantly— *"you can't subtract from it."*

Kleinsmidt whirled to glare at me. "Lawyer?" he asked.

I didn't say anything.

"Because if you're not," Kleinsmidt said ominously, "we don't like to have people practicing law without a license—not in this state; and when you presume to give advice to a person charged—"

He broke off abruptly, and I asked, "Charged with crime?"

He didn't say anything.

Kleinsmidt turned abruptly to Endicott. "Are you," he asked, "Paul C. Endicott?"

Endicott nodded.

"You're associated in business with Whitewell?"

"I work for him."

"In what capacity?"

"I'm in charge of things while he's gone."

"What do you do when he's there?"

"Keep them running smoothly."

"Sort of a general manager?"

"I guess so, yes."

"How long have you been with him?"

"Ten years."

"Did you know a young woman named Corla Burke?"

"I have seen her, yes."

"Talked with her?"

"Just briefly."

"Where?"

"One night when she came to the office."

"You knew she and Philip were going to get married?"

"Yes."

"When did you come here?"

"Yesterday afternoon."

"How?"

"With Philip."

"In his car?"

"Yes."

"How does it happen I didn't hear about you before?"

Endicott looked at him calmly. There was nothing of antagonism in that glance, nothing of submission. It was merely a disinterested, partially humorous, perhaps partially contemptuous appraisal. "I'm sure I don't know," he said with just the right inflection in his voice.

He was just the type to really run a business. Not simply caring for the details, but doing the executive work, and making the decisions. He wasn't a man who would get rattled. He wasn't one who could be frightened. He made up his mind as to what he was going to do, and he carried through his plans. All of that showed in that instant when the two men stood facing each other.

Kleinsmidt sensed what he was up against. He dropped his bulldozing manner. "Under the circumstances, Endicott, I'm going to want to know what you did last night."

"When?"

"Well, what were you doing around nine o'clock for instance?"

"I was in a picture show."

"Where?"

"The Casa Grande Theater."

"What time did you go into the show?"

"Oh, I don't know, around quarter to nine—perhaps a little earlier. Yes, come to think of it, I guess it was right after eight-thirty."

"How long did you stay?"

"Until I'd seen the entire show. I suppose around two hours."

"When did you first know about the murder?"

"Whitewell told me this morning."

"What did he say?"

"He thought there was some possibility he might be detained here, in which event he wanted me to take a plane to Los Angeles."

"Why the hurry?"

"Because the business has to be kept running."

"How do *I* know you went to the picture show last night between eight-thirty and quarter to nine?"

Endicott said, "I'm sure I wouldn't know."

"What was the picture?"

"Oh, a light comedy, something about a divorced husband who returned just as his wife was about to marry again. Some rather interesting situations in it."

"Can't you describe the plot any better than that?"

"No."

Kleinsmidt said, "I don't suppose there's any chance you preserved your ticket stub?"

Endicott said, "I may have." He started searching mechanically through his pockets. From a right vest pocket, he took out several stubs of tickets, looked at them, selected one, and said, "This is probably it."

Kleinsmidt walked over to the telephone, picked it up, and called a number.

"The theater won't be open this time in the morning," Endicott said.

"I'm calling the manager's house."

A moment later, Kleinsmidt said into the telephone, "Frank, this is Bill Kleinsmidt. Sorry I got you up, but a glass of hot water with a little lemon juice, and a brisk walk will do your waistline a lot of good. Now, wait a minute. Don't get sore— I want to ask you something about your tickets. I have the stub of a ticket that was sold last night. There's a number on it. Is there any way of telling when that ticket was sold? Oh, there is— Just a moment. Hold the phone."

Kleinsmidt raised the ticket stub, studied it, and said, "The number is six-nine-four-three— What's that? Yes, there is. Two letters. *BZ*. Oh, you're certain? Okay, thanks a lot."

"I'm afraid," he said to Endicott, "you're going to have to revise your time schedule somewhat."

Endicott tapped the end of a cigarette on a broad thumbnail, shaking the tobacco down. "Sorry," he said, and then after a second added, "I can't do it."

"Those tickets are keyed," Kleinsmidt told him. "They've had so much trouble with kickbacks on tickets, that they decided to tell exactly when the ticket was sold— at what part of the show in other words. So they worked out a time signal system. *A* is seven o'clock. *B* is eight o'clock. *C* nine o'clock, *D* ten o'clock. And *X, Y, Z* stands for fifteen-minute periods. For instance, *B* on a ticket means that it was sold between eight o'clock and eight-fifteen. *BX* means the ticket was sold between eight-fifteen and eight-thirty. *BY* means eight-thirty to eight-forty-five, and *BZ* means eight-forty-five to nine. They have an automatic stamp which is connected with the clock, and the letters are changed automatically."

"Sorry," Endicott said. "I still think I was in there before eight-forty-five."

"All right then, if you were in there *before* eight-forty-five, you could have got up and walked out."

A slow smile came over Endicott's face. "Afraid, Lieutenant, that I can't oblige you this time. I didn't realize how lucky I was, but if you'll check back on the show last night, you'll find that the feature picture ended about eight-fifty-five, and there was a drawing which took place immediately afterwards. The number of a ticket was called out. I somehow read my number incorrectly and started up to the stage. I saw my mistake. The audience gave me the ha-ha. You can verify that."

"Oh, yeah?" Lieutenant Kleinsmidt asked.

Endicott's voice held just the right amount of amused half-contemptuous tolerance. "As you so aptly express it—yeah," he said.

Kleinsmidt said, "That's an angle I'll investigate. I'll want to talk with you again."

"If you do, come to Los Angeles."

"Don't go to Los Angeles until I tell you to."

Endicott laughed. "My dear sir, if you want to ask me any more questions, you'd better ask them now, because within two hours I'll be headed for Los Angeles."

"Being independent?" Kleinsmidt inquired.

"Not a bit of it, Lieutenant. I simply happen to have a deep-seated aversion to letting an important business get at sixes and sevens merely because you want to hold everyone here in Las Vegas until you've finished your investigation. I can quite understand your position, Lieutenant, and I don't blame you in the least, but I have my own responsibilities."

"I can have you subpoenaed as a witness before the coroner's jury."

Endicott thought it over, nodded slowly, and said, "My mistake, Lieutenant, you can."

"And then you couldn't leave until the case was cleaned up."

"That's right—and the aftermath might be unpleasant. This is important business to you, Lieutenant. To me it's merely an unpleasant interruption, and I propose to see it causes me the least inconvenience."

"Suppose we compromise," Kleinsmidt suggested. "If I do nothing to interfere with your going, will you come back of your own accord if I send for you?"

"Yes—on two provisos. One, that it's really necessary; two, that I can adjust the business so I can leave it."

Endicott started for the door. "If it's all right with you, Arthur," he said, standing with one hand on the knob, "I'll leave here as close to ten o'clock as possible. That will get me in the office shortly after noon."

Whitewell nodded.

"Now, you wanted to write a letter of acceptance on that option given by—"

"Yes," Whitewell interrupted as though anxious to keep details from being disclosed in public.

Endicott took his hand from the door knob, nodded toward the writing-desk. "Just scribble a note," he said. "All you need is to mention the option. It was dated the sixteenth of last month."

Whitewell dashed off a note and affixed his signature with something of a flourish. Kleinsmidt watched him, studying every move he made.

"There aren't any stamps here," Endicott said suddenly. "I'll run down to the lobby and pick up some stamps. There's a vending machine—"

Whitewell said, "Don't bother, Paul. I always carry stamped envelopes ready for just such an emergency as this. Not quite as fresh perhaps as one you'd take from a desk drawer, but Uncle Sam will honor 'em just the same."

He took a stamped air-mail envelope from his pocket, slid it across the desk to Endicott, and said, "Fill out the address. You know where it is."

I glanced quickly at Bertha to see if Whitewell's habit of carrying stamped air-mail envelopes had registered. Apparently it hadn't.

Whitewell sealed the envelope, handed it to Endicott. "Rush this into the mail, Paul."

Endicott took the envelope, said, "I'm not certain of airmail connections out of here, but even if it has to go to San Francisco and back, it'll be there by tomorrow morning at the latest—which will protect you."

Kleinsmidt watched him, his eyebrows ominously level.

Abruptly he turned and smiled at Bertha. "So sorry, Mrs. Cool, I interfered with you so early in the morning. Try and overlook it. If you people can learn to accept these interruptions philosophically, it's going to be a lot easier on you."

He walked quickly to the door, turned on the threshold, and went out.

I looked over at Arthur Whitewell. He was no longer the flatterer, the somewhat muddled and very much worried father. He showed instead as a man with a quick, keenly incisive mind and the ability to reach snap decisions.

"All right, Endicott," he said, "you're going to be running the business. I'll stay here until this thing is straightened up. You get started for Los Angeles."

Endicott nodded.

"I'll be willing to bid up to eighty-five dollars a share to get that block of stock we were talking about last night. You understand?"

"Yes."

"I won't go over fifty thousand for that Consolidated outfit. I think there's a good prospect of oil in that underwriting proposition put up by Fargo. I'll go to seventy-five thousand on it, but I want my money to be the last in and the first out, with as big a slice of velvet as you can get. Understand?"

"You mean to tell them—"

"No. Listen. They're making the same mistake every new business makes—underestimating the amount of capital which is going to be required. Put in twenty thousand on their terms. Stipulate that the stockholders have to raise an additional twenty thousand. Then sit tight. When the shoe begins to pinch, they'll ask for small amounts, two thousand to five thousand dollars. Sit absolutely tight. Wait until they're desperate, then make them our proposition."

"Control?" Endicott asked.

"Control of the common and first preferred covering my investment. I want control *after* I've withdrawn all the money I've put in."

Endicott pursed his lips. "I don't think it can be done."

"It can if you go at it the way I've outlined. They're asking for thirty-five thousand dollars. Ask if they won't be able to raise twenty thousand dollars among themselves if I put in twenty thousand dollars. They'll do it—and they think that will be ample capital."

"I understand," Endicott said.

"Don't talk about this case," Whitewell instructed him. "If any newspaper reporters get in touch with you, laugh at them. I'm here on business. Point out very casually that I stopped off here several hours before the murder was committed. In other words, this is a business trip. My business here was important enough to cause me to take a plane and stop over for several days. Philip is here assisting me and learning certain details about the business. Understand?"

"Right."

"Now Philip is young, hotheaded, and impulsive. He's in love and worried sick over the disappearance of the young woman he was going to marry. You can appreciate the state of his nerves. Temporarily, he's estranged from me. We had an argument. I don't think he's apt to come around holding out an olive branch. I don't think the authorities here will let him leave Las Vegas. If they do, he'll come to you. I'm relying on you to keep him in line."

Endicott nodded.

"Under no circumstances is he to talk with the newspaper reporters. I think you can leave that to his good sense, but if you find him slipping, check him up. If you need anything, get in touch with me by telephone."

"How long do you expect to be here?"

"I don't know, perhaps for some time."

"But surely, you'll be in the office within two or three days. The investigation won't take—"

"I may be in jail," Whitewell said shortly.

Endicott puckered his lips and gave a faint whistle. "I think you'd better get started," Whitewell said. "There's a bare possibility your departure might be delayed."

"Not mine," Endicott said. "The time being stamped on those tickets and the drawing puts me in the clear. But it's all foolishness to suspect everyone who hasn't an alibi or who was anywhere in the neighborhood. That's a goofy way of going at the thing. Why don't they establish a motive and then start checking the time element."

"Because he's an overzealous cop in an isolated community," Whitewell said. "We can't expect metropolitan brains—and you're going to miss connections if you don't get started."

Endicott got to his feet, bowed to Bertha Cool, shook hands with me, flashed a quick smile at Whitewell, said, "Carry on," and hustled his big frame through the door. I could hear his heels pounding heavily on the corridor. Whitewell crossed over to the door and the sound of the clicking bolt in the lock made me realize that his approach toward me held some definite purpose.

"Now then, Lam, what can you do?"

Bertha said, "Arthur, you can trust the agency to—"

He didn't even turn toward her, merely motioned for silence with the palm of his hand.

"If you'll tell us—"

"Shut up," Whitewell said.

The command was so crisply authoritative that Bertha Cool mechanically lapsed into an uncomfortable and surprised silence.

"What about it, Lam? What do you want and what can you do?"

"Tell me what I'm up against first. Kleinsmidt knows about Corla now. That means some of the Clutmers' eavesdropping."

He said, "That girl is mistaken. I wasn't near Miss Framley's apartment."

I said, "I don't think she's lying."

"Neither do I. Don't you see what it means? There's a great family resemblance between Philip and me. She saw Philip. She had no reason to notice him closely, simply saw him as a passing pedestrian. If Philip had been here this morning, she'd have identified him, but he wasn't. She was anxious to make good for the police; she saw me, and there was enough resemblance— We must manage things so she doesn't ever see Philip."

"She's identified you now. She won't go back on that."

"Well, be sure she doesn't. Can you make any suggestions?"

"Sure. Let her see you a few times more, talk and move around in front of her. Then when she sees Philip, he'll register as a total stranger."

"Excellent."

"Does Philip have any alibi?"

"I wouldn't know. That's one thing I want you to find out."

"Shall I let him know that I'm working on that angle?"

"No. That's what I wanted to talk to you about. You mustn't let him know you're working on anything except Corla Burke's disappearance."

I said, "This is going to mean more expenses, you know, and—"

"That's all right."

Bertha Cool straightened up in her chair. "Pardon me," she said, "but—"

Whitewell's hand motioned her into the background.

Bertha said, "To hell with that stuff. Don't think anyone sets prices in this agency except Bertha Cool."

He suddenly became his old self, smiling at her. "Pardon me, Bertha," he said. "No one was trying to go over your head. I simply wanted Lam to understand what has to be done, because he's got to start immediately."

Bertha smiled up at him. Her voice was butter-and-syrup. "You know, Arthur, we have to charge more for working on murder cases than on other matters."

"How much more?"

Bertha looked at me and nodded toward the door. "All right, lover, *you'd* better get started."

Chapter Ten

THE STILL COLD of the desert night had melted under the impact of the sun's rays. The Dearborne residence seemed devoid of life. The brilliant desert sun caught the front of the building and turned the white stucco into eye-aching glare.

I sat in my rented car, parked across the street and in the middle of the block, waiting—soaking up the warmth of the sunlight and trying to keep from feeling drowsy.

I tried smoking cigarettes, but they only relieved the nerve tension, and made me feel even more relaxed. There was a mellow somnolence permeating the entire atmosphere. I closed my eyes to relieve them of the glare—and couldn't raise the leaden lids again. It might have been ten seconds or ten minutes. I snapped to reproachful wakefulness with a start, lowered a window in the door of the car, tried inhaling and exhaling as deeply and rapidly as possible, getting an over-abundance of oxygen in my blood. I tried to think of something that would make me mad. The door opened, and Ogden Dearborne came out.

He stood on the front porch for a minute, stretching his arms above his head. I slid down in the seat of the automobile so that only my eyes remained above the level of the glass in the door.

He looked up at the sky, down at the little strip of lawn in front of the house, straightened, and yawned again, a man without a care in the world, just an engineer working on a government job under civil service, pay checks coming in regularly, election over with, his party in power, and to hell with taxes. Then he casually went back into the house.

Within three seconds after the door had closed on him, it opened again, and Eloise Dearborne came out.

She wasted no time looking up and down the street or at the scenery. She walked with quick, firm steps, quite evidently headed toward some definite destination.

I sat in the car and watched her go. She turned a corner to the left, three blocks down the street. I started the motor, kept far enough back to be out of sight, and swung the car in close to the curb.

It was easy to keep her in view now. The district was becoming more built up, with little stores rubbing elbows. She went into a small grocery store, and I quit crawling along close to the curb, and shut off the motor.

I waited for nearly ten minutes, then she came out, carrying two large paper bags. This time she went only half a block. The sign on the door said, "Light housekeeping apartments."

I jumped out of the car, walked rapidly to the grocery store, bought a ten-cent can of condensed milk, went down to the rooming-house. A woman was sweeping the corridor. I held out the can of milk with an ingratiating grin, and asked, "Where can I find the woman who just came in with the groceries?"

The woman paused in her sweeping, looked up, saw the can of milk.

"What's the matter? Did she drop something?"

"Apparently so."

"I think she's in apartment Two-A," she said. "That's right upstairs and on the front."

I thanked her, climbed halfway up the stairs, waited until I heard the swish-swish-swish of the broom cease, and heard the click of a door. Then I ran back down, jumped into my car, tossed the can of milk into the back, and went to the telephone office.

"Long distance," I said, "station-to-station call. The

number of the B. Cool Detective Agency in Los Angeles. Make it snappy."

Elsie Brand came on the line almost as soon as central got the Los Angeles connection.

"Hello, Elsie. How's the sex appeal?" I asked.

"Rotten. How's the boss?"

"You won't believe it. She's slimmed herself down to around a hundred and fifty."

"What?"

"No fooling. What's more, she's getting coy."

"You're drunk. When are you coming back?"

"I don't know. Listen. Go down to a friendly newspaper office. Look in their morgue for all the dope on a man by the name of Sid Jannix who was a prize fighter. He was up somewhere near the top at one time. Either get some photographs or get a photographer to copy the pictures if you have to. I want them sent on here by air mail. Sal Sagev Hotel."

"Using your own name?" she asked.

"Uh huh. So's Bertha. We're both there at the Sal Sagev. Here's another one. Get hold of the Bureau of Vital Statistics, find out who Sidney Jannix married. See if there's ever been a divorce. Get that information and rush it to me by wire."

"Okay. There are a couple of people anxious to get some service at this end. One of them's a blackmail case, and the other's a hit-and-run. What'll I tell them?"

"Tell them Bertha Cool can't pledge the agency's unique service unless she receives a substantial cash retainer. See how strong they'll go. If it looks good—"

A feminine voice said, "Your three minutes are up."

I jerked the receiver away from my ear, and slammed it on the pronged cradle, but just before the receiver hit, I could hear the unmistakable click coming over the line that announced Elsie Brand had beat me to it. Bertha Cool would never have stood for overtime on a long-distance call. "It took me less than three minutes to tell my husband where he got off," she used to declare, "and nothing that's been said since has been half as important. So if *you* can't say what you want to get off your chest within three minutes, you've got to learn."

I walked out of the telephone office into a restaurant, had a pot of coffee, an order of ham and eggs, and then went over to the Cactus Patch. The attendant told me Louie Hazen wouldn't come on duty until five o'clock that night, but just as I was walking out, another man called to me to wait a minute. Louie, it seemed, was down in the basement, making repairs on some of the machines.

I stood around waiting while they sent for him.

Louie Hazen came up, looked at me dubiously for a moment, then as recognition showed in his eyes, his face broke into a grin. "Hello, buddy," he said, coming forward with his hand pushed out in front of him.

I reached for his hand, but his hand wasn't there. Louie wasn't there. He'd worked that fast shift, pushed my right hand over to one side, and when my eyes finally found his grinning countenance, it was within a few inches of my own, his right fist held gently but firmly against the pit of my stomach.

"You got to watch for it, buddy," he said. "You got to watch for it all the time."

I looked into his filmed eyes, saw the battered nose at close range, the broad grin that disclosed the two missing teeth over on the left side.

"You weren't watchin' for it, were you, buddy?"

I shook my head.

"You gotta be on your guard if you're ever goin' to make a fighter. I could make a fighter outa you, buddy, honest I could. I could teach you how to box, and you'd be dynamite. You've got what it takes. You've got nerve. You got that chunk o' courage in your guts that makes a fighter. I'd like to train you."

I took his arm. "We may do that some day. Where can we talk?"

He led me over into a corner. "What's on your mind, buddy?"

"I want you to do something for me."

"Tickled to death. You know I took a liking to you the minute I hit you. You know how it is, buddy. Some people you'll think you're going to like, but the minute you shake hands with them, you freeze up inside. The minute you touch him, there's some kind of electricity. Well, it was just like that, buddy. The minute my fist struck against the side of your jaw— Say, how is the jaw by the way?"

"Sore."

"You've got what it takes, kid. You've got what it takes. Gimme six months and I'd make a fighter outa you."

"Louie, I want you to do something for me."

"Sure. I already told you that. Just say what it is."

"Seen the morning paper?"

"No."

"Take a look at it."

"Why?"

"A man was killed last night."

"Killed?"

"Uh huh. Shot with a revolver."

Louie's eyes got big and round.

"You mean murdered?"

"That's right. Now, I've got a surprise for you. Guess who it was?"

He shook his head vaguely.

"The man who was in here playing the slot machines last night."

"You mean Sid Jannix, the one-round kid?"

"The police think his name is Harry Beegan."

"I tell you, he's Sid Jannix. I knew the minute I saw him swing that left shoulder up in front of his jaw, and wind up his right, it was the old Jannix crouch. Boy, that used to get 'em. He'd come plowin'—"

"Listen, Louie, I want you to do something."

"Oh, yes, sure. Sure, I'll do anything you want. What is it, buddy?"

"I want you to go down to the morgue and identify the body. Not as that of the man you had the trouble with last night when he was doctoring the slot machines, but as that of Sid Jannix, an old prize-fighter friend. Spread it on about how you fought him once—"

"But I never did."

"It wasn't a formal match, just an informal practice match that was arranged in the gymnasium."

"Jeeps, buddy, I don't want to go to no morgue."

"It isn't going to hurt you."

"I know it ain't goin' to hurt me, but it ain't goin' to do me no good."

"Oh, well, if you don't want to do it—"

"Now wait a minute, buddy. I didn't say I wouldn't do it. I just said I didn't *want* to do it."

"I wouldn't want you to do something you didn't want to."

"Sure, buddy. If you want me to do it, I want to do it. When do you want me to go?"

"Right away."

He adjusted his tie, hitched his coat up around his shoulders, and grinned at me with that snaggle-toothed grin of slap-happy, jovial friendship. "On my way, buddy. Lookin' at that stiff ain't goin' to make my breakfast set no better, but I'm on my way. Where'll you be when I get back?"

"I'll be in here a little later."

"Okey doke, ol' pal, I'll be seein' you. Remember now, I ain't kiddin'. I could make a fighter outa you. I tell you, you got what it takes."

"I'll think it over," I promised, and watched Louie Hazen walk down the long line of slot machines out the

136

front door, his head and neck resting on his shoulders with that unmistakable air of tough competency which characterizes a man who learned the hard way to take it and to dish it out.

I drifted over to the bar. When the bartender moved up and asked, "What'll it be?" I inquired, "Has Breckenridge come in yet?"

"Yeah. I think he's upstairs. Want him?"

"I'd like to talk with him."

"What's the name?"

"Lam."

"How do you spell it?"

"L-a-m."

He turned quickly back toward the mirror, looked at a piece of paper, and asked, "Are you *Donald* Lam?"

I nodded.

"The boss left a note about you. I wasn't on duty last night. He left word for the day shift. Anything you want in the place is yours. What'll it be?"

"Nothing right now. I just want to see Breckenridge."

The bartender caught the eye of a man who might have been an automobile tourist just sauntering around the place, looking the games over. The man's indolence immediately dissolved into fast-moving energy as he came over.

"Wants to see the boss," the bartender said.

Cold eyes stared at me, and the bartender said hastily, "It's Lam. The boss sent down a memo—"

The cold eyes were cold no longer. A well-cared-for hand with a big diamond on it was out in front of me. The man was pumping my hand up and down. "Glad you came in, Lam. How about taking a stack of chips and trying your luck, or—"

"No, thanks. I'd like to see Mr. Breckenridge."

"Right away," he said. "Come on up to the office."

He took me over to the door which led up the stairs. I

noticed there was a screen-protected diaphragm set in flush with the wall. My escort said, "Donald Lam's here, Harvey. I'm bringing him up—" The door swung silently open, and we walked up the stairs.

Somewhere near the head of the stairs, my escort unobtrusively removed himself to return to the casino, and resume his sauntering supervision. I didn't know exactly when he left me because Harvey Breckenridge was coming toward me with his hand outstretched, and a smile on his face. He gave the impression of a man who didn't smile often, and when he did, his thin, tight lips pressed secretively together as though willing to co-operate in the smile only on the condition the cause was kept a strict secret.

"Come in. Sit down."

I went in and sat down.

"Drink?"

"No, thanks. Everybody in the place has been urging me to have one."

"That's good. I looked you up, Lam. I'm awfully sorry about what happened last night. You were damn white about it. You know, you could have put us in quite a spot on that. I appreciated it."

"I gathered that you did," I said, motioning my hand in the general direction of the casino.

"Find everything all right?"

"Very much so."

"Anything you want, just ask for it. Tell the boys who you are, and the place is yours."

"I didn't intend to take advantage of you," I said, "but I have one request."

"What is it?"

"I may want to borrow one of your men."

The smile left his face. It was as expressionless as though he had just drawn a pat flush in a poker game. "Which one?"

"Louie Hazen."

His eyes softened, then he smiled, and, after a moment, laughed outright. "What do you want to do?" he asked. "Assassinate him?"

"No. I might have some use for him. Would it inconvenience you if I borrowed him for a while?"

"Good God, no! Take him with my compliments. I'll give you a quitclaim deed."

"I would, of course, pay his wages while he was—"

"Nothing of the sort. I'll give him a thirty-day layoff from duties and keep him on the payroll. Thirty days be long enough for you?"

"A week should be long enough."

"Take him for as long as you want. The poor devil. I hate to fire him, but—well, you know what he is. He's inoffensive and good-natured enough, but completely punch drunk. I suppose he'll get me into serious trouble if I keep him on here. I hate to just turn him loose. As a matter of fact, Lam, you'd be doing me a favor if you'd take him off my hands for a while. I'm going to try and find something else for him."

"You haven't had him long, have you?"

"Hell, no. I don't owe him anything. I should throw him out, but I can't do it. There's something about him that gets you. He's like a stray puppy coming around and wagging his tail, being so friendly and eager that you haven't the heart to kick him back down into the alley where he belongs. He'd be all right out on a ranch somewhere, and it might do him good, but he's permanently punch drunk. They pounded him enough so they jarred his brains out of plumb, got him so he thinks on the bias. When do you want him?"

"I may want him right away."

"As soon as he comes in, have him come up here and I'll tell him. What do you want him for, or is it any of my business?"

I met his inquisitive eyes. "I want him," I said, "to teach

me how to box."

"He's yours," Breckenridge said, but he was no longer smiling, and his eyes were squinted in concentration as I shook hands and walked out of the office.

Chapter Eleven

MY FIRST KNOCK on the door of apartment 2-A was a gentle, insistent tapping.

A woman's voice called, "Yes? Who is it, please?"

She seemed trying to keep the fright out of her voice.

I, said nothing, waited nearly twenty seconds, then knocked again, this time more insistently. The voice sounded from close to the door. "Who is it?" A note of panic had crept into the voice now.

I still didn't say anything, just waited—waited a good thirty-five seconds. Then knocked again, this time louder than before.

"Who—" Her voice broke.

I was raising my hand to knock for the fourth time when I heard the sound of a key in the lock, and the door opened a few inches. My shoulder pushed it the rest of the way. Helen Framley gave ground before me as I entered the room and walked toward her. Her face was chalk white. Her hand was on her throat.

"Well?" I asked.

"Close—close the door, Donald."

I half turned, stabbed at the edge of the door with the toe of my shoe, and slammed it shut.

"Well?" I asked.

"Sit down, Donald. My God, don't look at me like that!"

I sat down, took a package of cigarettes from my pocket, offered her one, took one myself, and held out a match.

She touched my hand in guiding the flame to her cigarette. I could feel her arm trembling. The tips of her fin-

141

gers were cold.

"How did you find me?"

"Easy."

"No. It couldn't have been."

"You forget I'm a detective."

"I don't care if you're the whole police force. It wasn't easy. I've been around enough to know how to take care of myself when I'm in a jam."

"All right, what difference does it make whether it was easy or hard? I found you, didn't I?"

"Why?"

"Because I wanted to hear your story."

"I haven't any."

"That's too bad."

"What do you mean?"

"The police won't like it."

"Donald, you're not going to—you're not going to *rat!*"

"The police will find you."

"No. They won't."

I just smiled, and I made it as superior as I could.

"The police haven't a thing in the world on me."

"Except that the murdered man was living with you in your apartment, and—"

"He wasn't living with me!"

"He spent most of his time there, didn't he?"

"Some of it, but he wasn't—wasn't living with me."

"Can you prove it?"

"Of course not," she said. "I don't take a notary public to bed with me."

I took the cigarette from my lips, and yawned.

"Donald, what's come over you? You don't think *I* killed him, do you?"

"Didn't you?"

"Don't be silly."

"Someone did."

"And he had it coming to him, too, if you ask me."

"The police would be interested in that statement."

"Well, the police wouldn't hear anything out of me. Do you think I'd squeal?"

"Probably not."

"You can bet your bottom dollar I won't."

"Got an alibi?"

"For what time?"

"Oh, around ten minutes to nine to about nine-twenty."

"No."

"Tough luck."

"Donald, listen to me. How did you find me? I thought this was absolutely airtight."

"Easy."

"Well, how?"

"That's a professional secret."

"I suppose you'd like to see me get a first-degree rap?"

"No. Believe it or not, I came to help you."

Some of the haunted, hunted expression left her eyes. "You're a brick."

"You can't stay here."

"Why not?"

"It's too easy to trace you."

"I didn't think they'd ever find me—not in a thousand years."

"They'd find you in a thousand minutes."

"What were you going to suggest?"

"I could get you out of town."

"How?"

"It's a secret."

"All right, what's your price?"

"I want to know what happened."

"Do you really want to take me out of town, Donald?"

"I'd do it for a consideration."

"You're a funny boy."

"I want something."

"What?"

"Information."

"That all?"

"Yes."

She pouted. "I don't believe I ever knew a man exactly like you. Tell me, are the police looking for me?"

"What do you think?"

"Why don't they get busy and find the real murderer?"

"They're looking for clues."

"Well, what am I going to do? Shake clues out of my sleeves, pull some out of the tops of my stockings, put 'em on a silver platter, and say, 'Here, Mr. Copper.' "

"That's between you and the police. If you don't tell what you know, it might put you in a serious position. You were the last one to see Harry Beegan alive."

"I was not. I broke up with him right after the fight."

"You ran away with him."

"I ran down to the alley. He came along after a few minutes. He grabbed my arm, and we ran almost to the end of the alley. There was a high board fence there. He picked me up and put me up to where I could reach the top. After I got up, I gave him a hand and he made it."

"And then?"

"We waited for a while until the cops had gone by. We could hear them talking, see their lights flashing, and hear them asking questions. A lot of people came along behind the cops. We made a clean getaway."

"Then what?"

"Then," she said, "I told him that he was a double-crosser, and that I was finished. He knew I meant it, too."

"And beat up on you?"

"Nothing like that. He begged and pleaded, promised he'd never interfere again, told me that he couldn't help but be jealous because he loved me so much, but that he'd

"Playing pool?"

"Two or three of them were."

"Did they look you over pretty carefully?"

"I'll say."

"Think they'd remember you?"

"Oh, I suppose so," she said, her voice showing her weariness. "The way they looked me over, if I'd had a mole the size of a pinhead just below the knee on my left leg, they'd have remembered it for twenty years. Does that answer your question, Mr. Detective?"

"It does. How about the second stories on those buildings? Was there a rooming-house or a hotel there in the block?"

"I don't know."

"Notice any lights in the windows above you?"

"No."

"Would you have noticed them if they'd been there?"

"I don't know. I was mad. When I'm mad, I don't notice things."

"Let's get back to Harry Beegan."

"Let's not. Listen, Donald, I want to get out of here. Can you get me out?"

"Yes."

"What do I have to do?"

"Exactly as I tell you to."

"For how long?"

"Perhaps two or three weeks."

"In order to get out?"

"Partly that. The rest of it is the price I'm charging for getting you out."

She looked puzzled. "Are you just making a cold-blooded proposition to me?"

"It isn't a proposition."

"What is it?"

"A business arrangement."

"What do you want with me?"

146

"I think you can help me."

"Do what?"

"Clean up a case I'm working on."

"Oh, *that!*" she said.

I tapped the ashes off my cigarette.

"All right," she said abruptly, "when do we start?"

"When can you get packed?"

"I'm packed. I didn't bring anything with me. There wasn't time for that."

"Not even a suitcase?"

"Just a little bag."

"When did you get it? I mean, when did you go to the apartment to get it?"

"Don't you wish you knew?"

"It'll come out sooner or later anyway."

"You can find out then."

"How about Eloise Dearborne?"

"What about Eloise Dearborne?"

"How long have you known her?"

"Where does she live?"

"Here."

"Here! Why, what does she do?"

"Her brother's an engineer out at Boulder Dam."

She shook her head. "I don't know her."

"Who," I asked, "was the redheaded girl with the bunny nose that you were chumming around with at the Cactus Patch?"

"I don't know whom you mean."

"Don't know anyone like that?"

"No. I may have stopped and passed the time of day with someone, but I haven't any friend who answers that description. How old?"

"Oh, twenty-three or twenty-four."

She shook her head.

I said, "Well, get ready to go. We may leave in a hurry."

"Okay."

147

"Now, one other thing. In traveling, we don't want to excite attention. There may be times when—when you'll have to—"

She laughed at me. "It took you a long while to get around to that, didn't it, Donald?"

I said, "Yes," got up, and walked out.

Chapter Twelve

BERTHA COOL CALLED, "Who is it?" in response to my knock.

"Donald."

"Come in, lover. The door's unlocked."

I opened the door. Bertha Cool was standing in front of the full-length mirror, looking back over her left shoulder at her reflection.

"What's the idea?" I asked.

She lashed out at me irritably, "I'm just looking at myself. Can't a woman look at the way her skirt hangs without you thinking there's something unusual about it?"

I walked over to a chair and sat down. Bertha Cool continued to study her reflection from various angles. "How old do you think I am?" she asked abruptly.

"I don't know."

"Well, make a guess."

"I don't want to."

"Good heavens, you've formed *some* opinion. A person always get an idea of how old anyone is. How old did you *think* I was when you first saw me? No, not then. How old do you think I look *now*?"

I said, "I don't have any idea how old you are. I don't even know how old you look. I came to tell you I was quitting."

She jerked her head around. Her hard, glittering eyes stabbed into mine. "Quitting!"

"That's what I said."

"But you can't quit."

"Why not?"

"Why—why, you're working on a case. You're—why,

149

what would I do without you?"

"You'd get along. You said just the other day that before you knew me, you were able to run a legitimate agency. That since you'd employed me, you were always in hot water."

"Why do you want to quit?" she asked, coming over to sit down where she could look at me.

"I'm going away."

"Going away?"

"Yes."

"Where? Why?"

"I don't know where. I'm in love."

"Well, why quit your job just because you're in love?"

"Because I think it would be better."

Bertha Cool said sarcastically, "You know, people have been in love and still managed to keep their jobs. Lots of them get married and still manage to work. Don't ask me how they do it, because I don't know, but it *has* been done; and if you're resourceful, you should be able to figure out some way. They tell me lots of men want to support their wives, and in order to do it, they have to work. Some men even put off marrying until they can get jobs. It seems a shame, but that's what actually happens. They claim there are statistics to prove it."

"I know," I said. "I'm quitting."

"And how are you going to support this little wren, or has she a fortune of her own?"

"We'll get along."

"Donald Lam, you listen to me. You can't pull out and leave me in the lurch this way, and what's more, you aren't in love. You've just fallen for some little trollop who's given you the come-hither eye. My God, if you knew as much about women as I do, you'd never even think of marrying one. Don't ever kid yourself. They want security, and they don't want to be old maids. They're hunters, Donald, ruthless, skillful, unprincipled, who talk mealy-mouthed and make sheep's eyes at you, but all the time in the backs of their heads they're thinking, 'Well, this man isn't exactly what I want, but he'll do in a pinch, and he's so soft-hearted and polite that if I just string him along, I can lead him into a proposal of marriage without his ever knowing he's had a ring stuck through his nose. He's too much of a gentleman to turn me down.' They—'"

"This woman isn't like that."

"Oh, no! No, of course not. *She's* different."

"She is."

"Well, why won't she let you keep your job then?"

"Because she doesn't like police. She doesn't like detectives. She wouldn't really fall for me if I kept on being a private detective."

"What's wrong with being a private detective?"

"Some people are just prejudiced, that's all. This girl has been on the other side for too long."

"Who is she?"

"You wouldn't know her."

"Who is she?"

"She's a nice kid, but she never did have the breaks. She—"

"Who is she?"

"She's the girl who had the apartment where Harry Beegan's body was found."

Bertha Cool took a deep breath, folded her hands on her lap, looked at me steadily, then slowly exhaled and shook her head. "You've got *me* stopped," she said. "I don't know what to do with you."

"Just get someone else to take my place."

"Donald, are you serious?"

"Of course."

"You realize what you're saying?"

"Naturally."

"You mean that you're going to give up your job simply to make a play for a little tart who plugs slot machines for a living, and who was living with a broken-down prize fighter?"

"We'll leave her out of it."

"Don't ever kid yourself, all she's in love with is your pay check. You quit your job, and she'll give you the air."

"Not that girl. You see, she knows who murdered Harry Beegan."

Bertha Cool said, "Now, listen, lover, you know as well as I do that— She what!"

"Knows who murdered Harry Beegan."

"How?"

"She was in partnership with Beegan. Naturally, he told her everything."

"In partnership!" Bertha snorted.

"That's right. They were partners. It was a business arrangement."

"Oh, yes," Bertha sneered. "A business arrangement. Of course, he lived in her apartment, but it was just a business arrangement. She's a dear, sweet little girl, and she couldn't think of marrying a private detective. Oh, dear, no. And because Beegan was her *partner* he told her everything. I presume that means he talked to her after he was dead."

"Will you lay off of her?"

"I'm just trying to keep you from making a fool of yourself. Within six months, you'll wonder how you could have been such a complete utter ass."

"I don't think so."

"Well, I do. I know it. I'll tell you something else. If that girl knows who murdered Harry Beegan, she'd better come through with the information. If you ask me, I think it's a stall. I think *she* murdered him. She must have. He was found in her apartment."

"Will you make out a check for what I have coming and quit talking?"

"I'll be damned if I do, not until you come to your

senses. I wouldn't give you your money if you were drunk, and I'm not going to give it to you while you're crazy. And what are we going to do about finding Corla Burke?"

"You can hire someone else to get on the job, someone who's had more experience than I have and who will be crazy to get the position."

Bertha Cool said, "I'm not so certain that Harry Beegan's murder isn't connected with Corla Burke's disappearance."

I said, "Helen Framley's a nice girl. She wouldn't know about that. All she knows about is Harry Beegan's murder, and you know how girls like that are. They won't rat. That's another reason why I'm quitting my job. She'll tell me all she knows. If I were working for you, I'd have to betray her confidence. I don't want to be in that position."

"Donald, you're crazy!"

"No. I'm in love."

"Well, being in love doesn't need to paralyze your brain cells. You don't have to—"

There was a gentle knock on her door. She called, "Come in, please."

The door opened, and Arthur Whitewell stood in the doorway.

Bertha Cool said, "Why, hel-lo, Arthur. Come in."

He said, "I thought you might want to take a little stroll around the city, and look in on some of the roulette games. After all, we can't let business entirely monopolize our time. All work and no play, you know. Is that a *new* dress?"

"Yes. I had it sent up. And it fits."

"I'll say it fits! It's wonderfully becoming."

Bertha said, "I never thought I'd see the day when I could wear ready-made clothes again."

Whitewell said, "You have a knack of wearing clothes. Anything you put on would look well. You have a marvelous figure—just the right proportions."

Bertha Cool said archly, "Flatterer!"

"No. I mean it. How about the stroll down the main stem, and risk a few dollars on the wheel of fortune?"

Bertha said, "Do you know what's happened to me?"

"No."

She said, "Donald wants to quit. Can you imagine that?"

"Quit what?"

"Quit working for me."

Whitewell looked at me. His eyebrows leveled. "*When* does he want to quit?"

"Now," I said. "Immediately."

"What's the matter?" he asked, looking from Bertha to me.

"He's in love," Bertha explained. "She's a dear, sweet, innocent little girl who—"

I got up and started for the door. "If you're going to discuss my private affairs," I said, "you'll probably feel more free to do so if I'm not here. And if you're going to talk about that girl, I don't want to listen. She's far too good for *you* to understand."

I pulled the door shut behind me and started down the corridor. I'd gone half a dozen steps when I heard the door jerk open, then Bertha Cool's voice saying, "Let him go, Arthur. It won't do any good. Once he's made up his mind, he—" The closing door cut off the rest of what she had to say.

I walked back to the Cactus Patch. Louie Hazen hadn't got back. I went down to the telegraph office and said, "I'm Donald Lam, with the B. Cool Detective Agency. I'm expecting a telegram from Los Angeles sent to me at the Sal Sagev Hotel. It—"

"Just a minute," the attendant said. "I'll take a look."

She came back in a few minutes. "It was just coming in over the wire when you came in."

"All right, I'll pick it up here and save you the trouble of taking it to the hotel."

She looked at me for a moment, then asked, "Do you have one of your cards with you?"

I gave her one of the agency cards.

She looked at it, opened a drawer, dropped it in, handed me the telegram. It was from Elsie Brand and said:

Sidney Jannix material being sent air mail. Married Elva Picard December fourteenth nineteen thirty-three. No record of any divorce. Find someone else has been looking up record. Believed to be detective representing some agency and interested in Elva Picard. Dietary complex may be due biological urge. Don't let her fall too hard she might not bounce.

I put the telegram in my pocket and walked over to the Cactus Patch to wait.

The floor man came up to me and tried to get me to take a stack of chips with the compliments of the house. He said Breckenridge would appreciate it a lot if I'd "make myself 'right at home.' "

I told him I appreciated the offer, but I was waiting for Louie Hazen to come in, and that I'd prefer just to stick around and watch the people.

He tried to get me to accept a drink, and seemed disappointed that I wouldn't let the house do something for me. Also, he couldn't seem to understand my attitude. After a while, he went away.

I'd been there about fifteen minutes when Louie Hazen came in.

"Everything okay?" I asked.

"It depends upon what you mean, okay. The bulls are nuts. Know what they're tryin' to do? The first rattle out of the box, they want to pin it on me."

"Pin what on you?"

"Killing Sid Jannix."

"You're crazy," I said.

155

"No, they are."

"How do they get that way?"

"Well, it's Jannix all right, see? I identified him, and they wanted to know how I knew. Seemed to think that just because I'd seen a man once in the ring I couldn't identify him when I saw him on a slab. So I told 'em I couldn't have picked him out if I'd just seen him stretched out stiff, but that I'd seen him and talked with him the night before, that I'd seen him in action. When you fight for a living, you learn how to look for little peculiarities in a man's fighting style, and once you've seen 'em, you remember 'em as long as you live. Well then, the bulls wanted to know all about where I saw him in action, and as soon as I told 'em, they started jumpin' on me, said that I had a grudge against him, that he'd been too good for me, and had got me in bad on my job, and that I'd sworn I was goin' to get even. They called up Breckenridge and asked him all about it, and asked him if I hadn't said something about getting even."

"What did Breckenridge say?"

"He told 'em I'd made some crack, but that they wasn't to pay any attention to me because I was slap-happy. Can you feature that? Louie Hazen, slap-happy! That's a joke!"

"Then what?"

"Well, they really went to town, gave me the works, yellin' at me that I knew I'd killed him and all that sort of stuff. Well, after a while I guess I convinced them that I didn't know anything about it, and they told me I could go. Cripes, I was working all the time the murder was being committed. I tell you they're nuts."

I said, "I've got a little dough saved up, Louie. Breckenridge says he'll give you a thirty-day layoff. How about really putting me in condition?"

"You mean for a fighter?"

I nodded.

His eyes lit up. "That's the talk! We could really do

something with you. You've got what it takes. You willing to go in the ring?"

"No. I just wanted to learn something about fighting."

"That's swell—but—"

"I've got this dough saved up, Louie. I'll pay you just what you're getting here. You won't be out anything, and your job will be here when you get back."

He said, "I could take you on right here. We could fix up a place down in the basement, and I could give you a little instruction every day, and—"

"No. I'm run down. I want to get out where I can be completely away from everyone. We'll go somewhere and put up a little training camp—some place up around Reno, perhaps. There'd be a girl with us."

"A girl!"

"Uh huh."

He blinked at me for a minute, then grinned in snaggle-toothed appreciation. "When do we start?"

"Right away," I said. "I'm going to pick up a second-hand car that will hold the outfit. We'll camp along the road, and take it easy. It won't cost us much."

"Say," he said, "I'm a swell camper. That's one of the things I'm good at, camp cooking."

I said, "Get your things together. We've got to get started in a hurry. I have an idea the cops may try to stop us if we don't get the jump on them."

For a moment, there was a flicker of fear in his eyes, then he said, "You can't get started too quick to suit me, buddy. I got some gloves, but they're pretty light. We'll want to get a heavier set for training. And we're goin' to need a punchin'-bag. I sold mine when I left Los Angeles, but we can get a good one for—"

"We'll pick it up in Reno," I told him.

Chapter Thirteen

I KNEW BERTHA would be laying for me at the hotel. So I never went back. What money I had saved up was in the form of traveler's checks, and I bought an ancient jalopy, picked up a heavy woolen shirt, some overalls, and a leather coat at one of the stores, purchased some bedding, a gasoline stove, cooking-pots, threw in a few canned goods, and was ready to leave by three-thirty that afternoon.

We looked like a typical bunch of dust-bowl refugees as we went rattling out of town. No one tried to stop us. We passed a carload of cops who looked us over and let us go on by.

We rattled out on the Beatty road, the car turning out a consistent thirty-seven miles an hour.

Along in the late afternoon, I pulled off on a crossroad which ran out into the desert, a pair of twisting ruts cut into the sand. After we were a couple of hundred yards from the main highway, I pulled out, picked my way through clumps of sagebrush, and stopped on a bare stretch of wind-blown desert.

"How about it?" I asked Louie Hazen.

"It's a swell place, buddy."

Helen Framley got out without a word, started lifting things out of the car.

"You got enough blankets," she said to me.

"We'll need them."

Her eyes met mine. "Two beds or three?"

"Three."

"Okay."

She spread the blankets down on the desert. Louie lifted the gasoline stove out of the carton in which it had come, set it up on the running-board, filled the fuel tank, and in a few minutes had a hissing blue flame under a coffeepot.

"What can I do?" I asked.

"Nothin'," he said. "Just stick around. You're the man of the family, the big boss. Ain't that right?" he asked, looking over at Helen Framley.

"That's right."

"What do I call you when it's time to come to meals?" he asked, giving her that snaggle-toothed grin.

"Helen."

"Okay. I'm Louie. There ain't no hard feelin's because of that slot-machine business?"

"Not a bit," she said, and pushed out her hand.

He folded his battered fist around her slim fingers, grinned once more, and said, "We're gonna get along."

He started moving around, picking out pots and pans, reaching into the grub box. There wasn't so much as a wasted motion. He didn't seem to be particularly in a hurry, but he accomplished things in an incredibly short time.

Helen and I tried once or twice to help, but he brushed us aside impatiently. "This ain't goin' to be no feast," he said. "We ain't goin' to set no table or have no style. We ain't got enough water to do a lot of dishwashin', and there ain't goin' to be many dishes, but the grub's goin' to stick to your ribs."

A few moments later, a breath of desert wind wafted an odor of beans over to our nostrils, beans with a touch of garlic and the smell of fried onions.

"Louie," I asked, "what is that?"

"That there," he said with pride, "is a dish of my own invention. You cut up a couple of onions fine, put 'em in a little water, and let 'em boil down to a dry pan. Then you add a little grease and fry 'em up. Put in a little garlic, then open a can of beans, and put in some syrup. That there grub will stick to your ribs, and it ain't goin' to taste bad."

Helen and I sat side by side on the blankets watching the western sky as some invisible artist went about painting a desert sunset, working swiftly with vivid colors, and a bold brush.

We were still watching the colors when Louie pushed steaming plates into our hands. "Here you are," he said, "all dished up. You eat it on the one plate, and what I mean is you clean it up." And he grinned at us.

We went to work on the grub. It tasted better than any cooking I'd had for months, with fresh sourdough French bread to sop up the gravy that was left in the plate after we'd cleaned out the mixture of beans, onions, and garlic.

Helen sighed. "I think that's the best food I've ever tasted. Donald, why didn't you think of this sooner?"

"I don't know. I guess I'm dumb," I said.

The afterglow faded from the west. Blazing stars came out to hang in the sky overhead.

Helen said, "I'll do the dishes."

Louie was insulted. "What does a nice girl like you know about doin' dishes? Not camp style, anyway. Look, sister, out here in the desert we don't have much water, see? I'll show you how it's done."

He took the dishes out to a place about fifteen yards in front of the car, turned on the headlights, squatted on his heels, and scooped up sand. He piled sand in the plates and started rubbing. By the time he'd finished, the sand had soaked up everything that had been left on the plates and scoured them clean. Louie poured boiling water over the dishes, just a few spoonfuls to each dish. The water cleaned off what was left of the sand, and left the dishes bright and clean.

"There you are," Louie announced proudly, "a lot cleaner than you coulda got 'em with a whole dishpan full of water. Now we'll stack 'em up on the running-board and be all ready for breakfast. What time you want to roll out?"

"I'll let you know," I told him.

Louie said, "I thought I'd pull my blankets over here and—"

"This is all right," Helen said. "I've got the three beds made, side by side."

Louie waited for a few minutes, then said, "Okay."

We sat around on the blankets for a while.

"How about a campfire?" Louie asked.

I said, "Someone might be looking for us along the road."

"Yes. I suppose so. How about a little music?"

"Got a radio?" I asked.

"Somethin' better," Louie said.

He pulled a harmonica from his pocket, tenderly wrapped his warped fingers and battered knuckles around the instrument, and raised it to his mouth.

It wasn't the sort of playing I'd expected. I'd been prepared for *Home Sweet Home* and some of the harmonica classics, but Louie gave us everything. The music which poured forth from that harmonica seemed somehow to blend in with the calm tranquillity of the desert night. It became a part of the darkness, the stretches of silent sand, and the steady stars.

Helen came over to lean against my shoulder. I slipped an arm around her waist. I could feel her steady, regular breathing, the warmth of her cheek, could smell the fragrance of her hair. Her hand stole into mine, slender and soft. I felt her shoulders heave as she took in a deep breath, then gave a long sigh.

The night was still warm. Twice within an hour we heard the distant snarl of approaching automobiles. Headlights danced vaguely up and down the main highway, casting weird shadows. The sound of the approaching car grew to a whine, then rapidly faded as the glare of the brilliant headlights gave place to the glowing red of a receding taillight. There were only those two cars within more than an hour. For the rest, we had the desert to ourselves.

Louie's music had the majesty of organ music. It was, of course, due in part to the environment, the desert, and the steady stars, in a sky which looked as though it had been freshly washed and polished by some cosmic housekeeper. Louie played by ear, but he was an artist, and he made that harmonica accomplish things one would have thought impossible.

Then, after a while, Louie quit playing, just let the music fade into silence, and we sat there, looking up at the stars, out at the dim outlines of the automobile, of the sagebrush against the sand of the desert, feeling the eternal silence.

Helen said softly in a half whisper, "It's close to heaven out here."

I could feel the warmth of her body through her clothes and mine, could feel the weight of her head settling down against my shoulder. Once or twice her muscles gave involuntary little twitches, as the nerve tension relaxed, and her body surrendered itself to drowsiness.

After a while, a breeze so faint as to be all but imperceptible stole over the desert, but that breeze was cold. The warmth simply vanished. The breeze grew stronger. You could feel the air moving now. Helen snuggled closer. She doubled her legs, and pushed her knees hard against my leg. For a moment, warmth returned, then the breeze came again, and Helen straightened with a shiver.

"Gettin' cold," Louie said.

"Bedtime," Helen announced. "Mine's the end bed. Donald, you sleep in the center."

She moved over to her blankets, slipped out of her outer clothes. It was too dark for details, but the starlight showed the general contours of her figure as her outer garments slipped down her smooth limbs. I watched her without curiosity and without self-consciousness. It was as though one were seeing a beautiful piece of statuary by starlight.

She slid under the covers, twisted and turned for a moment, slipping out of her underclothes, then sat up in bed to pull pajamas on and button them around her neck.

" 'Night," she said.

"Good night," I called.

Louie, slightly embarrassed, kept silent, pretending to think she had been talking only to me. She raised herself on one elbow. "Hey, Louie," she called.

"What?"

" 'Night."

"Good night," he mumbled self-consciously.

We waited a few minutes until she had settled herself in her blankets, then Louie and I got out of our clothes and snuggled down into our covers in our underwear.

I wondered how cold it was going to get. I could feel the tip of my nose getting cold. The stars were hanging in the sky directly above me. I wondered if one of them might fall, and if so whether it would hit me—then suddenly I opened my eyes, and an entirely different assortment of stars was in the heavens. The ground was hard underneath, and my muscles were cramped, but the clear fresh air, keen with the tang of dustless cold, had purified my blood, sucked the poisons out of me, and left me feeling as relaxed as though I'd been sleeping for a month.

I closed my eyes again. Once I woke up just before dawn to see the frosty glitter of bluish green where the sky was just beginning to take on color above a band of pale orange. I watched the orange grow vivid, saw a little cloud leap into crimson prominence. Listened to the rhythmic breathing of the girl on one side, heard Louie's placid snoring—thought about getting up at the "crack of dawn," and then snuggled down into the warmth of my blankets.

When I woke up, the sun was over the horizon, casting long shadows from the greasewood and sagebrush. A series of rippling contortions of the blankets next to me showed that Helen Framley was getting dressed. Louie was bent over the stove on the running-board of the car, and the fragrance of coffee stung my nostrils.

There has never been anything quite as soul-satisfying, quite as filled with the promise of life as the smell of coffee out in the open when the fresh air has done its work, and you realize that you're ravenously hungry.

Helen Framley came up out of her blankets, to stand slim and graceful. The golden rays of the early-morning sun touched the youthful lines of her figure with reddish orange. She glanced at me, saw I was looking up at her, and said naturally, " 'Lo, Donald."

" 'Lo," I said.

Louie turned around at the sound of her voice, then whirled back to bend over the stove.

There was quiet amusement in her eyes. "Hello, Louie," she called.

"Hello," he called back over his shoulder.

She finished her dressing, and said, "I could go for this in a big way. I wonder why someone didn't invent it sooner."

"It's been here longer than we have," I remarked.

She stood facing the east, the sun illuminating her features. Abruptly, she flung out her arms toward the sun in an impulsive gesture, then turned, sat down, and slipped on her shoes.

Louie said, "Half a basin of water apiece, and that's all, and breakfast'll be ready in five minutes."

We washed up, cleaned our teeth, sat on our blankets, while Louie gave us scrambled eggs, coffee that was golden clear, bacon cooked somehow so that it had a nutty flavor, crisp without being brittle. He had a little wood fire going, had let it die down to coals, and a screen propped on some small rocks over these coals was the grate on which he had browned thin slices of the French bread into golden-crisp toast with butter glistening on it.

Every mouthful of food seemed deliciously flavored

strength. I felt as though I didn't need boxing lessons, that I could stand up to any man on earth and blast him to the ground with my bare fists.

We sat around for a few minutes after breakfast, smoking cigarettes, soaking up the warmth of the sunlight. We finished our cigarettes. I looked at Louie. We looked at the girl. She nodded. We started rolling up the blankets, fitting them into the ancient jalopy. No one spoke much. We had no need for words.

Half an hour later, with dishes all done and put away, the car neatly packed, we were on our way, rattling across the desert, the motor full of piston slaps and bearing knocks, but managing to deliver its thirty-seven miles an hour. The sun rose higher. The shadow cast by the automobile shortened. The warmth gave place to heat. The right rear tire developed a puncture. Louie and I changed it. We didn't find it particularly annoying. We weren't nervous, and we weren't hurried. Everything went like clockwork—entirely different from those occasions when I'd been dashing around in Bertha Cool's agency car trying to get somewhere in a hurry. Then a tire would go flat, and nothing would work. The car would roll off the jack. The nuts would get cross-threaded on the bolts, and the rim never seemed to fit right on the wheel.

We didn't hurry. We had all the time in the world. Occasionally, we'd stop to just soak up the scenery.

We traveled all that day, camped at night on the desert, and got to Reno around noon the following day.

"Okay," Louie said, "here we are. What's the orders, skipper?"

The jalopy was covered with desert dust. I needed a shave. Louie had black whiskers sprouting all over his chin. All three of us were burned from the desert sun and wind, but I had never felt so serenely relaxed.

"An auto camp," I said, "while we get cleaned up, and find out what's to be done."

We found an auto camp. The woman let us have a cabin which had two rooms and three beds. We scrubbed under the shower. Louie and I shaved, then I left them in the cabin while I went out to reconnoiter.

I rang up the telephone company and inquired if Mrs. Jannix had a telephone. She didn't. I rang up all the hotels, asked them if a Mrs. Jannix was registered with them. She wasn't. I rang up the public utilities. They didn't want to give out any information.

I went back to the auto camp, picked up the other two, and we went out looking for a place to stay.

I finally found one just about dark, a place which was ideally suited for what we wanted. A man had a little filling station about seven miles out of town. He'd started to put up an auto court, but his finances had run out, and all he had was one big cabin back about a hundred yards from the highway.

We loaded the jalopy with provisions, and moved in that night. Louie played on his harmonica, waltzes, and Helen and I danced for a while. There was a little wood stove in the place, and we kept the cabin filled with that comfortable warmth which comes only from a wood stove in a kitchen.

Louie pulled me out of blankets early the next morning. It was time, he explained, for road work.

Helen smiled at me sleepily, said, "Have a good time," rolled over, and went back to sleep. I put on rubber-soled tennis shoes, tightened my belt, took a drink of hot water with a little lemon juice in it, and followed Louie out into the cold.

The sun was just getting up. The air stabbed through my thin clothing.

Louie saw me shiver. "You'll be all right in a minute. You're too light to do much sweating. Come on now, here we go."

He started off at a slow jog. I fell in behind him. A hundred and fifty yards, and the cold gave way to tingling warmth.

I realized there was quite an elevation here. My lungs began to labor for air. Louie, however, kept slogging along. We were on the pavement now. The steady *kloop—kloop—kloop* of his rubber-soled shoes grew monotonous.

"How much longer?" I asked.

"Don't talk," he called back over his shoulder.

I kept plugging along. My legs felt as though they were weighted with metal. We were jogging slowly enough so I could manage my breathing, but I was tired, terribly tired. It seemed as though we'd run miles before Louie swung around abruptly, looked me over with the eye of a professional trainer, said, "All right, walk awhile."

We started walking along briskly, sucking in great lungfuls of the cool, clean air. My legs were tired, but the change in muscular action was a relief.

After several minutes, Louie started jogging again, and I fell in behind him. The cabin showed up a quarter of a mile ahead. It seemed to take hours to reach it.

Louie wasn't winded. I could see that he was breathing more deeply, but that was all.

"Try opening up the bottom part of your lungs," he said. "Suck the air way down into the lowest part of your lungs. Okay, we'll go through a few moves now, just some of the preliminary stuff."

He brought out a set of sweat-stiffened boxing-gloves and put gloves on my hands. "Now then," he said, "the most deceptive blow and the hardest to deliver is an absolutely straight punch. Now, let's see a straight left."

I lashed out with a left.

He shook his head. "That ain't straight."

"Why not?"

"Because your elbow came up with the punch. Way out from the side of your body. Keep your elbow right in close to your body as you bring your fist up. First the left, then the right."

I tried again. Louie looked pained but patient. "Now look," he said. "Take off that right glove for a minute. I want to show you something."

And he showed me. And he told me, and then he kept me shooting out the left until I could hardly raise my arm.

"It ain't good," he said, "and it ain't bad. You'll improve. Now, let's try a straight right. Now when you throw a straight right—"

A voice from the window said in a sleepy drawl, "Wouldn't it be easier to take a licking than go to all that trouble, Louie?"

I looked up at the bedroom window. Helen Framley, her elbows perched on the sill, a kimono falling away from her throat, was watching us with an amused twinkle in her eyes.

Louie said, in all deadly seriousness, "There's times when a man can't afford to take a licking, Miss Helen— maybe he'd be fighting for you."

"Save it," she told him. "I like men with black eyes, and besides I have to clean my teeth."

She left the window. Louie turned to me with that grin pulling his lips back so that the missing teeth showed as black spaces. "There," he announced, "is a girl for you. Buddy, what I mean that's a girl!"

I nodded.

Louie was looking at me speculatively as though he wanted to say something else, perhaps wondering if he dared to try coaching me in something that wasn't fighting. But it was hard for him to find words. At length, he said, "Listen, buddy, you know where I stand. I'm your pal, see?"

I nodded.

"I'm backing your play. No matter what it is, I'm backing it."

Again I nodded.

He blurted awkwardly, "Well, don't pull no punches on my account. Come on, get your mitts up and let's go through that again. One—two—one—two—one—two—one—two—"

I was so tired I could hardly move when we finished. Perspiration was commencing to stand out on my skin. Louie looked me over. "No cold showers for you, buddy. That cold-shower stuff is all right for the guys that have a layer of fat under their skin. Even then it don't do 'em as much good as they think it does. You take a warm shower, not hot, now, just a little bit warmer than your skin. Get the temperature with your hands, then step in under it. It'll feel like a cold shower at first, and you'll want to turn on more warm water, but don't do it. Just stay under there and put on lots of soap and scrub off good. Then make the water just a little cooler, not enough to give you a shock, but just start cooling it down until you feel you'd like to get out and then get out quick. Rub yourself good with a towel, then get in on your bed and—well, then's when I take over."

I took the shower. The towels furnished by the man who owned the cabin were little thin things that became wringing wet by the time you were half through drying yourself.

Louie was waiting in my room when I stretched my damp body out on the bed. He had a bottle, and, as he sloshed some of the contents of the bottle into his hand, I thought I smelled alcohol, witch hazel, and bay rum. Then Louie went to work. He kneaded, pounded, massaged, slapped, rubbed, and then did it all over again.

I began to feel a delightful sense of relaxation. I wasn't drowsy, but I could feel new, clean blood coursing through my muscles, could feel my skin tingle and glow.

From the kitchen, I could hear the rattle of pans. Louie gave a little exclamation, strode across the room, jerked the door open, and said, "Hey, I'm the cook here."

I heard Helen Framley's deep-pitched distinctive drawl

saying, "You used to be. You've been promoted to trainer. I'm taking over the breakfast."

Louie came back to the bed. "A great girl," he said, stiffening his fingers and jabbing them into the muscles on each side of my spine.

It took Louie half an hour to get me massaged to suit him, then I got into my clothes, feeling slightly tired but not fatigued. Helen had the table set, with grapefruit, coffee, golden brown toast, thick ham steaks, and fried eggs. As we started eating, she got up to pour flapjacks into a big frying-pan.

I felt hungry, not particularly ravenous, just hungry, but the food I ate didn't seem to have any effect on my hunger. I ate and ate and my stomach refused to fill up.

Louie watched me approvingly.

Helen Framley said, "You'll have him so fat he'll waddle."

"He won't put on over three pounds," Louie said. "He's using up energy, and it takes food to supply that energy. He won't carry an ounce of fat, but, boy, oh, boy, will he get solid."

Her eyes searched mine. "Why the sudden desire to become proficient in the manly art of self-defense?" she asked.

I said, "I get tired of being a human punching-bag."

"And so you quit your job, hire a boxing instructor, and start right in with road work, massages, boxing, and regular fight training?"

"That's right."

"When you go after anything, you don't use any halfway methods, do you?"

"No."

"Some things, anyhow," she said, and turned away.

Louie said, "Now, buddy, after breakfast, you don't do nothing. See? You just sit back for an hour and let your food digest. You read the paper, and try to keep from moving. Don't do anything that will use up energy."

Nothing in my life ever felt quite so good as that hour of complete relaxation which followed. Then I announced that I had work to do. Louie wanted me to take some breathing exercises, and some "skull practice," but I insisted I had to go to town.

Helen said we needed some groceries, and handed me a list. Louie volunteered to go along and buy the groceries. Helen said she'd stay in the cabin and straighten things up.

Louie talked about her all the way into Reno. "A wonderful girl," he said. "She's got what it takes. She's championship stuff. Sock her one on the button, and her knees might be buckling, but you'd never know it."

I eased the car into a parking-space and told Louie to be back in half an hour.

"I'll be here," he promised. "You got that grocery list?"

I handed him the grocery list and twenty dollars. "Expense money," I said. "When it's gone, tell me and I'll give you some more."

His eyes held that same devotion you see in the eyes of a big dog looking up at his master. "Okay, buddy," he said, and pushed the money down into his pocket.

I went into one of the hotels, got a list of numbers, closeted myself in the telephone booth, and went to work. I called retail-grocer associations, credit bureaus, the dairies, and even the ice company. I was, I explained, from the Preferential Credit Bureau of San Francisco. I was trying to get some information on a Mrs. Elva Jannix. I knew they wouldn't have any credit applications, but I'd like very much to have them check their deliveries during the next few days, and if they got any information to save it until I called again.

That's a peculiar thing. No matter what kind of an alibi you use, you can't get information out of a business house unless you pose as a credit man, and then they'll turn everything inside out. They almost never ask to see any credentials. Simply tell them you're handling a credit matter, and the world is yours.

I made the rounds of the banks, told them I was trying to locate a stolen check, asked them if they'd had any business dealings with a Mrs. Jannix, either Mrs. Sidney Jannix, or Mrs. Elva Jannix.

Most of them fell for it. One of them didn't. The manager wanted to know more about me. Somehow, the way he went at it, I had an idea Mrs. Jannix might be a client of that bank. A man can tell you he hasn't the information you want without violating any ethics, but if he happens to have the information you're after, he gets a little cagey about giving it out.

I went back to the car. It had been an hour and ten minutes. There was no sign of Louie Hazen beyond a pasteboard carton filled with canned stuff, and two heavy brown-paper shopping-bags loaded with various staples.

I sat and waited for fifteen minutes. The sun crawled over the roofs of the store buildings, and sent warm rays glancing down into the streets. I felt drowsy. My muscles and nerves were all relaxed. I didn't give a damn for Bertha Cool or the detective agency or anything that concerned it. I closed my eyes to rest them against the glare of the sunlight—and woke up with a jerk from a sleep so sound that it took me a few seconds to realize where I was and how I had got there.

I looked at my watch.

It had been more than two hours since I'd left Louie.

I put a note on the steering-wheel, "Back in ten minutes. Don't leave," and went back to make some more telephone calls, plugging up a few loopholes I might have missed.

I came back and the note was still on the steering-wheel. There was no sign of Louie. I started the car and drove back out to the cabin. Helen had been sweeping. A handkerchief was tied around her hair for a dust cap. "Hello," she said when I'd brought the groceries in. "What did you do with Louie?"

"I don't know."

"What happened?"

"He went out to get the groceries. I told him to wait in the car when he came back, and to be sure and be there in half an hour. He wasn't there. I waited over an hour longer, and then came out here."

She took off her dust cap, put her broom in the corner, went into the bathroom, washed her hands, and when she came out, was rubbing some fragrant lotion into the skin.

She said, "This might be a good time to talk."

"About what?"

"Lots of things."

I sat down beside her on the little settee. She got up after a moment and moved over to a chair facing me. "I want to look at you," she explained. "If you're going to lie to me, I want to know it."

"That doesn't sound very encouraging."

She said, "I like you."

"Thanks."

"I liked you from the first time I saw you."

"Leading up to something?" I asked.

"Yes."

"Go ahead then."

She said, "The orthodox technique for a nice young thing is to be very demure and, if you take an interest in her, lead you along very, very gently. I don't do things that way. When I like someone, I go for them in a big way. When I don't like 'em, I just don't like 'em, and that's all there is to it."

I nodded.

"That first night out on the desert," she said, "was about the happiest night I ever spent in my life. The second night was almost as good."

"And now?" I asked.

"Now, I don't like it."

"Why?"

173

"I thought you were strong for me."

"I am."

"Phooey!" she said, with a little grimace. Then her eyes came up to mine. "It isn't because of what I was doing—that slot-machine racket—that you cooled off toward me?"

"I didn't cool off toward you. I like you."

"Yeah, I know."

She was silent for a few seconds, then she said, "Anyhow, being with Pug and working that machine racket, and having batted around on my own has made me feel that I'm on one side of the fence and the cops are on the other. There's no particular reason I should feel that way except I've had a lot of shakedowns in my time, and particularly on the slot-machine racket. Once or twice, Pug would get caught. The slot-machine man would pretend he was going to make a complaint and prosecute. We always knew it was a bluff, but the cops would hold us on their own and shake us down for everything they could get before they'd turn us loose. Well, I got to looking at cops as being—well, just cops."

I didn't say anything.

She averted her eyes once more, studied her shoe tip. "All right, Donald," she blurted at length, "if you think I know something about Pug's murder, and if you thought you could make a play for me because I was strong for you, pretend that you'd quit the detective business, and get me to tell you what I knew that way—well, Donald," she said, looking at me suddenly with the steady stare of slate-gray eyes, "I think I really could kill you if you're taking me for that kind of a ride."

I said, "I wouldn't blame you."

She kept studying me. "Going to say anything more?"

I smiled and shook my head.

She got to her feet abruptly. "Damn you, I wish I knew what it was you do to me, but I'm just telling you—I still say you're working on that case. Remember what I told you."

"I will. Where do you suppose Louie is?"

"Darned if I know. Did you give him any money?"

"Yes."

She said, "There's something wrong with Louie."

"What?"

"He's slap-happy."

"I knew that a long time ago."

"Yeah, I know."

"Something else wrong with him?"

"I don't know. It comes out of that condition of being slap-happy. They all get it sooner or later. I think Pug had some of it. It keeps them from seeing things the way you'd see them or the way I'd see them. Look, Donald, do you think that after a while, if you keep hanging around and I get nuts over you, I'll spill everything I know?"

"I just hadn't thought much about it."

"Well, think about it now then."

"All right, I will."

"If you ever try to pump me about that, I'll kill you. I— I'd not only hate you, but—but—but it would do something to me, Donald. It would jerk something out from under me. Please, Donald, give me a break on that. If that's the play, let's just call this little party off right now, and I can get over it—maybe. If I wait a few more days, I'll never get over it."

"Got any friends here?" I asked her.

"No."

"Where would you go and what would you do?"

Her eyes grew hard. "Say, don't you think you can frighten me with that line. Any time I need a man to live on, I'll take an overdose of sleep medicine. I can walk out of here right now with nothing but my bare hands, and— well, I'll get by, and I won't sell myself, either."

"What would you do?"

"I don't know. I'd find something. How about it? Do I start?"

"Not as far as I'm concerned."

She said, "I suppose you won't open up."

I said, "If you don't want to tell me anything you know about what happened to Pug, I hope you never do."

She came over to stand in front of me. "All right," she said, "I'll give it to you in words of one syllable. You can have anything you want out of me. You can ask me any-thing, and I'll do it. And if you ask me what about Pug, and what do I know about the night he was bumped off, I—well, I'd probably rat, but the minute you asked me that question, I'd know *why* you'd been doing all this," and she swept her hand in a gesture which included the auto camp. "And when I knew that you'd been doing it just to get me so that I couldn't say no to anything you'd ask—I'd be so sick inside, I could never feel clean or decent again, or think there was anything clean left in the world—ever. You got that straight?"

"Yes."

"All right then. What do we do next?"

I said, "I guess we go uptown and see if we can locate Louie in any of the bars."

She studied me a second or two, then burst out laughing, but there was a note of bitterness in her laughter.

I walked over to stand close to her. "Don't you see," I told her, "I don't want anything I'm not entitled to."

Her eyes narrowed slightly. "Go on from there."

"You're right about one thing. I'm a detective. I'm working. It isn't that I'm working for the B. Cool Agency. It's that I'm working on a case. I'm trying to see that some other people get a fair deal. They're depending on me, whether they know it or not. If I don't do the job, I don't think anyone else will."

"And so you want me to tell you what I know about—"

"I don't want you to tell me a damn thing," I said. "I'm

strong for you. I think you're one of the nicest girls I've ever met. But I'd never have asked you to leave Las Vegas and come out with me if it hadn't been a matter of business. I'm enjoying it. I'm happy. I like to be near you. I like the way you do things. I like everything about you. But I'm working on a job, and the reason I'm here with you is because it's along the line I'm following to make a success of that job."

"And when the job's over?"

I'd been dreading that question. I said, "I'll probably have something else tossed into my lap."

"And you're not going to ask me what I know about Pug?"

"No."

"Never?"

"No."

"And you didn't plan this so I'd spill what I knew?"

"No."

"And it's because you didn't want to take something under false pretenses that you've told—"

I nodded.

"And has it occurred to you that you've never even kissed me?"

"Naturally," I said.

Her eyes were on mine now, and there was a steady, shining light I hadn't seen in them before. She said, "I guess this is where we hit the jackpot, Donald."

Chapter Fourteen

ABOUT TWO O'CLOCK in the afternoon I found Louie. He was sitting at a table in the back room of one of the cheaper side street places. A bottle half full of bar whisky was on the table in front of him. The knuckles of the hand which held the glass were skinned and bleeding. His eyes were heavily glazed and staring with fixed intensity. He was mumbling as I came up to the table.

He looked up at me. "Oh, there you are," he said thickly.

I pushed the bottle of whisky to one side. "How about coming home, Louie?"

He frowned. "Say, thash right. I got a home, ain't I? I—Oh, my God." He stood up and plunged his hand into his trousers pocket, brought out two one-dollar bills and some chicken feed.

"You know what I done, buddy?" he asked, his glazed eyes surveying me with that fixed glassy stare. "I shpent that money you gave me—all that was left from the groceries 'cept this—booze. That's my failin'. I feel the cravin' comin' on every so often, and when it hits me, I can't—"

"Who was it you socked, Louie?" I asked.

He looked down at his knuckles and scowled. "Now thash funny. I *thought* I hit somebody, and then I thought it was jusht sort of an idea a man'll get when he's been drinkin'. It might 'a' been the last time. Wait a minute. Let me think.

"I'll tell you who it was. It was Sid Jannix. Was in line for a title once. A good boy—plenty good, but I give him the old one-two. Lemme show you how it goes, the old Hazen shift. I won the championship in the Navy—it must

178

have been the championship—sure, it was in Honolulu in—let me see now. Was it—"

"Come on, Louie, we're going home."

"You ain't sore about that money, kid?"

"No."

"You understand how it is?"

"Sure."

"You're the besh pal a guy ever had. The first time I socked you, I knew I liked you, jush like shakin' hands with a guy, shock him on the jaw an—awrigh', let's go home."

I got him out to the sidewalk, steadied him down the street, and into the jalopy. Halfway out to the cabin, the enormity of his embezzlement struck him. He wanted to get out of the car. "Lemme out, buddy. I ain't fit to ride in the same car with you. I can't face Miss Helen. Know what I did? I stole your money. I knew you didn't have much, too—just some money you'd saved up—an' I stole it. I wanna get out—serves me right if I hit my head and die. I ain't no good. I been hit too much anyway. I ain't got no—ain' got no self-control."

I put my hand on the arm that was over on the side nearest the door. His hand was fumbling with the catch. "Forget it, Louie," I said, driving the rattling car with one hand. "We aren't any of us perfect. I've got my faults, too."

"You mean you forgive me?"

"Sure."

"No hard feelings?"

"No hard feelings."

He started to cry, then, and was immersed in lachrymose repentance when I got him to the cabin. Helen and I put him to bed. "Well," she said, after we'd tucked him in and put a big pitcher of water beside the bed, "now what?"

"I'll stay with him," I told her. "You take the car, go uptown, and get your hair fixed at that beauty shop you were talking about."

She looked at me, hesitated a moment.

I said, "I'll have to give you a traveler's check. I—"

She laughed up at me. "Forget it. I've got money."

"All you need?"

"Sure. I lit out with Pug's bank roll. And listen, Donald, if you get short, I can stake you. I know you're paying for this show, and I know you're going to come out on it all right when you've finished up, but in case you find the shoe pinching, just let me know."

"Thanks, I will."

" 'By," she said.

"Be seeing you."

She started for the door, turned back to me, took my face in her hands, looked down into my eyes, and then kissed me. "The landlord was over while you were gone," she said casually. "He was calling me Mrs. Lam. So don't destroy his illusions. By-by."

She breezed out of the door. I sat down at the kitchen table, took a telephone directory, and made up a list of the places I wanted to call. I found some old magazines, read for a while, and then began to feel the effects of my unaccustomed exercise. I dozed off into a light sleep, waking occasionally just enough to realize that I should go in and see how Louie was getting along. But getting up out of the comfortable chair seemed too great an effort, and I'd drift off to sleep again.

I finally woke up enough to look in on Louie. He heard the door open. He opened bloodshot eyes, looked up at me and said, "Hello, buddy, how about some water?"

"In that pitcher right by your bed."

He picked up the pitcher, disdained the glass, and drank about half of the contents.

"You know I'm a heel," he said, putting down the pitcher and avoiding my eyes. "An' *I* know I'm a heel."

"You're all right."

"I wish you wouldn't be so damn nice about it."

"Forget it."

"I'd like to do some little thing for you, buddy—like a murder or something."

I grinned down at him. "How's the head?" I asked. "Aching?"

"It always aches. I guess that's why I take up the booze. I've had a headache so long now I'm used to it. I always tried to give the customers a run for their money. I'd stay in there and swap punches when I should have been down on the canvas, listenin' to the birdies. And now here I am, a drunken bum with a headache all the time."

"You'll feel better after a while. Want to go back to sleep again?"

"No. I'm goin' to get up and drink lots of water. What happened to the rest of that bottle of whisky?"

"I left it in there."

"It was paid for," he said regretfully.

"It's better in the saloon than in you."

"You're right," he said, "if I can get my mind off'n it, but I'm afraid I'll be thinkin' of that half bottle of whisky —you'd better kick me out, pal, before I get you in a spot. I ain't worth it."

"Snap out of it. You'll feel better when you get your stomach back into shape."

His bloodshot eyes stared up at me. "Tell you one thing," he said, "I'm going to teach you everything I know, every little trick of the ring. I'm going to make you a fighter."

"Okay. Now listen, I'm going to take a walk. Helen's in town. She'll be back in a couple of hours. You feel like keeping an eye on the place?"

"Sure."

"You won't leave?"

He said, "Where's my pants?"

"Over there on the chair."

"Turn the pockets inside out, take all the dough out, then I won't leave."

I said, "You gave me the change—what was left of it."

He heaved a sigh. "Okay then, that's fine. Go ahead." He punched the pillows back into shape behind his head, said, "Gimme a cigarette, buddy, and I'll be all right as soon as that water quits sloshin' around in my stomach."

I gave him a cigarette, and walked out to the highway. I hadn't gone over half a mile when a car stopped and gave me a ride to town.

A newsstand featured papers from all the principal cities. I found a Las Vegas paper. The police made much over the disappearance of Helen Framley. They had finally traced her to an apartment where she had been in hiding since the night of the murder. She had disappeared, and police, checking up on the activities of one Donald Lam, a private investigator who had been employed on another angle of the case, were convinced that she, an ex-prize fighter by the name of Hazen, and Lam had all left town together. The police were inclined to believe that Helen Framley had either been implicated in the murder or had highly significant information, and that the private detective, seeking to steal a march on police, was offering her a chance to escape in return for such information as she could give. There was a strong intimation that the officials would consider this a serious matter, and that Lam might well find himself prosecuted for compounding a felony. Hazen, it seemed, was also implicated. He'd positively identified the body as that of a former pugilist named Sidney Jannix.

Evidently, the police hadn't as yet linked me with the purchase of the secondhand automobile.

I rang up a few more places, handed them my regular line, cut out the article from the Las Vegas paper, left the rest of the newspaper in a telephone booth, and started back for the cabin.

I had to walk nearly a mile before I caught a ride.

Helen returned about an hour after I got back. Louie got the dinner, washed and wiped the dishes. The three of us went to a movie, and then went to bed.

Louie Hazen was pulling me out of bed before I hardly realized I'd been asleep. The air was filled with cold dawn.

"Come on," he said. "Get this road work in while it's cool. I don't want you to sweat."

I sat up on the edge of the bed, rubbed my eyes. "It's not cool, it's cold," I protested.

"You'll be all right when you get out."

He slipped a hand under my arm, lifted me to my feet. My legs all but buckled, the muscles were so sore.

"Gosh, Louie, I can't take it this morning. I'll have to rest."

"Come on," he said, and started pushing me around.

"Oh, forget it, Louie. I'm not training for any fight or anything. After all, we can—"

He opened the window, pulled off the screen, dropped it to the ground, tossed out my running-shoes, pants, and light sweater, and then, before I realized what he was intending to do, picked me up as though I had weighed precisely nothing, and tossed me out after them. Then he closed and locked the window.

The door was locked. It was cold out there on the ground. I picked up my clothes and moved around to the side of the house away from the highway, dressed in shivering silence, took a deep breath, and started jog trotting after Louie along the road. Every step was agony.

Louie kept watching me over his shoulder, looking at the expression on my face, the way I was moving my legs. He seemed to know exactly when the soreness began to leave me, and then again knew exactly when the breathlessness became acute.

We walked all the way back, taking deep breaths. I suddenly picked up Louie's trick of breathing with my diaphragm, sucking air way down, squeezing out every last bit of it before taking another deep breath.

Louie, watching me, nodded approvingly.

We went back to the house and put on the stiff set of fighting-gloves. Louie said, "I'm going to train you to throw a hard punch this morning. Now swing one right at this glove. Put everything you've got right behind it. No, no, no. Don't draw back."

It seemed interminable hours that we worked out there in the sunlight, and then Louie had me under the shower, was kneading and pounding my muscles again, and by the time I was up and dressed, Helen Framley had the kitchen full of the fragrance of steaming coffee.

Later that morning I got a lead.

A retail-credit association member had delivered groceries to a Mrs. Sidney Jannix in an apartment on California Street.

I went out to the place, parked the jalopy, climbed stairs, and pressed a buzzer.

The woman who opened the door was Corla Burke.

"May I come in?" I asked.

"Who are you?"

"A friend of Helen Framley."

She frowned at me. For a moment, there was quick alarm in her eyes. "How did you find me?"

"That," I said, "is something of a story. Do I tell it out here, or inside?"

"Inside," she said, and held the door open so I could come in.

I sat down by the window. Corla Burke, seated across from me where the light etched expression on her face, played into my hands by opening the conversation. "I simply couldn't have taken advantage of Miss Framley's offer," she said. "I wrote and told her so."

I adopted an attitude of being somewhat aggrieved.

"I don't see why."

"It wouldn't have been fair."

"I think it would have been a lot better than what you *did* do."

I could see that shot struck home. She said, "I didn't know, of course, what— Well, I couldn't look into the future myself," and she laughed nervously.

"Miss Framley felt she tried to do the square thing by you and that you hadn't been—well, suppose we say appreciative."

"I'm sorry. How did you happen to come here?"

"Why, this was the logical place to look for you."

"Why did you want to find me?"

"I thought perhaps something could be done to straighten things out."

"No, not now."

"I still think so."

"I'm afraid you're overly optimistic. Please thank Miss Framley for me and tell her that I certainly don't want her to think I was ungrateful, and I guess—well, I guess that's about all there is to tell her."

I glanced around, saw that a suitcase was open, that folded garments were placed on a table and on two of the chairs. On a small table in the corner by the window was a woman's hat, gloves, and purse. A stamped envelope lay on the corner of this table.

"Mind if I smoke?"

"Certainly not. I'll have one—"

I gave her a cigarette, held a match, managed to move so that I was at the edge of the table as I reached for an ash tray, and then grabbed for the letter.

She saw what was happening and flung herself at the table. I got my hands on the letter first. She clawed at it. I said, "If it isn't postmarked Las Vegas I'm not interested. If it is, I'm going to read it."

She redoubled her efforts, grabbed at my arm. I pushed

her away. I managed to avoid her, pulled the sheet of paper out from the envelope.

It was a hasty scrawl and read:

Donald Lam a private detective is on the job. He's contacted Helen Framley. Helen's boy friend, man by the name of Beegan, was murdered last night. You aren't safe in Reno. Hunt a deep hole somewhere else.

The letter was signed simply with the initials "A. W."

I said, "Let's be frank with each other and save time. I'm Lam. Arthur Whitewell hired me to find you—and saw that Philip knew all about it, of course. Now suppose you tell me your story."

She just stared at me, all of the fight had left her. She looked trapped and beaten.

I said, "I have a theory. I can outline it if it would help start the ball rolling."

She still didn't say anything, simply stood looking at me as though I was what was left behind after a cyclone.

I said, "I think Arthur Whitewell didn't want his son to marry you. He thought Philip could make a more advantageous marriage. But Philip was very much in love with you, and Whitewell is something of a psychologist. He knew that, after all, there wasn't much he could do about it. Philip was inexperienced and callow in some ways, but very much of a man in others. His father had never fully understood him, but he did realize there was a gap he had never been able to bridge. He knew that any attempt to come between you two would bring about a permanent estrangement. And then something happened to play right into his hands. He had the opportunity he'd been looking for. He manipulated things in such a way that you simply stepped out of the picture and left Philip to recuperate as best he could.

"And then," I said, "Philip took it so much worse than

his father had anticipated that something had to be done. It wasn't just an ordinary heartbreak. Philip is sentimental, sensitive, in his feelings and perceptions. He's never learned that people sometimes can't be taken at their face value. It was all too much for him."

She was crying now, crying quietly. She didn't try to say anything. She couldn't have talked.

I walked over to the window, looking down on a drab back yard which was pretty well filled with a litter of old boxes. A clothesline sagged dispiritedly between two poles. Little puddles reflected sunlight. A child's tin pail and shovel were standing on a pile of damp sand. I kept my back turned to the room so that she could have her cry out and regain her composure without feeling I was watching.

It was several minutes before she had herself sufficiently under control to speak. "Do you think that Mr. Whitewell expected you would find me?" she asked.

"I don't know. All I know is that he employed us to find you."

"But he stipulated with me that I must arrange my disappearance so that I could *never* be found. That was one of the things he insisted on."

"Exactly."

"Then hiring you would be just a gesture to pacify Philip?"

"That's it."

I could see she was clinging to a straw of hope. "But it costs real money to hire a good detective, doesn't it?"

"Yes."

"And you must be good—skillful?"

It was her party. If she wanted to kid herself along, it was okay with me. I said, "We think we're good."

"Can't you tell me something that would give me a clue as to how Mr. Whitewell really feels now?"

"Not until after you've told me what happened. Then I can put things together and perhaps find an answer."

"But you seemed to know. You knew all about Helen Framley."

"No, just that she'd written you a letter. I had to surmise what was in it."

"What did you think was in it?"

"I thought it was a trap."

"Set by this Helen Framley?"

"I don't think Helen Framley ever wrote the letter."

"But she *must* have."

"Suppose you tell me everything you know, and let me draw my own conclusions."

She said, "I suppose you know what caused me to leave."

"Sid Jannix?"

She nodded.

"Tell me about him first."

She said, "I was a little fool when I was a kid. I always had a savage streak in me. I liked fighting and fighters. I never cared much for baseball games, but loved football. Sidney was in school with me. He was on the football team. Then the school took up boxing, and Sidney was the best in our school. He became something of a hero. The boxing died out because there was too much parental opposition, but Sidney was the idol of every boy in school. And I guess he became the school bully. I didn't realize it at the time. It was our last year in high school.

"Well, I kept up with Sidney, and my family didn't like it. Sidney took up professional fighting, and adopted the attitude that he was something of a martyr, and I— Well, when Sidney was making enough to support me, I ran away with him and we were married." She shrugged wearily, then added, "Of course it was a ghastly, terrible mistake."

She paused for a minute as though trying to find some way of detouring what lay ahead, then she plunged once more into the recital.

"We lived together for just about three months. The

188

first two or three weeks I was completely hypnotized. And then, little by little, I began seeing him as he really was. He was a bully, and he was yellow. When he could handle anyone, he was ruthless in handing out punishment. When he couldn't, he was full of alibis. He got good enough to get almost to the top, and then, as he began to meet the better men—however, that's getting ahead of my story. At the time I married him, he was just coming up from the preliminary fighters, and beginning to attract attention. It went terribly to his head. He was emotional, intensely jealous. He began to treat me as though I were just so much personal property. I could have stood all that if it hadn't been for the little things—little places where the veneer scraped off, and I could see what was underneath."

"You don't need to go into all that," I said. "Just tell me what happened after you left him."

"I'd had some business training in school. I got a job. I kept trying to perfect my secretarial work, and I had the satisfaction of knowing I was succeeding. I kept working up."

"No divorce?"

"I thought Sid had got a divorce. That was the meanest trick he played on me. I told him I wanted to be free. He said that it would be better to wait for a year and get a divorce on the ground of desertion. He didn't want to have a lot of allegations of cruelty in the record. He said it would hurt his career.

"We started out to wait for that year to elapse. It was a big year for Sidney. He came a long way up for about seven or eight months of that year, and then he went all the way down in three months. I don't know all that happened, but his manager came to the conclusion he was yellow. He'd been a terror in the ring with the men he could master, but—oh, I don't know. It's a long story, and I think he did some crooked work—sold out his manager and threw a fight or something. I don't know enough of what happened to talk about it. I just heard rumors, but, anyway, about ten months from the date of our separation, he came to me. He was desperate then. He said that he'd never been able to get a grip on himself after I'd left. He said I'd taken the inspiration out of his life."

"That was after ten months?" I asked.

"Yes," she said, and her voice was bitter. "All the time he was going up, he was very patronizing toward me; but when the bottom fell out, he started begging for sympathy. Well, anyway, he told me that he was the sort of man who needed some woman to be his inspiration, that he knew he could never get me to come back, that he had met another girl, that he could never feel toward her as he felt toward me, but that she was desperately in love with him, and he sort of liked her." She laughed bitterly. "That was Sidney all over. She loved him desperately, and he sort of liked her."

"And what did he want?" I asked.

"He wanted to go to Reno and get a divorce."

"And suggested that you pay for it?" I asked.

She nodded.

"Why didn't you?"

"I did," she said. "And he told me the divorce went through."

"And the girl?"

"He married her. That's why I didn't bother to check the divorce records."

"And he hadn't got the divorce?"

"No. As it turned out, he'd simply taken the money I'd given him to make an impression on this other girl. He got her to marry him. She had some money saved. Sidney got that."

"That wasn't Helen Framley?" I asked.

"No. Her name was Sadie something. I've forgotten the last name, but I remember he kept talking about Sadie, and I was curious as to what sort of a girl she was."

"All right. Then what happened?"

"Absolutely nothing for years. I had entirely lost track of him, and I hardly ever even thought of him. He quit his ring career. I think the Boxing Commission had some evidence on him that made it impossible for him to fight again. I don't think he wanted to, anyway. He wasn't the type to stand up under punishment in a ring."

"And you met Philip?"

"Yes. I'd taken the name of Corla Burke so I could wipe out the past and begin all over. You see, my father—"

"I understand about the name now," I said. "Let's go on from there."

"At first, I—"

"You don't need to go into that. Just come to the Helen Framley part."

"I got this very queer letter from Helen Framley. She said that she had read in the paper I was planning to get married almost immediately, that she was friendly with Sidney, and had heard Sidney speak of me, that she wondered if I knew Sidney had never got a divorce. She went on to say that Sidney was very much changed from what he was when I had known him, that he had steadied down a lot and really wanted to make something of himself in the world. She didn't think he had the money to get a divorce right away, but if I didn't want to wait, she could fix things up so that I could go ahead with the marriage, and after I had married Philip, Sidney would go ahead and get a divorce. She said he'd had some bad luck, but within a few weeks he'd be in the money again. I could then pretend to my husband there had been some irregularity in stating my age or something of that sort in the license, and get him to marry me all over again, or just keep on living with him and it would be a common-law marriage."

" 'Queer' is right. How much money did he want?" I asked.

"She didn't even mention anything like that. Not as coming from me. She simply said that she thought that if he could get enough to set himself up in some business, it would be all he'd want, and I'd never hear from him again."

"Did you gather the impression that she was writing you at his request?"

"No. She told me that he didn't know anything about the letter she was writing, that he was intending to write to Philip Whitewell if it appeared that the marriage was going through, that he didn't want Philip to be placed in the position of making a bigamous marriage."

"Very considerate about Philip, wasn't he?"

"Well—oh, it was about what you'd expect of Sidney. This Miss Framley seemed very nice. She looked at it from my viewpoint."

"How had she found out you were really Sidney's wife? How had she found you under the name of Corla Burke?"

"She didn't say—just wrote this brief letter."

"I see. Now when the proposition was all boiled down, unless you promised Sidney Jannix enough money to start up in business, he was going to prevent your marriage. If you'd promise to take care of him from money you could get from your husband, he was going to sit back and let you become the goose that would lay his golden eggs."

"Well, if you want to look at it that way."

"It's the only way to look at it."

"Then you think this Helen Framley was—"

"I don't think Helen Framley ever wrote the letter."

"But she told me to reply to her."

"And you did?"

"Yes, of course."

"And that was the letter that Arthur Whitewell dictated?"

"He didn't dictate it."

"But he knew about what was in it?"

"Yes."

"I want to know about that," I said.

"Well, I had it coming to me. I deserved everything I got. I don't suppose I can ever explain it to you. I could never explain it to anyone, not even myself. But—well, I just had crossed those three months when I had been married to Sidney Jannix out of my life. I wrote them off as a bad experience, and—"

"By that you mean you didn't tell Philip anything about them?"

She nodded.

"And Philip knew nothing whatever about Sidney Jannix or about your having been married?"

"That's right."

"So this letter from Helen Framley dropped on you like a one-ton bomb making a direct hit?"

"Yes."

"And what did you do?"

"I took the letter and went to see Philip."

"Where?"

"At his office. We had a date for that night."

"But you didn't see Philip?"

"No. He'd been called out on a deal that was very important, and he left a note telling me he was awfully sorry but he just had to ask me to forget about the evening, that he'd been trying to reach me on the telephone, and couldn't. He said he'd give me a ring around eleven o'clock and see if I could have lunch with him the next day."

"Arthur Whitewell was in the office?" I asked.

"Yes."

"And knew from the look on your face that something was wrong?"

"No. I don't think so. He was considerate and very nice. He'd reconciled himself to the marriage. I'd known, of course, that he didn't exactly approve of it, but he'd been very tactful."

"But you did tell Arthur Whitewell the whole story?"

193

"Yes."

"And," I said, watching her narrowly, "I suppose it knocked him right off the Christmas tree?"

"It was a terrible shock to him," she said. "But he was perfectly splendid. He told me that at first he hadn't approved of me, but that he finally realized Philip was desperately in love with me, and that he had cared enough about his son so that he wanted him to have whatever would make him happy; that if Philip wanted me, then he had planned to take me into the family and had made up his mind that neither of us would ever know that he hadn't exactly approved. He was frank enough to tell me that. I was more attracted to him then than I ever had been. He was simply splendid. He comforted me, and—well, he was so wise and understanding and tolerant, and yet he looked at the thing from such a common-sense angle."

"What was his angle?"

"He said, of course, that now we couldn't go ahead with the marriage, and he told me what I'd known already, that if Philip realized I'd been married, that there was another man living who had been—the first in my affections, who had been my husband, who had lived with me, who—well, if you know Philip, you understand how he might feel about that. He's abnormally sensitive, and—his father confirmed my worst fears on that point."

"Go ahead with the rest of it," I told her.

"I showed him Helen Framley's letter. He told me how much he appreciated my being perfectly honest about it all. He said that many a woman would have been tempted to go through with the marriage and do exactly as this Miss Framley had suggested. But he said that I'd better write her and tell her that now the marriage was absolutely out of the question, so that Jannix wouldn't get in touch with Philip."

"Why did he want to keep Jannix from getting in touch

with Philip?"

"He didn't want Philip to be disillusioned so brutally. That was the idea back of the whole thing. I was to save face, but it wasn't on my own account. It was to protect Philip."

"Who suggested it?"

"Why, it was something we worked out together, sort of a collaboration. He said that for the time being, at least, I must step out of the picture in some way so that Philip would never know what had happened until after he had accustomed himself to my absence, and then we could let it come out. He said that sometime in the future, if I secured a divorce from Jannix and there was no reason why I couldn't marry, I could meet Philip again and explain everything to him."

"You didn't feel that you should go to Philip and tell him frankly—"

"Well, to tell you the truth, Mr. Lam, I did. That was why I'd gone to the office. I wanted to make a clean breast to Philip and explain things to him. I wanted to try and break it to him so it wouldn't hurt him quite so much. But his father told me he understood Philip better than I did, and that the thing for me to do was to disappear under such circumstances that it would appear something very unusual had happened to me. I really think he was thinking as much of himself as of Philip. You see, the announcements of the engagement had all been made and the wedding date was set; and if— Well, you know how it is. You simply have to make some explanation under those circumstances. The Whitewell family was in a peculiar position."

"In other words, Whitewell didn't want to go to his friends at the club, and have one of them say, 'Did your son get married today?' and have to say, 'No. After all, we found the woman had another husband living, so we called it off.'"

She winced.

195

I said, "I'm being brutal because I want you to see it from my angle."

"What is your angle?"

"I don't know just yet, but I *think* I know."

"What?"

"Don't you see? Philip would have forgiven you. He'd have insisted that it wasn't your fault, that you go ahead and get a divorce and his marriage with you would merely be postponed."

"I don't think Philip could ever have forgiven me for not having told him about my first marriage."

"I think so."

"Well, I don't, and I know him better than you."

"His father knows him pretty well," I said, "and his father thought so."

"What makes you say that?"

"Because his father used the opportunity to get you out of the picture, and to have you do something for which Philip never would forgive you. Don't you see? If you ever came back to Philip and tried to explain to him you'd be sunk. Philip could never forget the suffering he'd experienced when you disappeared under such circumstances that he didn't know and couldn't know what had happened to you. He's been tortured by thoughts that perhaps you'd been abducted and were in some danger. That—I'm sorry, I didn't mean to start you crying again, but I just want you to understand."

"But Mr. Whitewell promised. he'd tell Philip if it turned out that Philip became too worried about—"

"That," I said, "is all I wanted to know."

"What?"

"I said, "That means Whitewell took you for a ride."

"I don't see how."

"Don't you understand? If he'd ever explained it to Philip, he'd necessarily have to tell Philip how he knew, and in order to do that, he'd have to admit to Philip that he'd been a party to the deception, that he'd talked with you, that he was the one who had kept you from waiting to see Philip and telling him the whole story. Philip would probably have forgiven you—and something could have been worked out. Arthur Whitewell could have had some so-called important New York business deal take Philip back east. The wedding could have been postponed until he returned, and Whitewell could have explained to his friends that it was just a postponement. And during that time, you could have secured your divorce from Jannix. Philip will never forgive his father for handling the situation in this way. And if he knows the real facts now he'll never forgive you."

She said, "I can't understand. Why, I thought you were working for Mr. Whitewell."

"He employed me."

"Well?"

"But," I said, "he employed me to find you, to discover why you'd left, and what had happened to you. That was all I had to do, and I've done it."

She sat looking at me as though she were just recovering from a terrific punch on the jaw.

"But what are you going to do?"

"*I'm* not going to do anything. You're the one that's going to do it."

"Do what?"

I said, "You're going to trump the old man's ace."

"But I don't understand."

"You disappeared," I said, "under such circumstances that you might have had a sudden attack of amnesia."

"Yes. That was the way he wanted it to appear."

"He, of course, suggested you write Helen Framley, so Sidney wouldn't write Philip?"

"Yes."

"And gave you a sheet of paper and furnished you with a stamped envelope?"

197

"Yes."

"And while you may have thought you were collaborating, the essential scheme of this disappearance of yours was thought up by him?"

"Well—yes, I guess so. He told me I had to save the family's honor, and that it would be better and more beautiful to have Philip keep on loving me and always cherish the memory of our love, than to be brutally disillusioned and perhaps hate me."

"All right. You did just what you seemed to do."

"What?"

"Suffered a loss of memory."

"I don't understand."

"Go right through with it. You suffered a complete loss of memory. You were in the office. You reached for a pencil and—bingo. Your mind went blank. You found yourself out on the street without any idea of who you were or what your name was or how you happened to be there."

"What good would that do? How would that help?"

"Don't you see? You're picked up, suffering from amnesia. You're taken to a hospital, and the Bertha Cool Detective Agency finds you. You can't remember who you are. Your mind is a blank, but the good old Cool Detective Agency has tracked you down, and Philip comes to identify you. The minute you look on Philip's face, the shock of seeing the man you love brings back your reason and—"

"Stop it!" she screamed. "Stop it! I can't stand it."

"Why not?"

"You're tearing my heart to ribbons!"

"You're goofy," I told her. "I'm talking sense. Cut out the damn sentimentalism and get down to bedrock."

"Oh, it's absolutely impossible! It's out of the question. I couldn't deceive Philip that way."

"Why not?"

"Because it would be—it would be unfair."

"No, it wouldn't. You've already done the unfair part.

This would be just straightening it out. You should see the way Philip looks, the lines of suffering about his mouth, the shadows under his eyes, the hollow cheeks, the—"

"Will you *please* stop?"

"Not until you promise me to do what I've outlined."

"But I can't do it."

"Why not?"

"Well, for one thing, there's Sidney Jannix. Philip and I couldn't be married because—"

"Because what?"

"Because I'm a married woman."

I said, "No, you're not. You're a widow."

"I'm—what?"

"A widow."

"Then it wasn't true, that letter from the Framley girl? Sidney isn't living? He—"

"He was at the time the letter was written. He isn't now."

She studied me for a few seconds. "Look here," she said, "if this is some kind of a racket—"

"It isn't. I've come prepared to prove what I'm saying."

I took from my pocket the piece I'd cut from the Las Vegas newspaper and handed it to her. "Helen Framley's boy friend," I said, "was Sidney Jannix. You're not married to anyone. You're a widow."

She read it through carefully. I watched her eyes moving back and forth as she shifted them from one line to the other. After a while, they quit moving, but she kept them focused on the paper, pretending still to be reading, gaining time to think before she had to look up and face the situation.

Abruptly she looked up at me. "He was murdered then?"

"Yes."

"Who— Who did it?"

"They don't know."

"But you know, don't you?"

"I have an idea."

Her eyes shifted again. She pulled her lower lip in under her teeth, moved it slowly while she made biting motions. "Have you been employed to solve the murder?" she asked abruptly.

"No."

"Would you—well, if you knew who did it, would you necessarily have to—"

"No."

Abruptly she gave me her hand. "Mr. Lam," she said, "I think you're wonderful."

"And you'll do what I ask you to?"

"Yes."

"All right, remember you've had this apartment as Mrs. Sidney Jannix. You don't want to have any connection with this apartment. They must never be able to trace you to it. That would be fatal. Clean out of here. Ship your baggage or buy a ticket to San Francisco, check your baggage, and have the baggage checks in your purse. I suppose Whitewell gave you money enough to see you through, didn't he?"

"Yes. He insisted that I accept that so that I could leave all of my own money behind when I left. That was a part of the stage setting."

"If Philip had used his brain," I said, "that would have been the one clue which would have convinced him your disappearance had been planned in advance and financed. All right now, clear out of here. I want it so that no one can ever connect you with this apartment. Go out on the streets and start wandering around. Find a policeman. Ask him what town this is. Keep doing goofy things until someone picks you up, but whatever you do, don't take a drink of anything."

"Why?"

"Because if you have liquor on your breath, they'll throw you in as a drunk. If you're cold sober, and still act goofy, they'll call in a doctor. The doctor may try to trap you. He may smell a rat. You've got to carry it through. Think you can do it?"

"I can try. I'd do anything."

"Luck to you," I said, and shook hands with her again. "Where are you going?"

"I'm going to wait until you land in the hospital, and then I'm going to discover you. After that, I'm going to Las Vegas and report to Whitewell."

She said, "You're giving me a swell break, aren't you?"

I said, "I see no reason for throwing you overboard if I can bring the ship into port."

Her eyes were searching mine, and she was smiling somewhat wistfully. "You're trying to be tough and hard-boiled —and you're just a romanticist at heart. You remind me of Philip."

I started for the door. "Okay, try and be in the hospital by dark."

"I'll do my best."

I walked down the stairs and out to the street. The high elevation gave the shadows a slightly purplish hue. All about me the life of Reno flowed by in a steady stream. Reno claims to be the biggest little city in the world, and it might also claim to be the most distinctive. There's an individuality about Reno which hits you right between the eyes: cowpunchers clumping along the sidewalks in high-heeled riding-boots, disillusioned, bitter women waiting for their period of residence to expire, voluptuous cuties who are playing tag with life, and have dropped in on Reno during a period of transition, boldly looking for some temporary masculine contacts and not being overly particular. Gamblers rub elbows with tourists. Cowpunchers pass the time of day with the owners of dude ranches. Sunburned vacationists, enjoying the healthful climate, mingle with pale-faced tourists who are gawking about at the sights of the divorce capital.

I wanted a few moments in which to think things out

before I went back to the cabin. I drifted with the crowd through the doors of one of the more popular casinos, stood in a corner absently watching the expressions of the faces grouped around the wheel of fortune. Behind me, I could hear the steady whir of a slot machine. Intermittently, there'd be the tinkle of coins spilling into the cup.

I turned around to look.

Helen Framley, her back turned toward me, was busily engaged in milking one of the two-bit machines.

I walked quietly to the door and out into the street.

Chapter Fifteen

HELEN FRAMLEY CAME breezing into the cabin. "Gosh, I'm hungry. Anything to eat in the place?"

"Coming up right away," Louie said. "I've got some Spanish beans in the oven, keeping warm. I've had them simmering all day. Wait until you taste them."

"Boiled beans?" she asked.

"Not exactly. You boil 'em, then fry 'em, and mash 'em up into a meal with a little garlic. Don't tell me you've never tasted Mexican fried beans."

"No, but they sound good."

"I'll have 'em ready in just a jiffy."

Louie went out into the kitchen to busy himself over the stove.

Helen said to me very casually, "Donald, you were asking me about money. How are *you* fixed on cash?"

"I can get by."

"I don't believe it. How many traveler's checks have you got?"

"Don't worry. I'll get along."

"Let me see."

"I tell you, I'm all right."

"Come on, let me see. Where's the book of checks?"

I took out the book. There were three twenty-dollar checks left.

She laughed. "Chicken feed," she said, "for the expenses you're carrying. Listen, I want to pay some of this."

"Not a chance."

"Don't kid me. I'm dough-heavy, and I'm going to contribute. Try and stop me."

She opened her purse, pulled out a roll of bills, peeled

203

off three twenties which she put back in her purse and tossed the balance over to me.

I shook my head.

"All right then, it's a loan," she said. "You can pay it back."

"How much is in there?"

"I don't know. Three or four hundred dollars. Count it."

I counted it. There was four hundred and fifty dollars in the roll.

"Where'd you get it?" I asked.

"Oh, I had it in my purse. Remember, I had the roll when Pug and I came to a parting of the ways."

I put the money in my pocket. I didn't say anything about having seen her in the casino.

After dinner we drove uptown and took in an early movie. Louie seemed to be feeling very much himself. Helen didn't talk much. She had the quiet of calm contentment about her.

On the way home, she sang little snatches of popular tunes, and when we arrived at the cabin, had us stop to stand outside the door and look up at the stars. She said suddenly, "I know, of course, it's going to end. I'm afraid it's going to end soon, but it's grand while it's lasting, isn't it, Louie?"

Louie retorted, "Are you asking me? You know the way we're getting along, it seems like we all belong to the same lodge."

We laughed then and went inside.

I waited until Helen was in the shower, getting ready for bed, then said, "I think I'd better send a telegram, Louie. I'm going to run back uptown. Don't wait up for me, and tell Helen it may be an hour or so because I have to wait for a reply."

I made my voice sound casual, and it registered with Louie.

"Okay, buddy," he said. "Don't wander down any dark

alleys, and if anybody gets tough with you, remember the old Hazen shift. Give 'em the old one-two, and when you hit, remember to follow through."

"I'll remember," I assured him and slipped quietly out of the door and into the car.

Back uptown, I made a round of the hospitals. I was gravely professional and very casual—just routine leg-work, giving my card to the attendant at the desk and explaining that I was looking for a person who had disappeared, that there was a chance it was amnesia. If they had any amnesia cases, would they let me know.

"We had a case come in about half an hour ago," I was told when I stopped at the second hospital. "A young woman—"

I pulled the pictures of Corla Burke from my pocket. "Would she answer this description?" I asked.

"I don't know. I haven't seen her. But I'll call the floor nurse."

A few moments later, a stiffly starched nurse looked me over suspiciously, then looked down at the pictures and registered excitement. "Why, that's the girl!" she exclaimed.

"You're certain? We can't afford to have any mistake."

"No. There's no question it's the same one. Who is she?"

Instantly I became cautious. "I'm working for a client," I said. "I can't divulge information until I've consulted that client, but it's an interesting case. She disappeared almost on the eve of her wedding—overtaxed nerves. May I see her?"

"I'd have to ask the doctor."

I said, "Well, if you're absolutely certain it's the same person, we won't wait for any red tape. She doesn't know me, anyway. I'll get in touch with my client."

"But," the nurse said, "perhaps you could restore her memory by asking her questions, if you know who she is."

"I'd prefer not to take that chance. I'd rather let my

client get in touch with the doctor."

"That *may* be better," the nurse said dubiously, "but I'll want your name and address."

I gave her my card. The nurse at the desk said, "I already have Mr. Lam's business address."

I left the hospital, climbed in the jalopy and went out to the cabin. Helen Framley was sitting on the sofa in pajamas and kimono.

"Why aren't you in bed?"

"I'm waiting up. You knew you were going back uptown all the time, didn't you?"

"Yes."

She studied my face for several seconds, then she said, "It's all right, Donald. It's breaking up. I thought perhaps it was going to. You don't need to beat around the bush. When do we leave?"

I said, "I've got to catch a plane to Las Vegas. I should be back by morning."

"Want me to drive you to the airport?"

"Louie can do it."

"I'd rather."

"All right," I said.

She walked into her bedroom, chin up, shoulders jaunty. Louie came out and asked, "What is it?"

I said, "Louie, I want you to listen to me. This is perhaps one of the most important things you ever tackled in your life."

"What?"

"Keep an eye on Helen."

He showed surprise. "What about her? You don't think she's two-timing—"

"I mean keep an eye on her, protect her. I'm going to be gone tonight, but from now on don't ever let her out of your sight."

"Why? What's the matter?"

I said, "She's in danger."

"Of what?"

"Murder."

His filmed eyes became suddenly animated. "Buddy," he said, "you can count on me."

We shook hands.

Helen emerged from her bedroom, buttoning the sleeves of her blouse. She turned her neck to me, said, "Button me up the back, will you?"

I caught the snaps at the neck of her blouse, helped her into her coat. She turned slowly around as I raised the coat around her neck so that she was in my arms. Her eyes looked up into mine. Her lips were half parted.

"Yes," she said as I looked down at her.

I kissed her, felt the circle of her lips clinging to mine, then she drew away.

"All right, Donald, let's go."

Louie said, "I'll go along and drive the car back in case of a puncture."

She looked at him and shook her head.

Louie looked at me.

"It's all right now," I said, "but after she gets back, remember."

He nodded.

"What are you two talking about?"

"I told Louie to keep an eye on you and take care of you."

Her eyes showed she was hurt. "You didn't have to do that, Donald."

"It isn't on that account," I said. "It's something else."

"What?"

"Just something. I can tell you more about it tomorrow."

She didn't ask any more questions, simply got in the car and started the motor. Halfway to the airport, she said, "Please understand one thing, Donald. You don't have to explain anything to me."

I placed my hand on her forearm, squeezed it gently.

"The fact that you want to do anything is enough for me. It's all I want to know," she went on. "All I ask is that you tell me what I can do to help."

We didn't say anything after that until she pulled up at the airport.

The stars seemed like friendly, watching eyes suspended overhead, looking down at the world below. There was a chill in the air, but the dry atmosphere was invigorating. Once more she stood with me looking up at the stars. This time she didn't say anything.

I kissed her good night.

"Want me to wait until you get started?"

"I'd rather you didn't. It's cold."

"Would you mind awfully if I did?"

"No."

"I'd like to see you off."

"Okay, come on then."

We found a plane that was ready for charter. By good luck, it happened that the owner-pilot was on the field, chatting with one of the transport pilots who was waiting to board a ship for San Francisco.

When the fast cabin plane had been wheeled out, fueled, and tested, and the motor was warming up, Helen slipped her hand through my arm, stood watching the plane, outlined by the vivid lights against the black night.

The pilot nodded to me. Helen said to the plane, "Take good care of him, airplane," and then looked up at me. "Happy landings," she said and turned abruptly away.

I watched her as she walked off the field without once looking back. The pilot said, "All aboard." I climbed in and adjusted the safety belt. We taxied down the field, turned around, and came roaring back. I could feel the steady push of acceleration shoving me against the back of the seat. Then the ground abruptly fell away and tilted as we made a long, banking turn.

I looked down through the window of the plane.

Helen Framley was standing by the automobile, looking up at the lights of the plane. I could just make out the oval of her face, had a last flashing glimpse of the automobile, and then the turning plane swung her out of my vision. A few moments later, we leveled off, and the lights drifted astern. Down below was only the dark stretch of sage-covered plateau. Overhead were the steady stars. Behind us the lights of Reno drew together into a little twinkling cluster. A few minutes later, they had vanished altogether.

Chapter Sixteen

BERTHA COOL was evidently giving a party.

I stood in front of the door of her hotel room and listened to the sound of laughter. A babble of voices indicated that the room was well filled with people, and all of them were trying to talk at once.

I rapped on the door.

Bertha Cool called, "Who is it?"

I heard a man say, "Probably the boy with the ice."

The transom was open an inch or two, far enough to enable me to hear Bertha Cool's voice say, "Open the door for him."

A latch clicked on the inside of the door. I turned the knob and walked in.

It was quite a gathering. All three of the Dearbornes were there, also Paul Endicott, Arthur and Philip Whitewell. Bertha Cool was half reclining on a chaise longue, propped up with pillows. She was wearing a low-cut backless evening gown.

A table in the center of the room was littered with bottles. Glasses were scattered around the room. A silver pail of ice cubes held only an inch or two of water. Ash trays were well filled with cigarette stubs and cigar butts. The atmosphere of the room was pretty thick. The men were in dinner jackets.

Bertha Cool's eyes grew big as she stared at me.

The conversation came to an abrupt stop as though someone had turned off a radio when a mob scene had been playing.

Bertha said, "Well, fry me for an oyster!"

I stood in the doorway. People put glasses down as

though I'd been a prohibition officer making a raid.

"Well," Bertha demanded truculently, "where the hell *have* you been?"

"I've been to Reno. I've found Corla Burke."

The room became absolutely silent. You couldn't even hear the rustle of motion or the sound of breathing. Then Anita Dearborne gave a quick, sharp intake of breath. At the same time, Eloise sighed.

Philip Whitewell was coming toward me, hands outstretched.

"How is she?" he asked. "Is she all right? Is she—"

"She's in a hospital."

"Oh," he said, and then after a moment, "Oh, my God!"

"Mental," I explained.

He was staring at me as if I'd driven a knife into his chest.

"Amnesia. Doesn't know who she is, who her friends are, or where she came from, or what has happened. Otherwise, she's in good health."

"At Reno?"

"Yes."

Philip Whitewell looked at his dad. "We must go at once," he said.

Arthur Whitewell ran his hand up over his bald forehead, smoothed the hair on the top of his head, and repeated the gesture twice. He glanced surreptitiously at Ogden Dearborne, then back to me. "How did you do it, Lam?" he asked.

I said, "Helen Framley knew more than she admitted."

"How did you get it out of her?"

Bertha Cool came in with the answer. "Made love to her, of course. They go absolutely mad over Donald. What did she tell you, lover?"

"I'll make my report later on," I said, "in confidence, in writing, and to you."

I turned to look at Arthur Whitewell.

Philip said, "Come on, Dad. Let's get started. We'll have to arrange for a plane."

Whitewell said, "Yes. Naturally, we must leave at once. Is she—is there any chance of recovery, Lam?"

"As I understand it, her physical condition is all right. It's purely a mental reaction."

"From what?"

"The doctors say it could have been caused by shock, by overwork, by nervousness."

"Did you tell the doctors—"

"Not a thing."

Whitewell turned to Mrs. Dearborne, managed to make his remarks include Eloise and Ogden. "Naturally, this is quite a blow—that is, a surprise. I take it you'll understand."

Mrs. Dearborne got to her feet at once. "Certainly, Arthur. We only wish there was something we could do. We know there isn't. It's a matter that you must handle." Her eyes swiveled abruptly to me. She wrapped me in a cold stare until I felt like a barren tree limb the morning after an ice storm. "So you found her," she said.

I nodded.

She smiled frostily. "I might have known you would," she said. "Come, Eloise."

Ogden helped them on with their wraps. Bertha saw them to the door. Mrs. Dearborne paused to make the usual formal acknowledgment of a pleasant evening. Bertha Cool didn't take time wasting any words. She barely waited until they were out in the corridor, then turned, heeled the door shut, and said, "I thought there was something fishy about you running away with that woman. You were following a lead. How much money have you spent?"

"Quite a bit."

She snorted.

Philip said, "Please, let's not lose a minute."

Arthur Whitewell looked at his watch. "It's going to be

difficult to charter a good plane from here I'm afraid, but we can try. If necessary, we can telephone Los Angeles and arrange to have one leave at once. Philip, suppose you go down to the airport and see what you can do. Paul can go with you and give you a hand. We'll leave it entirely to you. Use your discretion."

"I have a plane which brought me from Reno," I said. "It will hold three passengers in addition to the pilot."

Bertha said, "That's fine. I'll stay right here. Mr. Endicott can wait with me. Arthur, you and Philip can leave right away, and go with Donald."

Endicott said, "Let's not rush the thing too much. After all, she's perfectly safe. They probably won't let us see her before morning anyway, and I for one think it's more important to have the right kind of a doctor on the job than anything else. Don't you suppose, Arthur, you could get Dr. Hinderkeld to take a plane and meet you in Reno? In cases of this sort, a sudden shock may revive the patient's memory. On the other hand, it *might* be disastrous. A great deal would depend on the condition of the patient."

Whitewell said, "You're right. Paul, you telephone Dr. Hinderkeld. Wait until you've found out what you can do here about a plane. If we have to get a ship from Los Angeles, Hinderkeld can come in on it, and we'll all go to Reno together."

Philip was standing at the door, his hand on the knob. "Come on, Paul," he said, and to his father, "You can do what you want about a doctor. I'm going to her now."

Endicott flashed Arthur Whitewell one searching glance, then he and Philip were out in the corridor.

Whitewell turned to me. "I suppose I have you to thank for this."

"For what?"

"As though you didn't know."

"You wanted me to find her, didn't you? I've found her."

He said, "You told Mrs. Cool that you thought I might

have dictated that letter, that I might have given her money. Evidently, young man, you don't have a very high opinion of me."

I said, "I'm employed to do a job. The letter she wrote Helen Framley was written on your stationery. The top had been cut off with a knife. Women don't carry knives. A woman cutting off the top of a letterhead would have folded the paper, and cut it with a paper cutter, or she would have used a pair of scissors, or she might have even tried to tear it off. She wouldn't have cut it with a sharp knife."

"Well, what of it?"

"The letter was written at night. It was picked up shortly before midnight. It was written on your office stationery. To my mind, that means it was written in your office."

"Well?"

"A man was present. She hadn't intended to write the letter before she went to the office. Otherwise, she'd have had the letter written—or else she'd have waited until she got back to her apartment to write it. She went to your office. She met some man. They had a conversation. As a result of that conversation, she decided to write a letter. For some reason, it was considered imperative that she write the letter then and there. She did so. The man cut off the letterhead. Someone furnished a stamped envelope. Corla Burke left very mysteriously the next day. The circumstances surrounding her departure were such that it was impossible to believe she hadn't left of her own volition. She'd left a purse on her desk with all of her money in it. Evidently, it was all the money she had. She couldn't have gone far without money. Therefore, it's obvious she was getting money from someone.

"There was enough in that letter to Helen Framley to show that she was leaving under her own power and because of some circumstance or development which she thought put her in a questionable light, particularly with the man she was to marry. You evidently knew of that letter. You evidently had a pretty good idea what was in it. You were willing to hire a firm of private detectives to start working on the case. You were very careful to see that the detectives met you in Las Vegas and started working from there. You were so afraid they might miss Helen Framley that you had her all ticketed, earmarked, and ready for delivery like a box of quick-frozen strawberries. And you carry stamped envelopes.

"Now you put all that together and see what you'd think if you were a detective."

, Bertha said, "Damn you, Donald. He's a client—and a friend."

"That's all right," I said. "I'm reporting. I haven't said anything to anyone else yet, have I?"

"That word 'yet' sounds like a threat," Whitewell said.

I didn't say anything.

"How much of all this about the amnesia attack is true?" Whitewell asked.

I said, "I somehow had an idea her disappearance might have had to do with a prior marriage."

"What gave you that idea?"

"She left under her own power. She tried to save her face, and she tried to save Philip's face. She wasn't the sort of girl who would have let you buy her off. Looking at it from any angle, the most plausible explanation was that a prior marriage was mixed up in it."

"So you went to Reno?"

"That's right. Persons who are suffering from unfortunate marriages and suddenly disappear are quite apt to go to Reno."

"And you made inquiries at the hospitals, I suppose," Whitewell said sarcastically.

"Exactly. There were two practical solutions, and only two. One of them was a prior marriage, and the other was an attack of amnesia."

"And if it had been a prior marriage, she'd have gone to Reno?"

"That's right."

"But why should she have gone to Reno if she had been suffering from amnesia?"

"It was a complication of both causes," I said, and grinned at him.

"And so you found her in this hospital! How nice!"

"Yes. When I made the evening round, I learned that a woman who answered Miss Burke's description had been picked up suffering from amnesia. I checked. It was Corla Burke, all right. That put me in a spot. The hospital authorities were trying to find someone who knew her. Naturally, they wanted to pump me. I kept my mouth shut."

Whitewell raised his left hand to the shining expanse of his high forehead, stroked what hair he had left with the palm of his hand. "If you'd uncovered Helen Framley," he said, "found that letter, turned it in, and then quit, your services would have been worth a great deal more to me."

"Then why didn't you tell me that was what you wanted me to do? You told me you wanted me to find Corla Burke."

He abruptly pushed his hands down in his trousers pockets. "I see by the paper," he said, "that the man who was living with Helen Framley was Sidney Jannix."

"He wasn't living with her. It was a business partnership."

Bertha Cool snorted.

Arthur Whitewell's eyes were narrowed. "Now that you have blurted out that you've found Corla, Philip, of course, will have to go to see her. Jannix is dead—murdered, very fortunately for her. She has no recollection of what happened. The poor girl was suffering from a nervous strain. Wouldn't it be just fine if the sight of Philip should restore her memory? She'd then have no recollection of what had happened from the time she walked out of the office and would be all ready to go on with the wedding."

I met his eyes. "I think that would make your son very happy."

He folded his arms. "Perhaps," he said, "I am more concerned with my son's happiness one year or ten years from now than in helping him gratify a brief infatuation."

"Quite possibly that's true."

"I don't suppose *you'd* have any ideas about that?"

"You hired me to find Corla Burke. I've found her."

Bertha Cool said, "He's right on that, Arthur. You should have taken us into your confidence. I told you Donald was very competent and a fast worker. He—"

"Shut up," Whitewell said without taking his eyes from me.

Bertha Cool came up out of that chair as though she'd been a rubber ball dropped from a twenty-story window. "Who the hell do you think you're talking to?" she demanded. "Don't you tell me to shut up. You—such a polished gentleman that butter won't melt in your mouth, filled with all your goddamn flatteries—and telling a lady to shut up! You hired us to do a job, and we've done it. Now get out your checkbook and settle up."

Whitewell completely ignored her. He said to me, "I suppose you'd also resort to a little blackmail?"

"About what?"

"Threatening to tell Philip unless you get the sort of settlement you want."

I said, "I'm reporting to Bertha Cool. She runs the agency any way she wants to. I don't have anything to say about that. However, if you're going to play ostrich and try sticking your head in the sand, you might remember that the police here in Las Vegas are going to be mildly interested."

"What business is it of theirs?"

"You forget the murder."

"You mean this mess is all going to come out in connection with the murder?"

"It might."

He frowned at me, and said, "By the time I unscramble that enigmatic remark, young man, I suppose I'll find a hook in it. That has all the earmarks of being the opening gun in a campaign of shakedown."

I lit a cigarette.

Bertha said, "You'd better come down to earth and realize you aren't done with *us* yet. You're going to need representation to keep this murder rap off your shoulders."

"Off *my* shoulders!" Whitewell exclaimed.

Bertha's eyes glittered at him, hard and greedy. "You're damn tootin'," she said. "Don't forget that girl who saw you."

Whitewell began to smile, a slow grin of amused triumph. "Well," he said, "isn't it going to be interesting to see what happens. Corla Burke has lost her memory. She doesn't know anything that happened from the time she finished taking dictation on the day of her disappearance. The next thing she remembers is when Philip walks into the hospital and says, 'Corla,' and the emotional shock suddenly brings back her memory. Rather a nice little master of ceremonies, aren't you, Lam?"

"Go ahead," I said. "Spill the rest of it."

"All right, I will. Corla Burke was an adventuress. She'd been married before, and she was concealing that marriage from my son. She'd trapped my son into a love affair. She was going to marry him. Then a few days before the ceremony, her husband makes a very inopportune appearance. Immediately Corla Burke disappears. Shortly thereafter, her husband is murdered. As soon as he has shuffled this mortal coil so that she becomes a widow and therefore perfectly eligible to make an immediate marriage, a private detective finds her in a hospital, suffering from amnesia.

And I won't insult your intelligence by intimating there's any chance she won't be promptly cured as soon as she sees my son, and I hope that you won't insult *my* intelligence by trying to make me swallow it as a genuine performance. But the point is, she was the one who had a motive for murdering Sidney Jannix. She wanted him out of the way. She had every reason to know that he could be located through Helen Framley. That's something for you to consider, Lam."

"Why?"

"Because if she doesn't know where she has been during the intervening time, she can't deny that she was in Las Vegas. She can't deny that she killed him."

"So what?"

"So," he said, "you have a plane here. We are getting a plane. If you started now, you could get back to Reno ahead of us. If Corla Burke isn't there in the hospital when we arrive, so far as I'm concerned, there won't be any temptation to associate her with the murder of her husband."

I said, "No soap."

Bertha Cool said, "What the hell do you take us for anyway?"

Whitewell made a little gesture with his hands. "All right, I'll approach it another way. Philip is my only child, my only living close relative. I realize that he is introspective, that he's abnormally sensitive, that he's inclined to brood. I know that his happiness doesn't depend entirely on himself. He's a young man who will be greatly influenced by his environment. That means that his marriage is going to be terribly important—getting just the right woman is going to mean a lot.

"Can't you give me credit for having some intelligence? Can't you realize that I know Philip better than any other person on earth? Don't you understand that his happiness is the primary consideration with me, that if I thought he could be happy with Corla Burke, I would move heaven and earth to bring the two together? Can't you realize that the only reason I didn't want him to marry Corla was that I knew she wasn't the woman for him? I knew the match was unsuitable. I knew that it was but the prelude to tragedy. She wouldn't stay with him. She isn't his type. She'd break his heart. Some persons can marry more than once. Some persons can't. Philip is one who can't."

I asked, "How is your son going to feel toward her when he finds she's been married before?"

He grinned. "What you're leading up to is how is he going to find it out? *I* can't say anything. That would be a giveaway. She won't say anything because she's had this very convenient loss of memory. Of course, it will come out after marriage, but that will be afterwards. Oh, I'll hand it to you, Lam. You're clever all right. It would have been a neat little checkmate. But it isn't a mate."

I saw the glitter in his eyes. "Don't forget that I can be absolutely ruthless when anyone crosses me. You either have her out of the way by the time Philip gets to Reno or she'll be arrested for murder, and then the whole thing will come out—and once she's pulled this amnesia business, she's licked."

I yawned.

He stood glaring down at me. "Damn you, you insolent little terrier, I mean it."

I reached in my pocket.

He crossed the room, picked up the telephone, and said to us, "I'm calling police headquarters."

I pulled out the letter I'd taken from Corla Burke's Reno apartment.

Whitewell took one look at that envelope and dropped the telephone as though it had been hot. I said, "I inquired for mail at Reno. I thought there might be a letter for her. There was."

He became very still.

"That was a breach of the postal laws. They can raise

hell with you for that."

I went on calmly, "I notice Paul Endicott seemed very anxious to mail your letter about the option. It's fortunate you accepted it. Evidently he's quite familiar with your business."

Bertha said, "Donald, what the hell are you talking about?"

I said, "Suppose Philip takes it right on the chin and still loves her, regardless of how many times she's been married? You're a man who likes your family, Mr. Whitewell. You're going to be pretty lonesome without Philip, and it's going to be quite a blow to you to be estranged from your own grandchildren."

If I'd given him Louie Hazen's one-two shift in the solar plexus, I couldn't have given him more of a jolt.

"If I were in your shoes," I went on, "I'd have considered the amnesia as just about the best break I'd had in ten years."

He said with conviction, "When he finds out how she's deceived him, he'll walk out on her. It will hurt for a while, but he'll walk out."

I said, "You're wrong. He won't find out. Personally, I'm going to get something to eat. I'll see you in about twenty minutes."

I walked out and left him alone with Bertha.

I strolled down the street to a bar, got a toothpick, and came back to Bertha Cool's room. She was alone. "Where's Whitewell?" I asked.

"Gone to get some things together. You really shouldn't have handled him that way, lover. You've always had a chip on your shoulder with him."

"I gave him a break with that amnesia business, and he was too dumb to realize it," I said.

"No, not dumb. Just confident that Philip will do exactly what he expects him to do."

"Philip is in love."

221

"Donald, what about that letter he sent. What was in it?"

"Nothing much."

She glared at me. The phone rang. She picked it up, listened a moment after she'd said, "Hello," and then said, "Okay, we'll be on our way."

She hung up. "Philip has chartered a plane. That and the one you brought from Reno will take us all. We start at once. Donald, what was in that letter?"

I started for the door. "Let's get going."

Chapter Seventeen

BERTHA WENT IN THE PLANE with me. The others followed in the plane Philip had chartered. At the last minute, Paul Endicott decided he'd go along, too, just for the ride.

The drone of the plane motor lulled me to sleep shortly after the take-off. Occasionally, Bertha would prod me into wakefulness with questions. I'd answer in muttered monosyllables and return to the warm comfort of sleep.

"You mustn't fight with Arthur Whitewell, Donald."

"Uh huh."

"You little devil, Bertha knew you weren't falling for a woman. You fall in love with them all right, and I mean *really* in love, but you're more in love with your profession than with any woman. Answer me, Donald. Isn't that right?"

"I guess so."

"Tell me, did Helen Framley kill that man she was living with?"

"She wasn't living with him."

"Oh, splash!"

"It was a business partnership."

Bertha snorted. "Pickle me for a beet."

I didn't say anything. After a few minutes, Bertha said, "You still haven't answered my question."

"What?"

"Whether she murdered him."

"I hope she didn't."

I didn't have to look up to realize that her glittering little eyes were searching every line of my face, trying to surprise some telltale expression. "Helen Framley knows a lot about who committed that murder."

"Perhaps."

"Something she hasn't told the police."

"Possibly."

"I'll bet she's told you what it is. You wormed it out of her, you little devil. My God, Donald, how do you do it? Do you hypnotize them? I guess you must. You can't give them the cave-man stuff. You make them come to you. I guess it's your readiness to fight at the drop of the hat, even when you know you're going to get licked. I guess that's it. Women love a fighter."

I felt my head jerk forward as I all but slipped into unconsciousness. Bertha pulled me back with her patter.

"Listen, lover, has it ever occurred to you what's going to happen next?"

"What?"

"Whitewell has money, influence, and brains. He isn't going to be pushed around."

I didn't say anything.

"I'll bet that Framley girl would do just about anything you asked her."

That didn't seem to call for any reply.

Bertha said, "I'll bet the person who did the job is sweating blood right now. Suppose this Framley girl really does know who killed him?"

I said, "I think she does."

"Then she's told you."

"No."

"But she'll tell the police—if they ask her."

"I don't think so."

"Donald."

"What?"

"Do you suppose the murderer knows that?"

"Knows what?"

"That she won't talk."

I said, "That depends on who the murderer is."

Bertha said suddenly, "Donald, *you* know who the murderer is, don't you?"

"I don't know."

"Don't know what?"

"Whether or not I know."

Bertha said, "That's a hell of an answer."

"Isn't it," I agreed and went sound asleep in the few seconds of glaring silence which followed. When I woke up, we were droning in for a landing at the Reno airport. It had been the change in the tempo of the motor that had wakened me.

Bertha Cool was sitting very erect and dignified, endeavoring to show her displeasure by a cutting silence.

We came circling in to a landing, and the other plane was right on our tail, following us in within just a few minutes.

Paul Endicott said, "I notice there's a plane leaving here for San Francisco within the next fifteen minutes. I see no reason for driving uptown with you and then rushing back. I've enjoyed the ride, and guess we're all straightened out now." He looked searchingly into Whitewell's eyes and said, "Here's luck, old man."

They shook hands.

Philip said, "I'm the one who is going to need the luck. Do you suppose she'll know me, Dad?"

Whitewell said dryly, "I have an idea she will."

Endicott gave Philip a handshake. "Keep the old chin up and take it in your stride. We're pulling for you, all of us."

Philip tried to say something, but his quivering lips mumbled the words. Endicott covered his embarrassment by keeping right on with a line of patter, never stopping, so Philip would not have to say anything.

We stood there in a little compact group waiting for the taxicab for which we had telephoned. I told them I had to telephone and excused myself. I wanted to check on Helen and Louie, but the Acme Filling Station out on the Susanville highway wasn't listed in the phone book. I

225

came back and stood around stamping my feet against the cold, waiting for the cab. At length, it drew up and we piled in. Arthur Whitewell stopped for a last word with Endicott, then they shook hands and Whitewell crawled into the jump seat.

"What's the name of the hospital?" Bertha asked.

"The Haven of Mercy," I told the driver, and glanced at Arthur Whitewell's face. It was set in expressionless immobility. He might have been posing for an old-fashioned time exposure, and concentrating on not even batting an eyelash. Philip was the exact opposite. He kept biting his lip, tugging at his ear, fidgeting uneasily in his seat, looking out of the window of the cab, trying to avoid our eyes, doubtless wishing that he could escape our thoughts.

We pulled up in front of the hospital. I said pointedly to Bertha, "This will be strictly a family affair."

Arthur Whitewell looked across at his son. "I think, Philip, you'd better go up alone," he said. "If the shock of seeing you doesn't clear things up, don't let it discourage you too much. We'll have Dr. Hinderkeld come up, and he'll get results."

"And if seeing me does clear things up for her?" Philip asked.

His father dropped a hand on his shoulder. "I'll be waiting."

Bertha Cool looked at me.

I said, "It gives me the creeps to wait around a hospital. I'll be back in an hour. That will be early enough in case I can do anything to help, and if I can't, it will give you time enough to get adjusted."

Bertha asked, "Where are you going?"

"Oh, there are some things I want to do," I said. "I'll keep the cab."

Whitewell said to Bertha, "It looks as though you and I were going to be left to pace the floor in the expectant-fathers department."

"Not me," Bertha said. "I'll ride uptown with Donald. We'll be back here in an hour. And then breakfast?"

"Excellent," he said.

Bertha nodded to me.

Whitewell said to Bertha, loud enough so Philip could hear, "I can't begin to tell you how much I appreciate— Oh, well, we'll talk about that later. I'm certain you understand." He placed his hand affectionately on Bertha's shoulder. "Your understanding and sympathy have meant more to me than you'll ever realize. And I'll expect you to control—the entire situation. You—" His voice choked. He gave her shoulder a quick pat and turned away.

Philip, who had been making inquiries at the desk, entered an elevator with a nurse. Arthur Whitewell was settling himself in a chair as Bertha and I went out into the cold chill of the mountain air.

"Well," I said casually, "we'll take the cab back uptown and—"

Bertha's hand clutched my arm. She swung me around so that I faced her, pushed me back against the wall of the hospital. "To hell with that stuff," she said. "You can stall those other guys, but you can't stall me. Where are you going?"

"Out to see Helen Framley."

"So'm I," Bertha said.

"I don't need a chaperon."

"That's what *you* think."

I said, "Use your head. She'll be in bed. I can't go out there and wake her up and say, 'Permit me to present Mrs. Cool—' "

"Nuts. If she's in bed, you're not going near her. You're not the type. You'd stand guard in front of the door. Donald Lam, what the hell *are* you up to?"

"I told you."

"Yes, you did. I'm getting so I know you like a book. You've got some trick up your sleeve."

"All right," I said. "Come along if you want to."

"That's better."

We walked down to the taxicab.

"What is it?" Bertha asked.

I told the cab driver, "I want you to drive out of town until I tell you to stop, then let us off, and wait until we come back."

He looked at me suspiciously.

"Set your speedometer at zero when you cross the railroad tracks. I'll want to get mileage from time to time. You'll get waiting time while we're gone, but I don't want the lights on or the motor running. Do you get me?"

He said somewhat dubiously, "I know you're okay, but on a trip out of town that way where we're left waiting by a highway, we're supposed to get—"

I handed him ten dollars. "That enough?" I asked him.

"That's perfectly swell," he said with a grin.

"Set the speedometer at zero as you cross the tracks."

"Right."

Bertha Cool settled back against the cushions. "Give me a cigarette, lover, and tell me what the hell all *this* is about."

"Who murdered Jannix?" I asked, handing her the cigarette.

"How should I know?"

I said, "Someone who was close to Arthur Whitewell."

"Why?" she asked.

"That's exactly it. Jannix had been playing the thing from the blackmail angle. Someone double-crossed him."

Bertha forgot to light her cigarette. "Let's get this straight," she said, leaning forward.

"The first part of it is a cinch. Helen Framley didn't write to Corla Burke. Someone did, someone who gave Helen Framley's name, and told Corla to reply."

"Well?"

"Get the idea?"

"No," Bertha said shortly.

"If Corla had walked into that trap, if she'd gone ahead and married Philip Whitewell, the marriage would, of course, have been bigamous. Her understanding would have been that Jannix would get a divorce. You know what would have happened. There never would have been any divorce. He'd have kept bleeding her white. Once she married Philip, she never could make a move to get the divorce. Jannix had her then where he wanted her."

"And you don't think Helen Framley wrote that letter?"

"I know she didn't."

"Why?"

"For one thing, she told me so. For another thing, it wasn't the sort of letter she'd have written to a woman in Corla Burke's position. Someone must have written that letter—and it was someone who was close to Helen Framley."

"How do you know that?"

"Because he told Corla to send the reply to Helen Framley at General Delivery."

"Why not send it to her at her apartment?"

"Because Helen Framley wasn't to get it. When she first went to Las Vegas, she'd been getting mail at General Delivery. Jannix had been picking it up occasionally, and probably held her written authorization to deliver any mail addressed to her."

"I get you now," Bertha said.

"The post-office authorities were *too* obliging. That was something the conspirators hadn't anticipated."

"I see, I see," Bertha said. "Go on from there. They delivered the letter directly to Helen Framley. It didn't make sense to her. But why did Jannix get killed?"

"Because Jannix was in on it, but he didn't think it up by himself. Someone was back of him, someone who wanted—"

"To cut in on the blackmail?" Bertha asked.

"No," I said. "That was the bait they held out to Jannix. But whoever did it was someone who knew Corla Burke well enough to know she'd never go through with the wedding under those circumstances. Therefore, it was someone who wanted to stop the wedding. It wasn't done for the purpose of blackmail."

"Who did it? Who was back of it all?"

"Any number of people, Arthur Whitewell, any one of the Dearbornes—or all three of them. It might have been Endicott, and it might have been Philip himself."

"Go ahead."

"It was a nice scheme. It worked perfectly. The only trouble with it was that after it worked, Jannix realized he'd been played for a sucker. He didn't like it. So Jannix threatened to talk."

"And got a dose of lead as a consequence?" Bertha asked.

"That's right."

Bertha said, "Arthur Whitewell wouldn't do anything like that."

"He hasn't any alibi."

"How about the Dearbornes?" Bertha pointed out. "They're a lean, hungry bunch of crusaders. I wouldn't trust any one of them as far as I could throw a bull by the tail up a forty-five-degree slope."

"That's okay with me."

The cab swung down the lighted expanse of Reno's main gambling street, jolted across the tracks, and headed out past the tree-lined residential district. Bertha said, "So you're going to go see Helen Framley and try to get the information out of her?"

"I'm going to leave her out of it. All I'm doing is making certain that the other person leaves her out of it."

"I don't get you."

"When I left you in Las Vegas, I was very careful to leave under such circumstances that you'd make a loud squawk. I wanted you to tell everyone who had any connection with the case just what a heel I'd turned out to be, that I'd run away with Helen Framley. That information wouldn't have meant much except to one person."

"Who?"

"The murderer."

"Fiddlesticks. I don't think there's anything to that. You're in love with that girl, Donald Lam, and because you are, you're worrying about her. But in case you're right, I'm going to be in on the finish."

I said, "You can wait in the cab if you want to."

"But no one could possibly get out there for a long while."

"I'm not so certain about that. Remember that Endicott stayed behind at the Reno airport; that Arthur Whitewell didn't go up to the room with his son; that Ogden Dearborne is a pilot and has a quarter interest in an airplane. He didn't say anything about placing that at Philip's disposal. Why?"

"Perhaps because he only owned a one-quarter interest."

"That may be, and then again he may have wanted to go somewhere in a hurry himself."

"Or with his sister?" Bertha asked.

"Or his mother."

Bertha Cool said, "Well, of all the saps! That's what comes of having a detective get lovesick. I'd have beer more comfortable waiting in the hospital. I think you're nuts."

"You don't have to come with me. I told you the cab would take you back."

Bertha Cool said, "That's just it. If I stay out here and shiver and freeze, not a damn thing will turn up. If I bawl you out for being lovesick, take the cab and go back to Reno, you'll trap the murderer within thirty minutes, make a big grandstand and have the laugh on me. Nuts to you, Donald Lam. I'm going to stay with the show."

"All right," I said, "suit yourself."

"You should know me well enough by this time to know that I always do," she snapped.

I cupped my hands up against the windowpane of the taxicab, and looked out, trying to get landmarks. We climbed a little hill, made the curve, started down on the other side. The gasoline station with the lone cabin a hundred-odd feet in the rear showed briefly as black splotches against the sky. Then they had swept on behind us.

I slid open the window. "Stop the car right here, will you?"

He swung the car over to the side of the road. "Don't race the engine, just cut it off, and switch out your lights."

"I don't get you."

"I want you to wait here."

He put on his brakes, shut off motor and lights, and said, "I think you got your distances wrong. There ain't a thing near here."

"It's all right," I told him. "I'll get out and look around."

Bertha got out with me. In the eastern sky there was a streak of dim light which as yet had no color. The desert chill seemed intensified after the warmth of the taxicab.

We started walking. The cab driver looked after us for a few moments, then turned back, settled down in his car, and huddled into his overcoat.

Bertha asked, "How much of this?"

"Half or three-quarters of a mile."

She turned abruptly. "I'm going back to the car. To hell with it."

"All right, take the cab back to town. I have a car that's good enough to get me where I want to go. I'll run back to the hospital as soon as I'm satisfied everything's all right."

Bertha turned without a word, started back to the cab. I had covered about fifty yards before I saw the lights flash on again on the cab. I swung to one side of the road as the cab swept into a turn, waited until the red taillight had become a ruby blot in the distance, and then started trudging along the pavement.

The streak of light in the east became more noticeable. There was enough light now to see objects as black blotches against a grayish background. Ahead of me I could see the gasoline station with the little house behind it, and then a hundred yards back from the road, the cabin. I slid into the shadows and waited.

The light in the east was growing stronger. A watcher concealed in the shadows could have seen me approaching along the road—not plainly enough to recognize me, but still I'd been too visible. It was cold. The air was as still as the reflection in a placid mountain lake. I could feel the tips of my ears tingling with the cold. My nose felt cold. I wanted to stamp my feet, yet dared not move. The sound of a car on the highway—remarkable how far you can hear a car snarling along the pavement. I tingled with anticipation. This would be my man. Now that I was here, I wondered just what would happen. Suppose Louie had been drinking again? Suppose the man who was coming had a gun and didn't waste time in argument? Suppose— The car swung around the corner. The headlights gleamed along the road. It didn't even slow down, but swept on past and into the distance. The sound of the car diminished into the frosty silence.

I pushed my hands under my armpits and hugged them. I was shivering now, and my teeth were chattering. My feet felt like chunks of ice. No other cars, no sound, just that still cold.

I looked at my watch. By holding the face toward the east I could see the time plainly. It would be three-quarters of an hour before the sun would shed any warmth. I simply couldn't stand that cold any more. I hadn't realized how the dry air of the desert will suck the warmth right out through your clothes.

I didn't want to waken the girl. I tiptoed around to the other window, and called, in a low, cautious voice, "Oh, Louie! Hello, Louie!"

There was no sound.

I picked up a little pebble and tapped gently on the window. Nothing happened. I ran the pebble quickly along the side of the house and gave a low whistle.

I waited, listened, and heard nothing.

The east was orange now, and the stars had drifted far back into space. I was seized with a paroxysm of shivering.

I tapped on the window with my knuckles and called, "Louie. Oh, Louie. Wake up."

The few seconds of silence after that seemed hours.

I walked around to the front door of the cabin and tapped on it gently. Then when I received no answer, I tried the knob.

The door was unlocked. It swung inward.

It had been cold outside, but the air was fresh. In here, there was a stale closeness to the atmosphere which made it seem even colder. I didn't think I'd ever get warm again. Louie shouldn't have left the door unlocked. I'd cautioned him particularly about that, and tonight of all times— I locked the door carefully behind me, tiptoed across the room. The boards creaked under my feet. The door of Louie's bedroom was closed. I turned the knob, opened the door gently, and said in a whisper, "Oh, Louie!"

Enough light was coming from the east now so I could see the objects in the room clearly. The bed hadn't been slept in.

I stood staring at that vacant bed as the significance of what it meant gradually dawned on my mind.

I whirled and strode toward Helen Framley's door. I didn't bother to knock, just turned the knob and kicked the door open.

Her bed was empty. It was half a dozen seconds before I

saw the white thing pinned on the pillow. I walked over to it. It was a sealed envelope with my name and address on the outside. There was also a stamp on it. Evidently, she hadn't been certain I was coming back, and in that event wanted the letter mailed to me.

I tore it open and read:

Darling—I guess this is the only way. You have your life and I have mine. The two never have mixed and never will. You're you, and I'm me. I've got to get out of town. That roll I gave you came from slot machines, and a dick spotted me. I got away, but they'll be looking for me. After you'd left, I talked with Louie. He's been around and he knows the way I feel. I can't work the slot machines without a man who's handy with his fists, and who knows the racket. Louie sees it the same way I do. Only remember, Donald, it's strictly a business partnership. That's understood. And I won't have trouble with Louie the way I did with Pug. Louie knows where my heart is—and he worships the ground you walk on.

By this time, I guess you know about Pug. I'm not certain that you didn't all along.

It was either him or both of us. He kept that gun in the bureau drawer where he had some of his papers and things that he didn't want to leave in his rooming-house. I told him I'd give him a drawer in the bureau. I knew there was a gun there. When he began to get so insanely jealous, I took the gun out and hid it in the dishpan in the kitchen. I knew he'd never look there. After he found us together on the street and had that trouble with the cop, he went directly to the apartment. He was wise. He turned off the lights and hid in the closet.

I came in a few minutes after nine, turned on the lights, and Pug pushed open the closet door. He was crazy. I couldn't do a thing with him. He swore that he was going to kill us both. He accused me of turning him over to the

235

cops. He hit me, and then made a dash for the drawer to get the gun. I ran for the door. He headed me off. I got into the kitchen and slammed the door. I didn't have time to lock it. We struggled for a minute at the door, and then he got it open, throwing me back against the sink. I whipped open the cupboard door and reached in the dishpan. He kept coming.

I'm not the least bit sorry. I had to do it. According to your code, I should have notified the law and stayed there and told them my story, let them probe into my past, ask me about my means of making a living, hold me in jail as a material witness, and all that bunk. Well, that's not my way of doing it. I walked across to the apartment next door and pounded on the door for Mrs. Clutmer—just to make certain that she wasn't home. No one answered my knock, so I just walked out, and left the door open. I ditched the gun where no one will ever find it.

I swore I'd never rat, but I can't hold out on you. There are some things you'll have to know. The girl with the rabbit nose is named Dearborne. She's strong for Philip Whitewell. Somebody in Whitewell's organization who didn't want the marriage to go through put detectives on Corla Burke. They uncovered her record and turned up Sid Jannix. I didn't know him by that name. I knew him as Harry Beegan, and called him Pug because he'd been in the ring.

I think Pug wrote the letter to Corla Burke and signed my name to it. He was pretty good at forgery. He wanted to get Corla Burke where he could squeeze her dry. She was too smart for him. Pug didn't think up the scheme. It was someone else who did, someone who didn't want the marriage to go through.

Philip's father knew about the letter to me. He wrote to the Dearbornes to look me up. The boy made the investigation, but his sister started cultivating me and trying to work me. She was suspicious of Pug. I don't know how she knew, but she did know he was connected with Corla Burke. She wanted to pump me. She was so obvious I just strung her along and didn't bother to take her seriously. I'd had the apartment where you found me for a week. I knew things were coming to a head with Pug, and I wanted a way to leave him for good when I walked out. I knew he'd never think of looking for me in another apartment in the same city.

But after the killing, I had to sit absolutely tight. I went out to get some grub—and darned if I didn't run into the Dearborne girl on the street. She knew I was hiding and offered to see me through. Why, I don't know.

Pug had taken the roll from me as soon as I came in, and I didn't have over thirty cents to my name. The Dearborne girl offered to get grub. Well, I let her.

We're taking your car for a few days. I have an idea you won't need it. When we get done with it, I'll drop you a note at your office telling you where you can find it.

I love you more than I have ever loved anyone in the world, and I'm taking a powder because I don't want anything to interfere with the memory of the time we spent together. I know it's finished. I know we can't go on. I know that if I try, something is going to happen to rob that memory of all its sweetness.

Louie doesn't understand all the details, but he knows enough to get the sketch. He says if there's ever anyone you want killed, all you have to do is put an ad in the personal columns of the Los Angeles papers, saying, "Louie, the guy's name is so-and-so." Louie would lay down his life for you. Louie says it's because you're a real champ, that people feel that way about you. I think it's because you're so darn clean and decent. Anyway, we're both for you and we're both saying—Good-by.

I was shivering with the cold and a nervous chill. My hand was shaking so I could hardly hold the letter. I turned on the hot water in the shower. When it was good and hot, I got out of my clothes and stood under the stream, letting the water run as hot as I could stand it. When I got out, I felt a little better. I rubbed myself with a towel, went out into the kitchen, and looked in the wood stove. Leave it to Louie to think of little things like that. He'd laid the fire with kindling and dry wood, so all I had to do was touch a match to it.

When the fire was roaring into flame, I lifted the cover from the stove and dropped in Helen's letter. I put on some coffee, and looked through the cupboard to see if, by any chance, there was any whisky. I couldn't find any. The warmth of the hot shower left me, and I was standing over the stove once more, shivering.

The east was splashed with vivid crimson, then the sun came up. The wood stove did its stuff, and my bones began to thaw out. The coffee started bubbling, and I had two big cups. By that time, I realized I was hungry. I broke some eggs into a frying-pan, scrambled them, made some toast in the oven, and had another cup of coffee with the eggs and toast. The kitchen was good and warm by that time.

I tried to smoke a cigarette, but the room gave me the jitters. Every article in it reminded me of her. The whole place was vibrant with memories—and desolate as a tomb.

I packed my bag and went out to stand in the sunlight. I couldn't wait in the house any more.

The man who owned the gas station came out, and unlocked his pumps, rubbing his eyes sleepily. I walked over to him and said, "I've got to leave by plane. The others have taken the car and gone on. There are some provisions in the house you can have if you want."

He thanked me, looked at me curiously, and said, "I thought I heard your wife and the other man drive away last night."

I started for the highway. I'd been walking about three

minutes when a car coming out from Reno swerved and slid to a stop. I looked up, my heart pounding in my throat.

Some woman was rolling down a window. Her arm concealed her face. I started toward the car, running across the pavement.

The window rolled down. The woman's arm came away so I could see her face. It was Bertha.

"Where have *you* been?" she asked.

"Getting things straightened out here."

"No one showed up, did they?"

"No."

"I didn't think they would. It sounded goofy to me. Well, come on. We've got work to do."

"What and where?"

"First we get back to Las Vegas. This man Kleinsmidt on the police force is raising merry hell, and you're the only one who can do anything with him."

"What happened with Philip and the girl?"

She snorted and said, *"Loss of memory!* Well, it's all right if he falls for it."

"They've made up?" I asked.

"Made up! You should have seen them."

"Where are they now?"

"Took a plane for Los Angeles. We've got to go back and square things with Kleinsmidt. Come on, hop in."

I climbed in the car with her, and she said to the driver, "All right, now we'll go to the airport."

A plane was waiting. We climbed aboard. I wouldn't talk. Bertha quit trying to pump me after a while. Then gradually the nerve tension left me. I dropped into a sound sleep.

A car met us at Las Vegas. "Sal Sagev Hotel," Bertha said, and to me, "You look pretty bad. Get a bath, shave, and then come to my room. We'll get Kleinsmidt up."

"What's eating him?" I asked.

"He thinks you spirited a witness away, and he doesn't like the way everybody pulled out of town last night without saying anything to him. He also thinks he should have questioned Corla Burke. He thinks the murder gave you some kind of a lead on her. You've got to square the whole thing. It'll take a good story."

"I know it will," I said.

We went to the hotel. I told Bertha a button was loose on my shirt, and asked her for a needle and thread. She became unexpectedly maternal, and offered to sew it on for me, but I stalled her along.

As soon as her door closed, I beat it for the elevator. It wasn't much of a walk around to the place where Helen Framley had lived. I stood at the foot of the stairs long enough to make sure no one was around, jabbed the needle into my thumb and squeezed out blood. I tiptoed up the stairs—and tiptoed down.

Bertha Cool was talking on the telephone as I came in. I heard her say, "You're certain of that? . . . Well, pickle me for a herring. . . . You've investigated at the airport? . . . That's right. We'll leave here on the afternoon plane. I'll see you in Los Angeles this evening. . . . That's fine. Give them my congratulations. Good-by."

She hung up and said, "That's funny."

"You mean that Endicott didn't show up?" I asked.

Her little eyes glittered hard at me. "Donald, you do say the damnedest things."

"Why?"

"How did you know he didn't show up?"

"Oh, I don't know. Something you said over the telephone."

"Nuts. You knew he wasn't *going* to show up. Where did he go?"

"I don't know."

"He didn't take that San Francisco plane out of Reno. He just disappeared into thin air."

I stretched, yawned, and said, "When do we entertain Lieutenant Kleinsmidt?"

"He's on his way up now."

Knuckles pounded on the door. I opened it, and Kleinsmidt walked in.

"You," he said.

"That's right."

"Quite a heel you turned out to be."

"What's wrong with me?"

"Taking a powder and putting me in Dutch, after the breaks I tried to give you."

I said, "I was out working for you."

"Thanks!" His voice was sarcastic.

"As I see it," I said, "all that interests you is the murder of Jannix."

"That's all, just a little minor matter like that, but the chief gets funny complexes. He's sort of riding me about it, and there's been a little criticism here and there, a few suggestions that your departure was rather abrupt, that I might have safeguarded the interests of the taxpayers a little better by seeing that you were provided with room and board. Where's that Framley woman?"

"I haven't the faintest idea."

"You went away with her."

"Uh huh."

"Where'd you leave her?"

"In Reno."

"Then what?"

I shrugged my shoulders and said, "Let's not talk about it. Another guy beat my time."

I felt Bertha Cool's eyes staring at me. Kleinsmidt said, "Who's the guy this time?"

"Man by the name of Hazen."

"The one who identified the stiff?"

"That's him."

"He didn't look like such a lady's man to me."

I said, "I made the same mistake, Lieutenant."

He said, "I think I'll do a little checking on that, Lam."

"Go ahead," I told him. "I can give you the name of the man who runs the gasoline station where we rented a cabin."

"What does he know about it?"

"He told me this morning that he heard my wife and the other man drive away in the night."

Kleinsmidt said, "Too bad. I don't think you're looking well. You need a good rest. We have the best climate in the west right here in Las Vegas. We'd hate to have you leave us again unexpectedly. I'm going to make arrangements to see that you don't."

I said, "Well, don't be in a hurry about it. Here's something for you to run down first."

"What?"

"Remember Paul Endicott, Whitewell's right-hand man?"

"Naturally."

"I don't know whether you heard Whitewell say so, but he was going to give his son a partnership interest when he got married. You know, the income-tax people get funny ideas about those things. When the new partnership was organized, they'd want an audit of the books, even if Whitewell didn't."

I saw Kleinsmidt's eyes showing interest.

"Keep right on," he said.

I said, "I wouldn't know, but if I wanted to make a bet, it would be that an audit of Whitewell's books would show the real reason Endicott didn't want the marriage to go through. That's why he got Helen Framley to write a letter to Corla Burke that would make her think the marriage couldn't go through."

"What was in the letter?" Kleinsmidt asked.

"I wouldn't know exactly, but it seems that Corla Burke's father walked out and left the family when she was about fifteen. I wouldn't want to be quoted, but I think the letter told her that her father had been arrested and was serving time in a penitentiary. Naturally, Corla wouldn't have gone ahead with the marriage under those circumstances. She wouldn't have thought it was fair to Philip."

"It's your story," Kleinsmidt said. "So let's hear the next installment."

"Corla got to brooding over it. She was on the verge of a nervous breakdown from overwork, anyway. She started out to investigate. Naturally, it wasn't anything she could entrust to anyone else, and she had to make a stall so she could get away and postpone the wedding until she could find out."

"That shouldn't have taken her long."

"It wouldn't have," I said, "if the shock hadn't thrown her off her trolley. They found her yesterday wandering around in Reno without the faintest idea of who she was or how she happened to get there."

Kleinsmidt's eyes narrowed into slits. He said, "Remember, Lam, I played ball with you once. I got my fingers hurt. Your pitching is full of curves. This time you've got to give me something that will stand up with the chief."

"What do you suppose I'm doing now?" I asked him.

"I'm damned if I know. And I'm a little suspicious."

I said, "Endicott was fighting for all the delay he could get. Jannix was to back his play. He was to be the witness who'd swear Corla's father was in the pen. Endicott was going to pay him. You know Jannix. He was hot tempered and a little suspicious anyway. Endicott made the mistake of coming to see him, and caught Jannix in one of his more suspicious moments. When he left, Jannix was dead."

"Very, very nice," Kleinsmidt said. "Only it's full of holes. It's bum stuff, even for a theory. You wouldn't, by any chance, have any facts to back up this fairy story, would you?"

"Lots of them."

Kleinsmidt said, "Well, you might begin by telling me how it happened Endicott could have done this at the exact moment he was sitting in a picture show. The chief would be interested in that. He's funny that way, the chief is."

I said, "If a woman had killed Jannix, he was killed between eight-fifty and nine-fifteen. If a man killed him, he might have been killed any time."

"How interesting!"

"The trouble with you," I said, "is that you got a theory and then tried to fit the facts to it. Your idea was that because the people who lived in the adjoining apartment hadn't heard a shot, the shot must have been fired while they were out."

"Try firing a shot in there without that old dame hearing it," Kleinsmidt said.

"Sure. She didn't hear a shot. She was out at the train. Therefore, the murder must have been committed while she was out."

"Well, what's wrong with that?"

"Suppose she hadn't gone out?"

"Then she'd have heard the shot."

"Would she?"

"Of course, she would."

"But suppose she hadn't?"

"I don't see what you're getting at."

"If she hadn't," I said, "you'd have tried to find out why, wouldn't you?"

"Naturally."

I said, "The body was found in an apartment. The people in the adjoining apartment had been out from eight-fifty to nine-twenty. This made it very nice for you. You were able to narrow the crime down to a thirty-minute interval and start asking questions accordingly. Well, if a woman had killed him, that would have been all right."

"Why does a man make it any different?"

I said, "A big, powerful man could have shot him in the alley or in an automobile or out in an auto camp, loaded the body into a car, parked in the alley, thrown the body over his shoulder, taken it up to Helen Framley's apartment and dumped it. Then he could have gone to a picture show and started building himself an alibi. Didn't it ever occur to you as slightly strange that Endicott dashed in to Las Vegas just to see a movie? He must be some little fan."

Kleinsmidt shook his head. "It's lousy," he said. "It stinks."

"All right, you wanted me to give you something you could take to the chief. Don't say I didn't do it."

"It's your story," Kleinsmidt said. "Even the way you tell it, it's full of holes. If *I* tried to put it across, it would rise up and hit me on the chin."

"Okay, it's your funeral."

"It may be my funeral," he said, "but you're going to be the chief mourner. Come on."

I said to Bertha, "You can address my mail care of Lieutenant Kleinsmidt."

"Like hell I will," Bertha said, getting to her feet. "Who the devil do you think you are?" she demanded, glaring at Kleinsmidt. "You aren't going to get away with this. I guess they've got lawyers in this town."

Kleinsmidt said, "Sure they have. You go right ahead and get 'em. Mr. Lam is coming with me."

Kleinsmidt took my arm. "Let's go quietly," he said.

We went quietly. Bertha Cool was standing in the doorway, saying uncomplimentary things to Kleinsmidt. He didn't pay any attention to her.

As we walked through the lobby, Kleinsmidt said, "I'm sorry, Lam. I hate to do this, but that story just doesn't hold water. Why don't you think up a good one?"

"Okay by me. Don't overlook Bertha, though. She won't take this lying down. Later on, when you have a chance to think things over, Lieutenant, this is going to be your embarrassing moment. You can write a prize-winning letter on it."

"I know," he said, "you're a plausible cuss, but if you talked me out of this, I'd never hear the last of it."

He took me down to headquarters. He didn't put me in a cell, but left me in an office with an officer standing guard. Around noon, Chief Laster came in.

The chief said, "Bill Kleinsmidt has been talking with me."

"That's good."

"And Mrs. Cool is waiting in the other room with a lawyer and a writ of habeas corpus."

"Bertha's a two-fisted individual. She makes her compromise with a club."

He said, "That theory of yours doesn't sound as crazy to me as it did to Bill Kleinsmidt."

"It's just a theory," I told him.

"You evidently had some evidence on which to base it."

"Nothing I'd care to discuss."

"But you had some?"

"No. It was just an idea."

He said, "I'd like to know just what gave it to you."

"Oh, just an idea."

He shook his head. "You had something more to tie to than just an idea. Did the girl tell you something?"

I raised my eyebrows, said with exaggerated surprise, "Why? Does *she* know anything?"

"That's not answering my question. Did she tell you something?"

"I'm certain I couldn't remember. We talked about a lot of things. You know how it is, Chief, when you're with a girl for several days."

"And nights," he said.

I didn't say anything.

He pinched his lower lip between his thumb and fore-finger, pulled it way out, then released it, and let it slide back. After a while, he said, "You're a queer one."

"What's the matter now?"

He said, "After Bill told me about that theory of yours, I went out and went over the premises inch by inch. We covered the stairs, taking each stair at a time. We found half a dozen drops of blood."

"Did you indeed?"

He said, "That knocks Endicott's alibi into a cocked hat."

"Have you asked him about it?"

"We can't. He's skipped."

"Is that so?"

"Yes. He went to Reno with you last night, and that's the last anyone has seen of him."

"Didn't he take the San Francisco plane?"

"No."

"What does Whitewell say?"

"Whitewell is saying a lot. I talked with him over the telephone. He's having auditors in."

I said, "Well, that's all very interesting, but I'd advise you not to keep Bertha Cool waiting. She's capable of sudden, unexpected action."

The chief got up with a sigh. "I wish you'd tell me what evidence you had to go on. It would help a lot."

"I'm sorry. It was just a theory of mine."

"You certainly had *some* sort of a tip."

"I don't see how you arrive at that conclusion. It seems to me it's a perfectly fair and logical deduction from the evidence. Just because a body is found in a certain place doesn't necessarily mean that the crime was committed there."

"When are you leaving Las Vegas?" he asked.

"As soon as I can get a plane out, and I'm not going to talk with any newspaper reporters, and as far as I'm concerned, you're the one who solved the crime."

He shifted his eyes and said, "Oh, I don't care anything about *that*."

"Well, I'm just telling you in case you did."

Chapter Eighteen

MY TELEPHONE RANG two minutes after the alarm went off. I picked up the receiver. It was Bertha on the other end of the line. "Are you awake, lover?"

"I am now."

"Bertha didn't mean to disturb you."

"What is it?"

"Mr. Whitewell called up. Apparently, he's stuck for about forty thousand dollars on the shortage."

"Too bad."

"He's asked me to meet him at my office at eight o'clock so he can make a complete settlement."

"Why so early?"

"He's going to have to go to San Francisco on the ten o'clock plane."

"I see."

"And I wanted to call you up to be sure I had all your expenses—that trip of yours to Reno, and all those incidentals."

"I made an account, itemized it, and put it in an envelope on your desk. You'll find it there."

"All right, that's fine."

"If you want to talk with me," I said, "you can call me at the Golden Motto. I'm going there for breakfast."

"All right, lover."

"You had breakfast?" I asked.

She said, "I'm only taking fruit juice for breakfast these days. I just can't seem to get my appetite back."

"All right, I'll be in the office after breakfast."

I hung up the phone, took a shower, shaved, dressed leisurely, and walked down to the Golden Motto.

The woman who ran the joint was looking rather groggy.

"Good morning," I said as I walked on through to the back room and took a seat at my favorite table.

The waitress came for my order. "Ham and, easy over," I said. "What's the matter with the madam?"

She laughed. "She's having a fit. Don't worry, she'll be around to tell you about it. Tomato juice?"

"A double tomato juice with a shot of Worcestershire. Bertha Cool may call for me. If she does—"

"Okay, I'll tell her you're here. I—here she comes now."

I looked up as Bertha Cool came marching through the door with that determined, bulldog set to her chin, her eyes glinting.

I got up and did the honors, seating her on the other side of the table.

Bertha heaved a sigh which seemed to come from her boot tops, smiled at the waitress, and said, "I have a hell of a disposition when my stomach's empty. Makes me feel like snapping somebody's head off. Bring me a double order of oatmeal, ham and eggs easy over, a big pot of coffee, and see that there's plenty of cream."

"Yes, Mrs. Cool."

The waitress moved silently toward the kitchen.

"Congratulations," I said to Bertha.

"On what?"

"You seem to have got your appetite back."

She gave a snort. "That old fool," she said.

"Who?"

"Arthur Whitewell."

"What did he do?"

"Tried handing me a lot of bull about how attractive I was."

I raised my eyebrows.

"I didn't mind it," she said. "In fact, I suppose I lapped some of it up, while it was just social, but when the damn fool tried to spread it on thick in order to wheedle me into making a low charge for our services, I saw through the old buzzard right away. I guess I've been a little foolish, lover. I guess a woman likes to hear those things, and if business hadn't entered into it, I might never have realized what a hypocrite he was."

"You got the dough all right?" I asked.

"Did I!" she said with her eyes glittering.

The waitress brought my tomato juice. I drank it, then while I was waiting, fished a couple of nickels out of my pocket and started over for the slot machine.

The woman who ran the place came rushing over to me. "Get away, get away," she said. "It's out of order."

"What's the matter with it?"

"I don't know, but a man and a girl came in here and played it about an hour ago, and won three gold awards inside of five minutes. Think of it. *Three* gold awards, to say nothing of the shower of nickels they dragged out of the machine. Something's wrong with it."

"Why," I said, "what makes you think there's anything wrong with the machine? You've always told me about the people who came in and won—"

"Well," she snapped, "this is different. I've telephoned for the service man to come over. You keep away from it."

I went back to my seat at the table.

"What is it?" Bertha asked.

"Nothing," I said, "except that someone will probably deliver my car to me today."

"Oh, it's already delivered," she said. "I forgot to tell you. The attendant at the parking-station said a girl had left a car there for you. It's an awful-looking jalopy, lover."

I didn't say anything.

The waitress brought food and placed it on the table. Somehow I didn't feel hungry. I kept thinking about the breakfasts on the desert and in Reno.

Bertha scraped the last yellow drop of egg yolk from her plate, looked up at me, and said, "What's the matter?"

"I don't know. I just don't feel hungry."

"Bah. You should always eat a good breakfast. You can't keep up your strength if you don't have food in your stomach." She snapped her fingers at the waitress. "Bring me a Milky Way," she ordered, and then turned to me to say, "I'll keep it in my purse in case I have that all-gone feeling around ten o'clock. Bertha's been awfully sick, lover. Awfully sick."

"I know it," I told her, "but you're completely cured now, aren't you?"

Bertha opened her purse, took out the blue-tinted check, and regarded it fondly.

"I'll tell the world," she said, "Bertha's all cured."

>>> If you've enjoyed this book and would like to discover more great vintage crime and thriller titles, as well as the most exciting crime and thriller authors writing today, visit: **>>>**

The Murder Room
Where Criminal Minds Meet

themurderroom.com